WHAT WE TAKE FOR TRUTH

What We Take For Truth

A novel
by

DEBORAH NEDELMAN

Adelaide Books
New York / Lisbon
2019

WHAT WE TAKE FOR TRUTH
A novel
By Deborah Nedelman

Copyright © by Deborah Nedelman
Cover design © 2019 Adelaide Books
Cover photo © by Barbara W. Ingram

Published by Adelaide Books, New York / Lisbon
adelaidebooks.org
Editor-in-Chief
Stevan V. Nikolic

For any information, please address Adelaide Books
at info@adelaidebooks.org
or write to:
Adelaide Books
244 Fifth Ave. Suite D27
New York, NY, 10001

ISBN-10: 1-950437-18-3
ISBN-13: 978-1-950437-18-4

Printed in the United States of America

To the forests

Contents

Section 1: Parrot   9

             Chapter 1   11

             Chapter 2   26

             Chapter 3   40

             Chapter 4   61

             Chapter 5   78

             Chapter 6   91

             Chapter 7   106

Section 2: Charlie   123

             Chapter 8   125

             Chapter 9   139

             Chapter 10   153

Section 3: Secrets   167

             Chapter 11   169

             Chapter 12   180

             Chapter 13   188

Chapter 14   *202*

Chapter 15   *213*

Chapter 16   *220*

Section 4: Lost and Found   *229*

Chapter 17   *231*

Chapter 18   *239*

Chapter 19   *250*

Chapter 20   *260*

Chapter 21   *268*

Chapter 22   *276*

Chapter 23   *294*

Acknowledgements   *309*

About the Author   *311*

SECTION 1: PARROT

Chapter 1

May 24, 1991

My dad's advice: if you're caught in the forest when a cloud descends, move slow, feel your way. Your eyes are useless. Sound is distorted. You have to trust your instincts.

But now, one instinct says stay still, wait for things to clear and another says everything is falling apart around me, get away.

Could it be easier to be an orphan in the city than it is here? Orphan artist. Alone in the big, bad city.

(Below the last line is a sketch: the skyline of a savage city, buildings roofed with jagged, hungry teeth and a tiny figure in the corner in a red cap, a paintbrush in her hand.)

Grace "Parrot" Tillman opened the drawer of her bedside table, laid her diary inside, and pulled out the tattered bird book she'd inherited from her mother. The cover was torn, the title only partially readable, the pages yellowed and brittle. She ran her forefinger over the faded signature on the inside of the front cover. This ritual of searching out the subtle indentations from the pressure of her mother's hand had long ago smoothed them away, but Grace still found it comforting. She laid the spine of the book in her flattened palm and let it fall open where it would—the closest she came to an act of divination. The answer appeared as she knew it would: *Li-lac-Crowned Parrot* Amazona finschi *(Mexico):Red forehead, lilac crown, green cheeks, pale bill. Resident of western Mexico from southeastern Sonora to southern Oaxaca. A number have been sighted in the San Gabriel Valley of Southern California.*

That had been her mother's dream: seeking those tropical birds, going south to the sun. But despite the nickname her mother had bestowed on her, Grace was a Pacific Northwesterner. The tropics called to her, but a cautious inner voice told her she'd be lost without rain, without evergreens.

A piece of paper, worn thin from handling, slid from its hiding place between the book's pages and fell to the floor. Grace picked it up and tenderly unfolded it. The crayoned picture of a parrot wasn't bad for an eight-year-old. *For Mommy, From Parrot* was printed in childish letters at the bottom. Grace had spent a childhood full of rainy afternoons making drawings of the birds in that book. The sketch pad that lay on the bed beside her was full of more recent efforts to capture the lushness of the tropical fantasy her mother had described to her when she was toddler. Sure, folks had told her she had talent. Even her art teacher at Cooper High had encouraged her to take herself seriously and go to art school. But supporting herself with her art? That was crazy. Grace shook her head, slid the drawing back into its hiding place, and closed the book.

Pulling open the drawer to put the book away, Grace glanced quickly over the slick, wildly colored brochure that lay tucked in the back. Stenciled across the top of the brochure were the words *Instituto Allende*. That glance was all it took, and Grace was lost once again, conjuring up its pictures of painters at easels and sketchers sitting in front of Mayan ruins, working to capture their faded power on paper. Hugging the bird book close to her chest, Grace whispered "Momma, I wish you were here. I don't know what to do."

There would be no answer to her plea. Grace knew this, and she also knew it was time to get to work. Leaving her sketchbook and pencils scattered across her bed, Grace grabbed her jacket and her red watch cap from its hook and headed down to the post office.

The chill bit against her cheeks as she stepped out of the house. She tugged her cap down over her ears and stepped onto the gravel road, the same road she had walked all her life. The recent rush of change, though, had left a ragged wake through the familiar terrain.

The Nybergs, who'd lived next door as long as Grace could remember, had packed up their truck and pulled out two months ago. Already their house had the look of long abandonment. The gutters sagged along the front edge of the roof and black ice slicked the porch steps. Bits of old newspaper and frozen litter were piled up in the flowerbeds where Mrs. Nyberg's dahlias lay rotting underground.

How many did that make? It was getting to the point where counting the empty houses and storefronts took longer than counting the ones where someone still kept the lights on. Grace held her right hand out in front of her, turned her face away and swept the vision of her neighbors' empty home out of her sight. As a kid, she'd held her hands over her ears to shut out her father's angry voice; she'd buried her head under blankets when the scary demons of the dark invaded her sleep. She might be an adult now, but Grace knew that if she allowed herself to feel each loss—let her eyes and ears absorb it—she'd be just as paralyzed as she'd been at four.

Patches of snow huddled in the mucky shade. There was a groggy resistance in the air. On days like this, Grace pictured the green soul of the forest as a defiant teenager refusing to rise from its icy dreams, pulling a gray blanket over its tousled head. The cajoling May sun was not strong enough to win this fight. Grace wanted to believe that spring meant things would improve, but if she were honest, she knew this season . . . it was a tease, a cheat, and a damn liar.

And yet. This morning the sight of a cluster of yellow tips poking through the dirty crust of ice along the road edge ambushed her. In spite of her eighteen years of experience—of knowing how wobbly spring could be, retreating back into the arms of winter many times before finally setting its course—seeing newly sprouting crocuses made her heart jump. A towhee, hidden in the brush, chittered its suppressed giggle of delight and she was hooked again. She inhaled the frigid air; her shoulders relaxed in the thin rays of sun, and a smile bloomed across her face.

Then she took a single step forward and landed on a transparent veneer of ice. She slid, uncontrolled, until her boot shattered the treacherous barrier, spraying freezing mud into her face.

Dammit! I've got to get the hell out of here. Face it— art school in Mexico isn't going to happen. I could never afford it. Seattle isn't Mexico, but at least there you can catch a bus instead of sloshing through icy mud to get to your job. There it doesn't matter if the snow still weighs down the cedar branches in mid-May. Nobody has to race the sun to finish hauling out that last tree before the winter closes the whole town down. Seattle is full of people doing all kinds of things all year long—everyone isn't a logger or married to a logger!

This thought was like holding the key to a treasure chest in the moment before lifting the lid, when anything was possible. Wiping the mud from her face, Grace sighed. Her cautious inner voice taunted her again, reminding her that the city was more like Pandora's box than a treasure chest. Yes, plenty of folks had moved away from Prosperity and, yes, she knew some of them had made a life in the city, but the model for escape that burned most brightly in Grace's memory was her mother, Annie.

Annie had poured her own dreams of running off to exotic lands into the bedtime stories she told her young daughter. But when Grace was four, Annie had disappeared into the shadows of an early death instead. More than disappeared, really. Because after she was gone, no one ever talked about her. As Grace grew, she was haunted by the sense that her mother had vanished not just from the earth but from everyone's memory as well, so that Grace was left mourning someone none of the other people in town even remembered. In Grace's child mind a connection formed between the terror of disappearing and the world outside of Prosperity. There lay monsters.

Ridiculous. Here it was, 1991. She wasn't going to vanish off the face of the earth if she left this town. Prosperity. Even the name of the place was a bitter joke. The only life it offered her was that of a worn-thin wife of a pitiable lumberjack. Her father, Warren, had loved this town and it had loved him back; maybe all he'd ever wanted was to be a logger, or maybe he'd never had any other choices. But Grace was a high school graduate and she had her own dream.

For the hundredth time in the last week, Grace recommitted herself; she was going to get out of here. One more week and she'd be gone. Away from this dying town, these hovering mountains, and all this heavy green. Concrete. Traffic. The buzz of the city. An apartment with her two best friends, the first step to a new life of possibility. With the same gesture she'd used to block the evidence of Prosperity's decline from her vision, Grace held her hand out in front of her, her fingers spread wide, palm out. With one full sweep of her arm across the horizon, she pushed the images of tropical jungles filled with brilliantly colored birds out of her mind. Seattle was far enough, and Seattle was real.

Standing in front of the small bank of post office boxes a few minutes later, Grace dug into the pocket of her jeans. Her fingers located the metal key ring and tugged it out. It held two keys—one to the mailbox and the other to the door of the Hoot Owl Café. Three miniature plastic birds strung together on a woven cord also dangled from the ring. The largest of the birds, about an inch long, was a green parrot with a spot of red on his yellow bill; he was connected to a tiny black toucan and a mini scarlet macaw. As usual, the cord that held the birds to the ring was wrapped around the post office box key and Grace had to unwind the mess before she could get to the pile of bills waiting inside number 1013.

So many times she'd thought about walking down the street to Sherman's General Store and getting a new key ring, or at least removing the birds so the keys could dangle free. But she could never bring herself to do either. Her mother had attached those birds and the two keys to that ring. And, despite all the years since she'd last felt the warmth of her mother's hand, when Grace held on to that ring, she felt connected to her.

Inserting the key into the post office box lock, Grace opened the door and removed the small stack of windowed envelopes. She didn't look at them; they would only depress her. She wasn't going to let the state of the café or her aunt's financial woes make her reconsider her decision. Only one more week of this and she'd be gone!

"Hey, Parrot!" Kev leaned against the post office door. "Got magazines?"

Startled, Grace turned toward the familiar voice. Another sign she needed a change of scenery—Kev, in his perpetual Day-Glo sweatshirt, had become invisible to her. She grinned at him and registered how much the ten-year-old had grown in the last year. Grace had been like a big sister to Kev since he was born; more than once she had cradled him in her arms while his mother begged the doctor for solutions to the puzzles of Kev's body. There had been few answers, but Kev was one determined kid. Though the doctors had predicted he might never do so, Kev learned to walk, and though school presented major challenges, his memory was phenomenal, and he kept close tabs on all the goings on in town. As long as things stayed constant in Kev's world, he managed well. When something disrupted the routines of his life, though, Kev and all those who cared about him suffered until a new equilibrium could be established.

Grace knew that her plans to move would rock Kev's foundation, but she couldn't let that stop her. She couldn't stay in Prosperity for Kev. He had parents. He had this whole town.

Grace reached into the back of the post office box and pulled out the Bargreen's restaurant catalogue.

"Here's something for you, Kev." On the slick cover was a photo of a chef smiling behind a glistening stainless-steel cooktop. No need for this. Aunt Jane would just toss it; she'd be lucky if she could manage to replace half the chipped coffee mugs at the Hoot Owl by the end of the year. Kev, on the other hand, would pore over the catalogue. It would occupy him all day.

"Yay! Bargreen's," which sounded like "bah gweens" when mangled by Kev's rebellious tongue.

"OK, Kev. I gotta go to work." Grace locked up the box and walked over to the door. She held it open as Kev shifted his weight and made his way out of the post office.

"But no school no more! You all done with school now." Saliva sprayed from Kev's mouth as he gave Grace a huge grin.

"That's right. I'm done. Graduated. Never thought I could do it, did ya?" Grace grinned back.

"Maybe, maybe not." It was Kev's favorite phrase; he'd repeat it in a mechanical tone whenever he didn't like what he was hearing.

Grace ignored this comment and waited for him to step down the stairs and out to the muddy street. As Kev walked across the intersection, Grace turned her eyes away from the boy's awkward gait to look up, over the tops of the buildings into the deep green of the Cascade Mountain Range that hugged Prosperity tightly in its snowcapped grip. There wasn't much to Prosperity; turning her head from right to left Grace could almost see from the mill at one end to the cemetery at the other. It was a withering nothing of a town only a couple of hours from Seattle. Yet, all her life Grace had heard folks talk as if that journey was much more effort than it was worth. The common sentiment had been, if you could manage to stay in Prosperity, why would you ever go to the city?

Grace didn't want to think about what she'd be leaving behind: the dew rising from the tops of the trees on a fall morning, making the woods smell like life starting anew; the smooth solidity of the boulders along her favorite mountain trail, where she'd found solace for so many losses; the wild pitch of the eagle's call as it soared across the valley. But most of all she didn't want to think about Patrick.

She clenched her jaw, sealing her lips tight. She wouldn't think about the marriage she'd refused, and she wouldn't listen to that voice, the one that always asked "what would Momma want me to do?" There was never an answer.

It would be so much easier to leave if it didn't feel like she was turning her back on her mother somehow. If Grace left Prosperity, who would even think of Annie again?

As she and Kev made their way across the empty street, Grace tried not to notice how the faded blue paint on the front of Jarvis Hardware store was peeling off the wooden siding. But a wedge of memory managed to slip between the slamming doors of her mind and hold her at nine years old for a brief moment, clapping for joy when Norma Jarvis chose to use a bright color, so different from the drab grays and browns of the other places in town. Things were brighter in general in those days. People were optimistic. The mill was busy. The timber waiting to be cut seemed endless.

No one was going to repaint that building now. Months ago, Tim Jarvis had sold off his stock to Sherman's and boarded up the windows before he left town.

Once inside the café, Kev settled himself at his favorite table next to the window and spread the Bargreen's catalogue out in front of him. Grace headed to the back to get her apron. She plopped the stack of mail next to the cash register and pushed through the swinging door into the kitchen. Her aunt stood in front of the sink, scrubbing the pots.

"Nothing important, just bills." Grace reported this as she opened the refrigerator to find a piece of chocolate cream pie for Kev. His order never varied.

"You can file them for me then. They all go in the round file." Jane's deep smoker's voice barked across the pass-through from the kitchen into the café.

Grace placed Kev's pie in front of him and he rewarded her with a smile. Two grayhairs, Larry and Al, sat at the corner table solving the problems of the world—at least the world minus Prosperity.

"Nice to know you keep good track of your paperwork, Jane." Larry's voice was strong and deep enough to be heard over the running water in the kitchen. "It'll make it easier for the bank when they foreclose." He winked at Grace.

Larry and Al had been regulars since Grace started working at the Hoot Owl when she turned thirteen. Both men had long ago retired from their jobs as cutters, though they still wore overalls and drank their coffee black at the crack of dawn. Grace picked up the coffeepot and walked over to them.

"Mornin', guys. Want anything?"

"Nothin' we can afford." Al sighed. "Listen, you hear about that Green River killer, Parrot? You gotta be careful in the city. I don't like to think of you all alone there."

Grace put her hand on her hip and cocked her head, looking at the old logger. "You think I'm gonna let a little ol' murderer stop me from leaving when I've had to put up with down-and-out loggers and mill workers all my life?"

Larry nodded. "Parrot's got a point, Al."

"And by the way, my name's Grace. Annie, my dear departed momma, named me Grace Annable Tillman and if any of you gentlemen should ever call me Annable that will be the last cup of coffee you ever drink in the Hoot Owl. If you need me quick you can still call me Parrot, but I prefer Grace. I've decided when I move to Seattle I'm going to be Grace, so I'm starting now."

"Maybe, maybe not!" Kev bellowed from his seat. The men hooted.

"You finish up your pie, Kev. Near time to get back home." Grace knew how Mary worried about her son even though his solo trip to the Hoot Owl in the morning had been part of Kev's routine for nearly a year. "Momma's waiting for you."

Kev crammed a large mouthful of chocolate cream into his mouth and pushed his plate away. He scraped his chair back from the table and rose.

"See you tomorrow, Kev," Grace said as he made his way out the door.

"Maybe, maybe not," the boy repeated and let the door slam behind him.

"That boy's going to miss you," Larry mumbled from behind the sports section.

"Give me a break, guys." Grace walked back behind the counter and returned the coffeepot to the heat.

Jane stuck her head through the opening to the kitchen, "Don't let those old coots make you feel guilty. They're just jealous cause they know this town is dead and they don't have the gumption to move on themselves."

Grace sighed. Shaking her head, she walked over to pick up Kev's empty plate just as the door slammed open, admitting the husky form of Burt Samson, heavy-booted and overall-clad with a greasy baseball cap that declared "I.W. of A." in faded letters.

Red-faced, Burt demanded, "What kind of shit is this? I'll be goddamned if birds are more important than people! You hear the news?" he asked the open space of the café. "That goddamned judge is shutting down timber sales in national forests. All to save a fuckin' owl."

"Yahoo! Point for the good guys!" Jane screamed from the kitchen.

"Shut up, Jane." Al had gotten up from his chair; his brow furrowed as he leaned against the table. "Warren's turning over in his grave; it's our loyalty to your brother keeps us coming in here. You keep talking like that and you won't see another customer in this café for a long time." He looked over at Burt.

"What's Jackson say? You guys still got some contracts on private land, right? Like to see 'em try and stop that!"

"Let's take this to the tavern, Al. Don't feel too logger friendly in here." Burt looked at Grace as he said this. "And I shouldn't even be talking' to you, little lady. All because of you I got a mopey-eyed, do-nothin' son to deal with now. He's so screwed up he's not safe in the woods." He shook his head. "Can't understand how a girl bred and raised in Prosperity could turn her back on my Pat. You think you're gonna find a better man in Seattle? That's a joke." He turned on his heel and stormed out of the café with Al and Larry in tow.

Grace sank into the nearest chair and watched the men cross the street to the Bullhook. If she didn't get out of here, she'd have to deal with Burt Samson and every other logger in town treating her like a traitor.

"Hell, Parrot. Patrick is a fool and his daddy is no better. Don't let those cretins get to you." Jane had come out of the kitchen to stand beside her niece. Her orange hair stood in short spikes around her head, its color mirrored in her glossy fingernails. The flour-dusted apron she wore over her tie-dyed T-shirt said *Hoot Owl Café* in orange embroidered letters. "You'll find better men than Pat in about five minutes in the city."

Grace looked up into her aunt's face. The sharp line of her jaw, the deepening wrinkles around her eyes, the fierce clamp of her lips. Time and stubbornness were skillful carvers.

"Don't worry. I'm going. It's gonna to take more than a few remarks from Burt Samson to stop me." She sighed and pushed herself up to stand next to her aunt.

Jane fished in her apron pocket and pulled out a quarter, walked over to the jukebox in the back of the café and dropped it in the slot. "We need a little dancing music, don't you think?"

She Drives Me Crazy poured from the speakers and Jane grabbed Grace's hand and began swaying and bouncing to the music.

"That boy is crazy. But you didn't drive him to it." Jane grinned. "He's got that deluded logger mentality, just like every man in this town. They just can't face reality."

Grace stood rooted in the center of the empty café. She dropped her aunt's hand. "I know. It's just . . ."

There'd been a time—hell, most of her childhood—when everyone in Grace's world spoke about Prosperity and logging with pride. But it was all different now. Ever since the government put the spotted owl on the endangered species list and started to restrict where trees could be cut, there'd been a war brewing in the woods: you were either a crazy tree-hugging radical or a shortsighted, tree-killing redneck. And that war was killing her town.

In spite of everything, Grace loved Prosperity. She loved it almost as much as she hated it. How many places were there where you could walk one block from your house and be in an old-growth forest? Where you could fall asleep to the sound of owls calling to one another? Where everyone knew everyone— for better or for worse. And beyond all that, Prosperity was home to her mother's spirit.

"Damn it, Parrot. If you aren't going to dance with me, I'll go back and finish those salads." As Jane headed toward the kitchen, she put her hand on her niece's shoulder and whispered in her ear, "Stay here and you're stuck being an out-of-work logger's wife. Don't be a fool. You know this town is dying. Run for it and don't look back."

Years ago, when Jane, who'd always pushed against the grain, began talking about how people couldn't keep clear-cutting the trees without screwing up the whole balance of life,

Grace was curious. She knew how much her daddy loved the woods, just like she did. It confused her to know that he "killed trees," as Jane put it. But Grace saw how the town, even her daddy, had laughed at Jane. Then three years ago, Warren was killed in a logging accident, and Jane's passionate environmental spirit twisted her grief into an anti-logging rage.

Warren's death had rocked Grace's world too. The conflict between those who were fighting to keep every tree alive and those whose own lives depended on cutting them down wound itself into Grace's grief. Much of the time she wouldn't have been able to say if she were mourning her father or the forest.

It wasn't long after Warren's death that a group of hippies set up camp in a stand of old growth—a bunch of tree-huggers who threatened to put their bodies in the way of any woodsman's chain saw. The Hoot Owl had always welcomed the short-lived summer "crowd" of hikers but relied on local loggers to pay the bills. Once Jane made it clear she sided with the environmentalists though, the locals began shunning the café.

At the same time Pat had begun pushing Grace to take him to the spotted owl nest Warren had shown her, so he could destroy it. The Northern Spotted Owl was a shy, finicky bird that could only live in healthy forests; it needed a diverse habitat. The government was convinced it had to save the owls by keeping loggers out of the forests where the birds lived. Pat argued that, without a local nest, the government wouldn't limit logging in the nearby national forest. His plan was ridiculous, but Grace couldn't get Pat to see that. Instead he'd made it into a test of her love and loyalty. A test she was failing big-time.

It might mean abandoning her mother's memory but getting out of Prosperity felt like the only way Grace was going to survive this crazy battle that was killing the town.

Grace grabbed a wet rag from behind the counter and began wiping down the tables.

"You go on home and start packing." Jane called from the kitchen. "Knowing you, it'll take you a week just to decide you aren't going to need your hiking boots in the city."

"Don't you want help with breakfast?"

"Ummm. There any customers out there waiting to order?"

"No, not yet."

"Right. The crowd could show up any minute, I forgot." Jane pushed open the door from the kitchen and stood looking at her niece. "I said, go. If I get more customers than I can handle, I'll climb up on the roof and yell."

Grace dropped the dishcloth on the counter and stomped out, letting the door slam behind her. *Damn Aunt Jane. Damn Patrick.*

Chapter 2

The echo of the café door slamming shut still rang in the empty street and Grace stood with her hands balled into tight fists, her nails digging into her palms. She looked across the road and considered the tavern. The Bullhook was going to outlast everything else in Prosperity. There would always be thirsty loggers, and the worse things got, the more there would be. Here it was, not even nine o'clock in the morning, and the sign was lit. She didn't need to look inside to know who sat at the bar. How much time had her own father spent on one of those stools?

Without making a conscious choice, Grace found herself wandering up the street toward the mill—the opposite direction from Jane's house, the house she'd called home since she was four. She walked past Sherman's General Store, not yet open for the day, and the few houses that stood between the tiny business district and the elementary school. Mrs. G, the postmistress, lived in the first of these and worked hard to keep encroaching desolation at bay. Hers was one of the few homes in town with windowsills painted bright white and pots of purple azaleas blooming boisterously next to the steps. A porch swing with a yellow cushion beckoned by the front door. Grace looked away from this point of cheerful welcome and lifted her eyes to the steep slopes covered with cedar and hemlock. When she got to the corner across from where the ancient, long-empty log cabin stood, she turned up toward the mountains and the sawmill.

Dyer's Mill sat on the largest area of flat land in Prosperity. Most places in town were up or down from one another, except for the few establishments that ran along Main Street: the café; the post office; the tiny police station where Kev's father, Kevin Bigley Sr., drank his coffee and saved his energy for Saturday nights; Jarvis Hardware with its empty windows staring out at the street like shocked victims of some horror; and Marlene's Do It Again, the thrift shop run by the few church ladies left. It was a steep step up across the street from the café to the Bullhook Tavern and Sherman's General Store. Prosperity Grade School, with its four narrow classrooms and its empty bell tower, occupied a smaller square of level land downhill from the mill. Those who still believed there was a point to it made a hilly trek to the opposite end of town to reach the old clapboard church on the one Sunday a month when Reverend Foster appeared.

The tallest structure in town was Dyer's drying kiln, an inverted metal cone that mimicked the shape of the volcanic peaks from Mount Baker down the spine of the Cascades to Mount Shasta and, like them, it periodically spewed plumes of steam into the air. When the mill was hard at work, the kiln emitted clouds day and night. Lately, the rusty miniature volcano was quiet most of the time and functioned primarily as a landmark for the occasional hiker who needed directions to the old logging trail that led to the ridge.

Children had never been allowed inside the mill, but when Grace was a toddler Warren had insisted that his daughter would understand the work it took to produce good lumber.

One day, in spite of Annie's objections, he carried his baby girl like a shining bouquet of spring wildflowers tucked in the bend of one massive arm and walked into the metal-walled milling shed. No one had interfered with them. The piercing whine of the saws and the rumble and pound of the sorting machines terrified Grace. The child threw her hands up and clamped them over her ears. She sobbed, "Daddy, the trees are crying."

That first impression had never completely left her.

She walked up to the chain-link fence that outlined the mill yard and stood looking at the small pyramid of branchless tree trunks, each stripped of its green by the buckers who'd used their chain saws to trim them down to these red logs. They lay waiting their turn to be ripped by the hungry blades and tamed into lumber.

Like all the residents of Prosperity, Grace had seen the slow and steady decline, the shrinking dimensions of the logs. When she was a kid, her daddy had hoisted her onto his shoulders to give her an idea of how big the trees were that he cut—a single giant lying on its side filled the extended bed of a logging truck and towered over the cab. Grace had reached out instinctively to touch it, feeling a mixture of awe and terror as she inhaled its scent. The perfume of red cedar still sent shivers through her.

Lately, the log trucks that passed through town heading to the mill carried piles of tree trunks, each far thinner and younger than that giant. Those majestic old-growth trees were scarce now, and men were cutting huge swaths of the spindlier second growth to get the wood they needed, keeping the buckers busy.

Grace knew if she were ever going to get out of this town, she would need to buck herself—strip away the innumerable limbs that extended out from her to intertwine with the community. She would have to stand on her own, stop leaning on those who loved her, on the people who had always been there surrounding her with support. She would have to say goodbye to the Dyers.

The early morning mist thickened as Grace stood at the mill fence. No one was at work yet, and the machinery was quiet. Rain began falling in earnest, heavy drops landing on her head and sliding down the silky shafts of her black hair. Still she stood, occasionally wiping the water from her face, letting pools form at her feet. Her arms tingled from the accumulating cold, but she couldn't turn away, her mind flooded with all the stories of how she and her parents were tied to this place.

Mill owner Jackson Dyer and his wife Rose had been close to Annie and Warren from the early days, when Grace's parents were love-struck teenagers. They comforted Annie during the months when Warren was away in Vietnam, responding to her fears with stoic calm. Once Annie was gone, Rose Dyer stepped in to help Warren and Jane care for little Grace. The older couple reveled in the role of doting grandparents, filling the void left by Annie's and Warren's own deceased parents.

Since she was a sophomore in high school, Grace had spent at least one evening each week making dinner for Jackson and Rose. And with each of these meals Grace's branches had knotted themselves more tightly among those stretched out from the Dyers' sturdy trunks.

The whole thing started when Grace was sixteen. She had been waitressing at the café in the afternoons for nearly three years.

Jackson came into the Hoot Owl one day, as usual, for his afternoon coffee. The café was empty but for Grace sitting at the counter trying to finish her homework. He made his regular comment about not wanting to take her away from her important work and headed behind the counter to pour a cup for himself. This afternoon, though, something in his voice made her look up.

He was standing across the counter from her grinning like a kid with a naughty secret. The smile started in his squinted eyes and lit up his whole grizzled face. Jackson was normally a serious man; his thin gray hair and salt-and-pepper mustache revealed what the years of running the mill and bearing the responsibility for the whole town's welfare was doing to him. Seeing him like this, almost giddy, made Grace jump off her stool.

"What? What? You look like you're going to burst. Tell me."

"Well," he tried to pretend a studied calm, but it came out like a giggle, "I have an idea." He leaned across the counter and lowered his voice, even though there was no one else in the place. "This is a secret, OK? Just between you and me." He was getting more excited as he talked.

Grace nodded. All this buildup was ridiculous. Jackson was the most predictable man she knew. He was probably going to tell her he'd decided to have banana cream instead of his regular apple pie or something.

"Next Saturday is our anniversary—me and Rose. And I want to do something special."

Wow. Jackson, a romantic? No wonder he wanted her to keep it a secret—imagine what they'd do with this at the mill.

"You're a great cook, Grace. You like to make different things—things not on Jane's menu, right?" Again she nodded. She'd been experimenting for a while; when it was slow Jane let her use the café kitchen to try new recipes. Sometimes she'd let regulars taste her creations. Jackson had been a guinea pig more than once.

"Well, how'd you like to make a special anniversary dinner for me and Rose? I could take her over to the river for the day and you could cook in our kitchen. Then when we got home, it'd be all ready and she'd be so surprised!" Then he straightened up and became the serious businessman for a moment, "'Course I'd pay you. You'd be like a caterer." And he waited, his eyebrows raised in anticipation.

"Jackson, I think that's very romantic of you." How could she refuse such an offer? Getting a chance to do something she loved for people she loved and getting paid for it! "Sure. I'd love to do it."

Rose had been eating at the café for years and Grace knew what she liked. But designing a meal for her that wouldn't be limited to what was on the two sides of the Hoot Owl menu was a new adventure. It got Grace excited.

The hard part was hiding it all from Rose. Grace loved Rose and could never have lied to her. If she'd asked what was going on, Grace knew she wouldn't be able to stop herself from blurting it all out. Fortunately, even if she had an inkling something was up, Rose never asked. Things worked out just as Jackson had planned.

Grace treated the meal as an opportunity to create something beautiful as well as delicious. She let her artistic sensibilities take over. She borrowed Jane's truck and made a trip to Everett for supplies.

When the couple came home that evening, the table was set with candles and a crisp white cloth. On each plate, spring-green asparagus sat next to curried carrots and rice darkened by slivers of wild mushroom; slabs of pink salmon were sprinkled with minced red pepper and parsley, slices of lemon on the side. The green salad was topped with orange nasturtiums and purple pansies, and for dessert Grace had drizzled raspberry sauce over a caramel custard. It was a work of art.

Rose stood before it all with her mouth agape. She looked from her husband to the young woman she regarded as a granddaughter.

"How? Did you—?"

Grace and Jackson nodded in unison.

"Oh, my, how lovely! And how delicious everything smells." Behind her glasses, Rose's brown eyes sparkled with tears. Rose was a sturdy woman who was not used to being taken care of. She immediately insisted that Grace sit and share the meal with them.

"No, no. Rose. I loved every minute of making this for you. Please sit and enjoy it. It was Jackson's idea and he paid me for it. Happy Anniversary."

Grace left the couple and retreated to the kitchen. As a child, she'd papered the Dyers' walls with drawings and brought in bouquets hand-picked from Rose's garden. But ever since she'd started working at the café and earning her own money, Rose had refused to accept any gifts from her. "You need to save your pennies," she'd tell her. "You never want to be financially dependent on someone else." Though this message belied Rose's own life choices, Grace understood it as hard-won wisdom.

That had been the beginning of the tradition of Grace making weekly dinners for the older couple. Tonight would be the last of those meals.

The crunch of tires along the back road signaled the arrival of the first of the mill workers for the day. Grace turned away from the fence and headed back, retracing her steps past the café with its still-empty tables, and ran the short, wet blocks back to the house.

Grace had lived in this house for fourteen of her eighteen years, but aside from a few books and a box of art supplies, little that she owned seemed right for the city. She pulled her favorite jeans off the hook on the back of the closet door, folded them and laid them on top of the underwear she'd strewn across the bottom of the suitcase. Two minutes later she lifted them out and hung them back on the hook.

Grace would never share Shauna's excitement over things like clothes and makeup. They'd remained tight, in spite of what would have an unbridgeable gulf had they lived in a community that offered the luxury of such differences. But in Prosperity, and even at Cooper High, Shauna could roll her eyes in frustration over her best friend's lack of fashion awareness without running any risk to either of the girls' social standing.

Just three months ago, Grace and Shauna had been standing in front of the mirror in the girls' bathroom at Cooper. Their next class started in five minutes. Shauna had her makeup arrayed across the narrow space between the sinks and was taking meticulous care with her eye shadow. Grace quickly washed her hands and barely glanced at her face in the mirror. As usual, the paper towel holder was empty. Grace impatiently wiped her wet hands on her pant legs. "You and Jen are going to spend all your money on clothes. That's ridiculous."

"Well, at least people aren't going to assume we're ignorant rednecks from the mountains when they look at us. First impressions, you know." Shauna shook her finger at her friend.

Grace looked away, pulled her hair back from her face and tied it with a scrunchie. "I'm from the mountains and I'm not ashamed of it. Anyway, I'll probably get some waitressing job where I have to wear a uniform."

"It's a start." Shauna carefully outlined her lips in coral. "Once you've gotten used to Seattle, you'll probably be wearing four-inch heels and tight skirts."

As she was about to shut her suitcase, Grace grabbed the jeans and stuffed them inside.

It was four o'clock—time to head up to Rose's. Grace climbed into Jane's old pickup and drove to the end of Hope Street and up the one-lane gravel road that wound through Jake Oliver's forest—the ancient stand of trees surrounding the town, unlogged by order of Jackson's maternal grandfather, the man who gave Prosperity its ironic name. The road ended at the Dyers' place.

Grace had planned an Italian dinner and was soon in the kitchen mincing garlic and chopping tomatoes for Jackson's favorite pasta dish. Rose sat at the table fighting the urge to get up and help. It had been a stumbling process, convincing Rose to let Grace do the cooking alone. In time they settled on this: Grace cooked, and Rose kept her company, never gossiping (which Rose referred to with disdain), but, inevitably, sharing stories about their neighbors.

"I hate how everyone in town is riled up over this spotted owl thing." Grace moaned.

"Oh dear, yes. Some days I think it's going to kill Jackson. I hate to even talk about it. It's as if you can't just love the forest anymore. You have to either be for logging or against it."

"That's exactly it!" Grace put down her knife and turned to Rose. "That's why Pat broke up with me. I wouldn't pick a side." She wiped her hands on the dishtowel slung over her shoulder. "Which, according to him, meant I had picked the other side."

Rose put her idle hands flat on the table in front of her and looked sternly at Grace. "I have to admit I am disappointed. My garden is going to be so beautiful for a summer wedding."

Grace grimaced. As a child she'd played dress-up in Rose's garden, creating an elaborate fantasy wedding under the wisteria vines. She sighed.

"He wanted me to take him to that spotted owl nest my dad showed me. He would have destroyed it. I just couldn't."

Rose tilted her head and took a long look at the young woman who was as close to a granddaughter as she'd ever have. "Jackson always said that Patrick had the makings of a good woodsman. Maybe too good."

"It's all these regulations and everything. He's changed." Grace stirred the sautéing vegetables, turning the flame down to let the onions release their juice slowly. Then she slumped into the chair opposite Rose.

Grace had known Pat as long as she could remember. They'd spent their childhoods in the tiny Prosperity Grade School, ignoring, then hating, and finally flirting with one another. Their relationship had bloomed through high school and everyone in town had expected them to marry.

"I don't think I'm ready to settle down anyway. Shauna and Jennifer are going to Seattle to find jobs and I'm going with them. They've picked out a house for us to share." She kept her eyes on the stove. "It'll be kind of fun."

Rose nodded slowly. "I wondered how long it was going to take for you to tell me. Jennifer's sister is the bookkeeper at the mill, Grace. Did you think I wouldn't find out?"

Rose's voice took on a particular tenderness whenever she called her Grace.

Grace flushed and shrugged her shoulders.

Rose reached out and took Grace's hand. "If you aren't ready to get married, then going to the city and getting a job, that's a good option." Rose searched the young woman's face for a moment, then turned away to look out the window. The sauce was beginning to bubble and the kitchen was filling with smells of basil and oregano.

"I wanted to tell you, but it just felt so . . . final, I guess. Once I told you, then I'd have to go." Grace was surprised by a sudden sense of loss. These were just onion tears, weren't they? "My dad would have wanted me to stay."

Rose turned sharply back. She stood and walked over to place herself between Grace and the stove. "Now that's just silly. This isn't about what I think or what your parents would have thought. Sure, Warren loved this place. He would have stayed forever. Your momma? She always talked about going somewhere warm—somewhere where there were parrots." Rose smiled. "Now it's time for you to make your own decision."

Rose was the one person who ever mentioned Annie, and when she did there was always sadness in her voice. But rather than answering Grace's questions, Rose would always say things like, "Your momma was a sweet girl," or "Annie loved her baby girl." These references to her mother comforted Grace, and she sensed that by pushing Rose to tell her more she'd be causing her pain.

Grace had lost her mother before she was five years old. And just three years ago they'd buried her father in the town cemetery after a jagged stump of hemlock kicked back as he tried to wedge it into a straight fall. The remnant of that tree stood somewhere on this mountain, red and raw like a bloody sword. The unmistakable finality of her father's death had resurrected old memories of her mother's disappearance, and now as Grace yearned for some parental advice, she was heartened to think how well Rose had known Annie.

"Right. Momma loved parrots, didn't she? Maybe I should save my money and go somewhere tropical."

Rose shook her head and threw up her hands. "That wasn't what I meant, and you know it. Your mother was a daydreamer, but she loved Prosperity almost as much as she loved you. She never ever wanted to leave you." She shook her head as if to erase her next thought and then took Parrot's face in her hands and looked her square in the eyes. "Nobody can tell you what's best. All I know is whether you go or stay, Prosperity won't go back to the way it was. All this spotted owl rigmarole is changing us. That's what happens. We all change. You can't avoid it." Rose turned toward the stove, unable to stop herself from turning down the flame just a tad. "And, one more thing, young lady." She turned back to face Grace. "I think it's high time you started claiming your proper name. Grace is a beautiful name. And it doesn't come from some foolish bird book. You are Grace Tillman."

Grace smiled and put her arms around Rose. She'd never cut her ties to this woman, but that didn't mean she had to stay in Prosperity. Did it? The aroma of the sauce called her back to work. She began to mix the meat for the meatballs when the phone rang. Rose picked up the receiver.

"Hello, this is Rose Dyer. No, he's not home yet. Oh, yes?"

Grace let the sound of Rose's conversation fade into the background. Rose was right, this place was changing; it was useless to try and fight it. And she was ready to be Grace, even if no one else in this town would call her that.

A shift in Rose's voice got Grace's attention. She turned to see her Rose slump down in the chair as she said into the phone, "Thank you for calling, Doctor. I understand. I'll tell him right away." She hung up and the look on her face made Grace drop the knife from her hand and rush to her side.

"Rose, what's wrong?"

Rose stared at the phone. After a long moment she whispered, "You can't tell anyone. The town would panic."

"What, what are you talking about?"

"I mean it, "she shook her head. "You have to keep this a secret. He'd be furious if he knew I'd told you."

Grace nodded and sat down next to Rose, "OK, sure."

"It's been so hard to keep this to myself. He's been sick for a long time." Tears puddled behind Rose's glasses. "I keep trying to get him to talk about it, but you know how Jackson is."

A rope of fear knotted in Grace's stomach.

"Some of the guys may already suspect. He's been taking time off to go to Everett for tests." She stopped talking and sighed. She pulled a handkerchief from her pocket and began wiping her eyes. "Well, now there isn't much time left."

When Rose looked up, Grace recognized the all-too-familiar face of grief.

One day in the early fall, when Grace had gone up to the Dyers' to make dinner, Rose was sitting by the living room window looking out at the garden. In her hand was a black-framed photo of a baby.

"Hey, Rose, what's up?" As usual, Grace's adolescent exuberance bustled with her into the Dyers' home. But as soon as Rose looked up, Grace saw this wasn't a usual day. Rose's eyes held a sadness Grace had never seen in them before.

"Today is Jake's birthday," Rose said. "He would have been thirty years old." Rose and Jackson had had a son they'd named after his grandpa, Jake Oliver.

He had been just a baby when he got sick. The doctor told them to get Jake to the hospital. It was winter. The road down the mountain was bad. They probably shouldn't have even tried, Rose said.

"Maybe we could have kept him warm enough at home, maybe the fever would have broken." But they got out on the highway and there was black ice everywhere. Jackson could barely see through the thick snowfall. She held the sleeping baby on her lap and she felt him get hotter and hotter.

"Sometimes I can still feel that—his little body burning up. He cried so pitifully. I didn't know whether to unwrap him, it was so cold in the car." As she told the story, she continued to stare out the window. "Then he got quiet. I thought that was a good sign." She stopped talking. After a while she turned to Grace. "Oh, that was such a long time ago. I'm sorry. You go on and fix dinner, dear."

They never talked about Jake again. But Grace imagined it must all be coming back to her now.

Jackson was dying. Grace could barely allow herself this thought.

No more losses. She just couldn't take it. She couldn't imagine facing the empty hole of Jackson's absence.

As she put her arm around Rose and murmured comforting sounds, something inside Grace began to shut down. By the time she set the table and served the older couple their dinner—averting her eyes from Jackson's face, smiling with a forced cheer—she'd gone numb.

It was as if her home were disappearing beneath her, one person at a time. What was left to hold on to?

Chapter 3

May 30, 1991

A weird dream kept me tossing all night. I was a little kid, crying out for my mommy. There was a crowd of people and I knew Mommy was there, too, somewhere. I was in a forest of legs. I tugged at different pants and skirts. Some hands reached down and patted my head, but no one said anything to me. Garbled talking above my head. Couldn't understand a thing.

That feeling—not scared exactly, but lonely, confused, wanting my mother—that was real. I can't remember anyone ever sitting down with me and explaining what happened to my mother. People don't talk about death. Maybe it's just these people, just Prosperity—there are so many losses. Everyone grieves silently. A glass raised in memory or a hand on the widow's shoulder.

Rose doesn't want to talk about Jackson's illness. But it's all over her face.

(Here a sketch of a dead tree with a flock of parrots sitting in it; all around the perimeter of the page, the name "Grace" is written in various script.)

Grace jumped up gratefully when the phone interrupted her.

"I finally got a call back from the landlord about our place in Seattle—oh, I love saying that!" Shauna's voice practically bubbled out of the phone into Grace's ear. "He says we can move in Saturday! So, this is it. We need to know for sure. You're coming, right?"

Grace swallowed and nodded her head firmly. "Yes, Shauna. I'm doing it." The words were so simple, but as she said them the ground beneath Grace's feet seemed to vanish. "Shauna?"

"What?" Shauna's need to leave Prosperity was fueled by the daily sight of her own father, whose once-powerful hands had set choke, chaining the fallen timber so it could be hauled out of the woods. He'd lost the thumbs from both his hands and now was barely able to hold his beer. Shauna couldn't wait to put Prosperity behind her.

"Do you want me to come over and help you pack?"

Grace reached her hand out and leaned against the wall. She took a deep breath. "No. Thanks. I'll be ready on Saturday."

"Great! I promise you, you won't regret this. The place is so cute! You'll love it. I bet you'll be the first one to get a job with all your waitressing and cooking experience."

"We'll see. I'm just hoping folks in the city believe in tipping. See you Saturday." Grace hung up the phone.

Without giving herself another moment to think, she crammed the contents of her small dresser into the half-filled suitcases, not bothering to fold anything or even consider whether she needed it. She pulled her flannel shirts and jeans off their hooks and threw them on top. She slammed the cases shut, dragged them off her bed and set them by the front door.

The lack of business at the café didn't seem to upset Jane, and Grace wasn't sure what to make of that. Over the last weeks, her aunt had been almost as preoccupied as Grace herself. It was probably a good thing they hadn't been busy; only last week Jane had let three pies turn to cinders before she pulled them from the oven.

Grace was leaning on her elbows at the kitchen table when Jane came home. She'd been sitting there since late afternoon, memorizing the gouges and cup rings that embellished the massive plank her father had cut and sanded. It was now well after dark.

"Thought you'd come by the café for dinner." Jane sank into the old couch where the contours of her butt were clearly imprinted.

"Wasn't hungry." Grace's lips barely parted; her head didn't move. "I'm going to Seattle."

"So you say." Jane had heard this before.

"No, I mean it this time." Grace sat up and pushed her chair back, the legs scraping on the linoleum. "Moving on Saturday."

"'Bout time you figured it out." Jane closed her eyes and propped her feet on the coffee table. "What have I been telling you? This place is dying. You need to get away. Hell, *I* need to get away." And Grace knew it was true.

Since the moment she'd learned about Warren's accident, Jane's hatred of logging had consumed her. Nearly every day she had some sort of confrontation with one of the men she'd known all her life, men who had treated her like their own sister, men she'd gone through school with, even men she'd slept with. At first, they gave her room, ignored her verbal slaps in their faces. They knew how close she'd been to her brother. Hell, they felt his loss like a deep wound themselves. But time didn't seem to be mellowing Jane's rage.

Clett Tolfson, Shauna's dad, had confronted Grace one evening when she'd stopped by to see Shauna. "You tell your aunt she can't hope to make it without no loggers, Parrot. That's bullshit she's spouting. She needs to shut up or folks are going to forget who she is." This wasn't a surprise, but it stung just the same. She knew her aunt wouldn't care, but Grace never passed the message along.

"Hey, wait. I've got something I've been saving for you." Jane roused herself from the couch and began rummaging through the drawers in the kitchen. Grace felt a sudden chill.

"I think I'd had a one too many beers when I wrote this, but hey. Here it is." Triumphantly, she pulled a sheet of crumpled paper from the back of the junk drawer. "Your recommendation."

Grace felt her shoulders drop and realized she'd been holding her breath. How ridiculous. Annie'd been gone fourteen years. If her mom had left something for her, Grace would have found it long ago. And Warren had had little that wasn't already his daughter's. Anyway, Jane didn't have a sentimental bone in her body; she would never have kept something of Annie's all these years. What had she been thinking?

"You wrote me a recommendation? When?"

"Oh, I don't know. I was just playing around. Dreaming of the day we—by that I mean you—would move on." Jane handed Grace the paper and picked up a pack of cigarettes from the counter.

Grace A. Tillman has worked as a waitress and sous chef at the Hoot Owl Café in Prosperity, Washington, for __ years. This café is a venerable institution in the Cascade Mountains where connoisseurs of true American cuisine come from miles around for a fine meal. Grace has long been an essential part of the ambiance that makes the Hoot Owl an exceptional dining experience. Customers have regularly commented to the management that while they enjoy the food, it is Grace's inviting and courteous manner that brings them back. Any establishment where Grace works will be enriched by her presence.

Hire the girl. You won't be sorry!

"Jane! I never realized you knew so many big words. And you even used my proper name!" Grace laughed. "I especially like the last line. That's sure to get me a good job!"

"Like I said, I think I'd had a bit to drink that night." Jane grinned. "I left the number of years blank—I was hoping it wouldn't be more than five. But the rest is all true, isn't it? I especially like the 'venerable institution in the Cascade Mountains.'" She made quote marks in the air with the first two fingers of each hand and raised her nose to point toward the ceiling. "We serve 'true American cuisine,' don't we?"

She opened the refrigerator and pulled out two bottles of beer, handing one to Grace and with a heavy finality plopped herself into the chair opposite her niece. "Anyway, we did. I think we should drink to the damn Hoot Owl." She twisted off the beer cap and raised her bottle. "It's the end of an era. All wrapping up neat and tidy. I'm finally getting out of here and so are you. The Hoot Owl can just die a natural death. No tears for that one."

Grace stared at her aunt. She opened her mouth, but nothing came out.

"You OK?" Jane leaned across the table and looked closely into Grace's face. "Honestly, this can't be that big a surprise to you."

"I know. But if you go, and the Hoot Owl closes, what can I ever come home to?" Grace immediately regretted having let this slip out—it was too raw, too real. Too honest.

Jane leaned back in her chair and took a long swig from her beer. "Oh, hell, Parrot. This whole town is your home, your family. You know any time you show up, they'll throw a party. Not like me. Once I leave, they're going to seal up the entrance. They'll be so glad to see me gone, it'll be a town holiday. And, believe me, I ain't ever coming back. And, you might as well know, Sherrie Thomas is getting evicted from her house and that woman needs a break. Since there's no way I'm going to sell this place, she's going to move into your room as soon as you leave. I don't know, maybe she'll want to take on the café. But I doubt it. Once I get my shit together, though, I'm out of here and I'm renting this whole place to her."

So that was it. Grace was about to cross a threshold and once she was on the other side of it nothing would be the same. Ever. It was time to grow up. A twinge of panic raced through her.

"Wow." Grace walked into the kitchen and stared out the window into the trees.

"Come on, kid. Let's celebrate!" Jane called to her.

Grace turned back to her aunt and drank a deep swallow of her beer.

"Here's to Seattle!" Jane shouted.

"Bye, Momma. I'm sorry," Grace whispered to herself.

Grace woke early on Saturday. Her friends wouldn't be by to pick her up till noon. If Shauna had her way, they'd all be up, packed, and on the road by dawn. But Jenn, who slept fitfully, was not a morning person. The three friends had long ago reached a compromise that was uncomfortable for all of them but allowed them to be a trio—Shauna and Grace would wait, Jenn would hurry, and everyone would complain. This friendship may have looked odd from the outside, but without it none of them would have made it through high school.

Both Shauna and Grace had had serious boyfriends who had threatened to tug apart this feminine connection, but the three had forged a bond as children and annealed it in early adolescence through the fires of family tragedies and limited options.

Jane was already at the café. The hollowness of the house made Grace restless. She needed to walk. She grabbed her day-pack, always filled with a sketchbook and pencils, and went to take a last inventory of her hometown.

Folks moved away from Prosperity with some regularity, but newcomers rarely moved in. Houses, even empty ones, became stand-ins for the families whose lives unscrolled within them: the Nybergs; the Parkers; Mrs. Sammy and George; Paul and Fiona; Mary and the Kevins, senior and junior; Doc Janson.

When the Nybergs left, Mel Parker and his wife, Casey, tried to keep both their houses up for a while. "Can't let the whole street fall to ruin or none of us will ever be able to sell," Casey grumbled when Grace saw her mowing the Nybergs' lawn. But that didn't last long.

"It's hard enough keeping the forest from taking back your own yard," Mel had told Jane as he sat drinking coffee in the café and staring out at the gray mist.

George Sammy had to put his mother into a rest home down in Cooper when she started swearing at him and re-fusing to eat. He'd never been much for home maintenance and once his mom was gone, he didn't bother at all. The mo-torcycle he'd won in a poker game still leaned against the side of the house, its seat green with moss and blackberry vines winding through the spokes.

Doc Janson, who wasn't a real doctor but had trained as a medic in the war and could set your arm if you broke it in the woods, spent his time making chain-saw statues of bears and eagles. Not the artfully carved totems of the Makah or Tlingit—coastal Northwest Indians who used hand tools to carve myths from sacred cedar. Doc Janson yanked his Husqvarna into action and tried to make something out of the stub ends of trees he cut for Jackson. These splintered caricatures crowded his yard—the wilderness viewed through a fun-house mirror.

As she passed each house, Grace rehearsed this litany of the neighborhood. Taking much greater care than she had with her clothes, Grace gathered these belongings, these scraps of memory from each of the homes she knew so well and stuffed them down in the bottom of her bags. You never knew when you might need the comfort of George Sammy's rusted bike to get you through the strangeness of the city.

The trail climbed steeply through Jake Oliver's woods. After half a mile, it leveled for a stretch that ran snug along the side of a granite boulder, a giant piece of Ice Age litter. This was where she had felt the pain of her father's death settle deep inside her; the day after the funeral she and Jane had sat here together, each leaning against this cold stone, as they began to face life without Warren. This was where Grace had recognized the depth of the sibling bond between her father and her aunt.

In the fog of her grief, Jane had told Grace the rambling story of how, as a six-year-old, Jane had wandered alone into the thick dampness of this same forest. A curious child, Jane loved all those small, scurrying things—the chipmunks and mice, spiders and garter snakes, and especially the rummaging birds jabbering in the brown cedar bows that carpeted the floor of the woods.

It was a day like so many in her childhood, neither parent watching over her as she wandered among the trees. Creatures were twittering and scratching and Jane followed the chit-chit of one bird—the insistent, irritated, raspy one—that seemed to have something to tell her. She followed as it darted among the fallen leaves and detritus. The sun sparkled off bare

47

branches. She moved deep into the shadows before she started to feel cold, before she realized she was lost.

It was Warren, her big brother —only seven at the time— who missed her. And it was Warren, her hero, who tracked her childish whimpers into the darkening forest, and it was Warren, her only real guardian, who led her back home. No one registered her absence until he was gone too. Their mother lay in bed as always, calling for them.

"Daddy was in his usual drunken stupor, and when he couldn't find either one of us, he started in on Mom; he didn't need much of an excuse. By the time we crawled out from the trees, Dad's yelling and beating on Mom had roused the neighborhood and there were a lot of folks standing around calling our names."

As the Jane and Grace sat leaning against the boulder that day, Jane talked on and on about Warren. Grace had been a willing receptacle for her aunt's memories, yearning as she always had for pieces to the puzzle of her family.

"Your daddy should never have gone to Vietnam. He wasn't cut out for it and it changed him. Sure, he was tough, star of the football team and a logger, all that. But if anyone had encouraged him, he could have been a doctor or something.

"When I was a kid, I'd get carsick at the drop of a hat. Warren kept a handkerchief and a jar of water in the backseat of that old car we had. Our daddy would insist on driving us down the mountain on some drunken adventure and Warren would sit next to me, holding my hand. When I started to feel sick, he'd wet the handkerchief and put it on my forehead. Daddy wouldn't even stop the car."

"What happened to him in Vietnam?" Their shared grief made Grace bold. If she could keep Jane talking, maybe she'd finally learn why her father never spoke about Annie.

"Oh, same thing that happened to all those poor jerks who went over there. None of them should have gone. At least he came back in one piece. We were all grateful for that. And now, after all that, I just can't believe it was a goddamned tree that took him." Jane began to sob then, and the opening Grace had sensed slid closed on the flood of her aunt's tears.

Now, as Grace lowered herself to sit beneath the firs next to the boulder, she took her sketch pad from her back and began to draw. Over the next hour Grace filled the paper with a scattering of images: George Sammy's motorcycle, the trees around her, the boulder, but also a hand—rugged and strong, hinting of violence—and a small female figure with long flowing hair that covered her face.

When she got back to the house it was almost noon. Shauna's old pickup pulled up in front just as Grace opened the door. Shauna shouted to her from the cab, "There's some room near the tailgate. Throw your stuff back there. You said you didn't have much, so we took you at your word."

Jenn laughed and jumped out of the truck. "Don't listen to her. There's plenty of room. Give me that." Jenn, looking awkward in her thin-heeled sandals and sheer yellow dress, ran up the steps to grab a bag from Grace. "Can you believe it? We're finally getting the hell out of here."

Jenn swung Grace's bag up into the truck bed, betraying her attempt to look delicate and girly. Of the three of them, Jenn may have had the greatest need to get out of Prosperity. Confrontations with her alcoholic father had grown increasingly violent in the months since Warren's death. The two men had served together in Vietnam and Grace's dad had been the only one in town who could calm Glen Huff down when he was on a tear. Grace was afraid for Jenn and had more than once thought she'd rather have lost her father than have to endure what Jenn was faced with.

"Hold on just a sec," Grace called to her friends. "I need to say goodbye to Jane." At that moment, her aunt came out of the front door looking stricken, her face flushed. "Parrot, Rose is on the phone for you."

"What is it? I told her I'd call as soon as we got settled." Grace looked over her shoulder at her friends. "I just wanted to give you a hug, Jane. We've gotta go."

"I know. But you need to take this call. I'm sorry. It's important." Jane sighed. Her words came out heavy with disappointment. For a moment Grace stared at her aunt, bewildered.

"Oh no!" Grace's heart began to thud with dread. She took the two porch stairs in a single leap and dashed into the kitchen.

"Girls," Jane continued down the walkway toward the truck. "I'm afraid she won't be going with you, at least not today." She reached into the truck bed and pulled out Grace's bag.

Inside the house Grace stood holding the phone to her ear, her forehead pressed against the kitchen wall.

"He did what? Oh, Rose, I can't believe it. I'll be right there. I'm coming right now." She hung up the phone.

Jackson Dyer was dead.

Grace was bent over, a withering powerlessness engulfing her, when Shauna and Jenn came into the kitchen.

"Oh, my god. Jackson's dead? Shit. My folks are going to go nuts. This whole town is." Shauna grabbed Grace by the shoulders. "I know you loved him, but we can't let this stop us, Parrot. We can come back for the funeral, but we have to go now or we'll lose our place."

"Look," Jenn's words poured out in a panicked rush. "If Jackson is dead, we really need to get out of here before the shit hits the fan. This town is dead for sure now."

Grace shook her head. "I can't. Rose needs me." Tears were running down her face now. "Dammit," she whispered.

Shauna grunted. "Listen to me, Parrot. Rose a great lady, but you can't let this stop you from leaving. If you have to stay right now, stay until the funeral. We'll be back for that and we'll take you with us when we go back to the city. The next day. You hear me? Your room will be waiting." She bent down and pressed her forehead against Grace's. Then the three young women threw their arms around each other and hugged. Grace closed her eyes and tried to soak in the energy from her friends. She was going to need it.

Jenn broke away first.

"I'm so sorry, Parrot." Then she looked at Shauna. "We gotta go. My dad is going to use this as an excuse to stop me from going, I just know it. I can't stay."

"Yes. Go. I'll see you at the funeral."

Jane stood away from the group. At her feet were her niece's belongings. "Let's go," she said. "Rose is up there by herself."

Grace nodded, turned away from her friends. She grabbed her bags and threw them in the bedroom. "Yeah. Let's go."

When Grace and Jane arrived at Rose's house, they found her sitting on a stone bench at the back of the garden where an apple tree's newly sprouted leaves held individual drops of the previous night's rain suspended, like tears unwilling to fall.

Rose stared into those leaves, weariness coloring her face. Jane put her hand on Rose's shoulder. "I'm going in the house and clean things up, Rose. Parrot'll stay with you." Grace wrapped her arm around Rose and let her own tears flow. Rose held out her open palm to collect the droplets as a breeze passed through the branches of the tree.

"We planted this tree the spring after Jake died." She spoke without lifting her head. "Jackson loved its apples. Always said they were little Jake's gifts to us." She sat up straighter and turned to face Grace. "He refused to go through the pain, the slow dying. He didn't want me to have to watch that. There was nothing I could say."

Grace nodded silently. Everyone knew once Jackson had decided on a course of action, no one could talk him out of it. Rose sighed. "If he hadn't been so worried about the mill and all that, maybe he would have hung on. He kept up a good front, but he lost faith in himself."

Rose's words were inflected with doubt and confusion. "'Let the young guys figure it out,' he said. When I heard that, I knew he was done."

The two women sat silently until the stone's chill worked its way into their bones. "How did he . . .?" Grace asked, as they stood and headed back to the house.

"Oh, I should have known he wasn't taking those pain pills the doc kept prescribing. He never took pills, not even an aspirin. I just fooled myself. He must have stored them up somewhere." The exasperation in Rose's voice was heartening to Grace. "I hate to think about telling people."

"He was sick and there wasn't anything the doctors could do. That's all they need to know." Grace knew how the Prosperity telegraph worked, though, and how impossible it would be to keep the truth from getting out. Rose turned her eyes to

Grace's, searching for something. Apparently, whatever she'd feared or hoped to find wasn't there, and she turned away, taking Grace's hand. The two made their way up the steps to the front door.

"I called Kevin just after I called you. I guess Jackson told him about being sick. He didn't ask me any questions, just called the mortuary."

"The town is going to want some sort of funeral." Grace knew well how Prosperity honored its dead.

Rose sighed. "I know. But you know Jackson; never one for church.

"Rose was looking tired now and Grace opened the door and guided her to a chair."

Reverend Foster can do something at the cemetery. I'll take care of it." Grace heard the calm, efficient tone of her own voice, and stiffened. She had been a little girl when she first learned to turn off her own grief.

Someone had taken down the old wire gate that used to hang at an angle and needed to be lifted in order to get the rusty latch to catch. They'd cut down the tangle of blackberry vines. Outlining the void left where the gate had been was a clean metal arch that framed a view into the cemetery.

Since her father's death, Grace had rarely visited this spot, though the graveyard had been one of her favorite places as a child. She first saw it shortly after Annie died. She remembered how the gravestones looked like little houses from her childish perspective. "Is this a little town? Can I play here?" she'd asked Jane when they'd walked up the wooded trail to the old gate. It had taken awhile for Jane to explain that dead people slept under the ground here and that their names were carved in the stones. Grace could still feel the disappointment when her aunt told her, no, her Momma wasn't here.

"But this is where the angels live, isn't it? And Momma is an angel!" Grace remembered calling, "Momma, Momma!" and then thinking, "She's playing hide-and-seek. But she can see me!"

Today, the sun broke through the clouds, a thrush called from its hiding place in the cedar hedge, just as Grace stepped through the gate. Even as she walked Rose to Jackson's gravesite, Grace relived that first day in the cemetery and a temporary calm came over her. She still had the feeling her mother was here, somewhere, watching over her. There was no grave with Annie Tillman's name on it, but Grace had learned not to question this. Her father had responded with silence and had withdrawn into himself whenever anyone mentioned Annie's name; Grace had made that mistake rarely. Her own need to know what had happened to her mother had gradually dissolved beneath her need to show her loyalty and love for her father. Grace felt her mother's presence here in this grave-yard and that had been enough. Over the years Grace had had picnics on the cemetery grass and wove stories about the folks whose names she read on the markers. But since Warren was laid to rest here three years ago, the cemetery had become a place of sadness and confusion. Grace had avoided it.

Now a large crowd was beginning to gather around Jack-son's freshly dug grave. Several people were scattered among the headstones, paying their respects to others buried there. Grace turned to look down the row of graves to the clean, up-right stone that read, "Warren Tillman, 1950-1987."

"You go ahead, dear," Rose said, seeing the direction of Grace's gaze. "We won't start without you."

As Grace walked across the grass to where her father lay, she heard someone step up behind her.

"Thought you were going to escape this place, eh? No such luck." Grace recognized the voice immediately.

"Hi, Patrick." They hadn't spoken since she refused to show him the owl nest.

"You've got another chance to do the right thing." He'd stepped up close to her, the way he used to when he was preparing to give her a kiss. She looked away.

"Parrot!" Shauna and Jenn approached the couple, and Pat stepped back.

"You know you want to be on the right side of this, Parrot," he said as he turned and walked away.

Shauna threw her arms around Grace and whispered, "What the hell was that about? You really need to get out of here, if he's still after you!"

Grace smiled and returned her hug. "First time I've talked to him since we broke up. No worries. Tell me, is it great?"

Jenn nudged her way into the hug. "Are you packed? We're going back tonight. I'm afraid to stay any longer."

Grace nodded. "I actually never unpacked. But I don't know about leaving tonight. Rose might need—"

"What did I tell you, Parrot? She's got lots of support. You can't let this stop you, and we *have* to leave tonight." As Shauna said this, Grace looked at the faces of her two friends and she knew she they were right. Rose would manage.

"OK. I'll talk to you after this is over. Rose is waiting." She turned her head toward her father's grave and silently promised him she'd be back. Then she returned to Rose's side.

During the service, Grace held the widow's shaky hand and looked at the pale faces around her. The lives of everyone here—everyone in town—were knotted up with the fate of the mill. Grace saw their blank, staring eyes and their shoulders slumped with grief—and something that looked more like fear. Not one of them had known Jackson was ill. Rose may have thought she could prevent panic by keeping it a secret, but Grace now saw how wrong that choice had been. This was a town in shock.

Everyone knew how hard Jackson had been working to keep the mill alive. With the logging restrictions, the mill hadn't been able to fulfill a couple of big contracts and it had cost them. The word got out—Dyer's Mill couldn't be counted on. Their customers had quickly turned to other sources. There was little loyalty these days. Even Grace knew how Jackson had worried over their best customer, a Japanese firm that bought nearly all their cedar. If that firm pulled out, there was no point in keeping the mill open. But they hadn't. No one was sure how Jackson had pulled it off.

Now what was going to happen? Rose wasn't prepared to run the mill.

As they lowered Jackson's body into the earth, Clett Tolfson mumbled, "You was good to us, Jackson." Everyone knew the story. After Clett's accident, Jackson made sure the Tolfsons had enough money to keep their house and then he fought with the insurance company to get Clett the treatment he needed. Shauna stood between her parents. Her mother nodded. "He was a good man."

The crowd pressed close, gathering their communal strength. Grace felt the warmth of a body behind her, then a tug on her shirt, "You didn't go." Kev's loud, unmodulated voice rang through the hush.

Grace smiled and reached her free hand back to the boy. "Not yet, Kev," she whispered. Dammit, she hadn't prepared him. When he walked into the café tomorrow morning and she wasn't there, he'd be distraught. She'd have to talk to Mary and Kevin, let them know that she was going to abandon Kev, just like Jackson abandoned this whole town.

A wave of anger spread through her. Why had Jackson insisted on keeping his illness a secret? *Why didn't he prepare us?* In her head Grace composed a eulogy of her own. *Jackson Dyer may have been a good guy, even a good boss, but in the end, he let you all down. He knew he was sick and he could have told you, helped you prepare. This didn't have to be another sudden loss. He didn't need to leave you all in shock. In the end he abandoned all of us.*

Dammit, Jackson! You knew this town was dependent on your mill. How could you be so irresponsible? We loved you. You can't just disappear.

Rose reached across and put her free hand on Grace's arm. "I'm OK, Grace. You can let go."

Grace looked down to see her own hand squeezing Rose's so tightly that the older woman's fingers had turned white. She felt her face flush and she released her grip. "Sorry," she whispered. Rose nodded and returned her gaze to the grave.

Grace took a deep breath and stepped back to let Rose say her private goodbyes. Kev grinned up at her. "You didn't go. I said, 'maybe, maybe not.' And it was maybe not."

"But Kev, I *am* going. I'm leaving tonight." The tears she hadn't cried for Jackson were now welling up in her eyes.

Kev refused to listen. "Maybe, maybe not," he sang and turned away. "I'm going home now." And he shuffled over to where Mary stood waiting for him.

Before Grace could collect herself, she felt a hand on her shoulder and turned to see Henry Martin standing behind her. "He was a great guy. We're going to miss him," Henry said.

"Yeah," Grace agreed. She motioned Henry over to stand with her away from the crowd. Henry was younger than her father, but the two men had had each other's backs in the woods. Grace knew Henry as a reliable friend, one she trusted to be honest with her. "What's going to happen with the mill, though? Rose can't run it. This town is screwed!" She tried to keep her voice down.

"Oh, Jackson took care of that. I mean, sure, these are bad times. But Jackson set things up awhile ago. Rose doesn't have to worry." He was so sanguine about it Grace was caught off guard.

"What?" she blurted, more loudly than she intended.

Henry's answer was interrupted by Shauna, who came up to them and motioned to Grace. "I think Rose might be ready to leave." She gestured toward where the older woman stood surrounded by the whole town.

Grace saw the overwhelmed look on Rose's face.

"Oh, no!"

She rushed to Rose's side and managed to extricate the widow from the crowd of sympathizers. "They loved Jackson. They don't know what to do with their grief," Rose said as she stuffed a crumpled tissue into her pocket. "None of us do, I guess."

Grace took hold of Rose's arm and guided her back to the truck.

"Well, you don't have to take care of them. At least not today and not all at once. Right?" Grace loved that about Rose. The older woman always saw the good intentions beneath people's sometimes not-so-good behavior.

As soon as they were settled in the truck, Rose put her hand on Grace's knee. "Grace, I need to talk with you."

Grace tensed. *If she asks me to stay*, she thought, *how can I say no?*

"Jackson left something for you. It's his gift and he hoped it would make your life easier, not more complicated. We talked about it when he was preparing his will. I told him it might be more of a burden for you than a benefit, but he was adamant." Rose paused.

Grace let out a sigh. She was relieved that Rose wasn't asking her to stay, but after all her angry thoughts about Jackson, learning he'd left something sent a wave of guilt through her.

"He left you Jake's old cabin."

Grace felt the blood drain from her face.

Rose searched Grace's face, as if looking for reassurance. "You know that old place was always a bit of a thorn in Jackson's side. He'd wanted to tear it down so he could expand the mill."

"What do you mean, he left it to me?"

"He wanted you to have your own place. Some place in Prosperity you could always call home and come back to if you ever left. Since the cabin can't be torn down by the stipulations of Jake's will, he had two choices. He could leave it to someone who would value it and preserve it, or he could give it to the Parks Department and let them turn it into a museum. Jackson was always one to choose life over—" Rose went silent and pulled back from Grace, stiffening.

"Grace, just make it live again. There's enough money in the bequest for you to make that place livable. It'll take a while for all the legal falderal, but it's yours. Stay here long enough to bring it back to life, and then go if you still want to." The widow now opened her purse and pulled a key from its depths. She handed it to Grace. "Do that for me. Will you, dear?"

The key lay innocently in Grace's open palm. As she folded her fingers over it, Grace felt her heart open. Dear, stubborn Jackson. How could she say no to this? A home of her own. It didn't mean she had to stay in Prosperity, just fix it up a bit like Rose asked and then go. But she'd always have a place to come back to, a place where she could keep Annie's memory alive. How could she have been angry with him? He hadn't abandoned the town, and he hadn't abandoned her. "Of course." Then she clenched her fist around the key and whispered, "Thank you."

Grace had fantasized about what it would be like to live in Jake's old cabin since she was a little kid. It was right next door to the sawmill. You could see it from the schoolyard. She'd passed it hundreds of times when she went to meet her father at the end of the day. Other kids had told stories about it being haunted, but she'd always thought of it as a magical place and dreamed of the fantastical creatures that lived inside. Jackson kept a huge, forbidding lock hanging from a thick chain strung across the door.

Jackson.

Grace caught her breath, "Rose, did you know that Jackson had made some sort of arrangements for the mill in case he died?"

Rose looked over at her. "Of course he did. He started turning the whole business over to the crew, well, I guess it was a year or more ago. I wasn't so sure about it at first, but he knew what he was doing." Rose took a deep breath. "I think I'd like to be alone now. Can you just take me home?"

"Yes, yes." Grace's hand shook as turned on the ignition and put the car in gear. She kept her eyes on the road and lifted her left arm to her cheek to wipe the tears as she drove away from the cemetery.

Chapter 4

The truck's tires sent gravel ricocheting off the trees as Grace and Rose wound their way up the road to the Dyer home. It was a striking house, alone in the only clearing in Jake's preserve. The terms of Jake's will allowed his grandson to cut enough trees to make space for one house, but that was the only exception to the logging prohibition. Jackson had used the old-growth timber to make a home with the rustic look of a cottage, but large enough for the family he'd hoped to raise there.

Rose had begged Jackson to push the edge of the forest as far from the house as the restrictions would allow so she could plant the flowers that brought her joy. It had been a challenge to place the plants precisely where they could benefit from the scarce sunlight.

Over the years Rose's garden had developed its own blooming schedule that differed from the houses farther down the mountain. In the heart of Prosperity, the pale tips of daffodil and tulip buds promised to burst any day into shocking color. In Rose's garden, trees were just beginning to leaf out. Ice still caked the edges of dark flowerbeds and small mounds of snow still owned the shadows.

"Thank you. I'll be fine now," she said as Grace helped her out of the truck.

Grace nodded and leaned in to kiss Rose on the cheek. "I'll come by tomorrow with some food."

"No, no. Please, no." Rose waved a dismissive hand and turned to walk up the path to her front door. "I've more than enough food. Casseroles I'll never touch, soups, breads. The women have taken care of all that. Just leave me be, dear. I'll be fine." She looked back at Grace. "Take care of that cabin," she said firmly. Then Rose got out of the car, went in to her house and shut the door.

The click of the lock.

Grace let her shoulders droop and she leaned her head against the steering wheel. The reality of her situation was setting in. *Dammit.* That cabin was going to take weeks to fix up. How long could she expect Shauna and Jen to keep her room open? She sighed and turned the truck around and headed back to Jane's.

She'd dressed in a dark skirt and sweater for the funeral and, as usual, these clothes made her feel awkward and uncomfortable. Grace grimaced recalling the six-inch heels and miniskirts Shauna had foreseen for her. At least she could put that off for a while.

As soon as she got back to Jane's, Grace ran to the bedroom, kicked her pumps into the corner and started to pull off her skirt. Jane stood in the doorway looking puzzled.

"How's Rose doing? I thought you'd stay at her place for a few nights."

"No, she wants to be by herself. She was really clear about that." Grace grinned. "I won't be here long, though."

"Right," Jane nodded. "Shauna called and said they'd be by around eight."

"Um. Jane?" Grace took a deep breath letting her skirt drop to the floor and stepping out of it. "I'm not going to Seattle. At least not for a while."

"You're not going to Seattle? You're not moving in with Pat after all? I saw you two talking at the funeral." Jane shook her head in disbelief. "Damn it, Grace, how dumb can you be?"

Grace laughed, "Well, not that dumb, apparently." She realized in that moment that Jackson must not have expected her to marry Pat or he wouldn't have given her the cabin. Or at least he'd wanted her to have an option. "I am now the owner of my own place." Grace stood tall and straight and skirt-less before her aunt. "Jackson left me the old cabin."

"You've got to be kidding." Jane sank down onto Grace's bed.

Ignoring her aunt's deflated tone, Grace dug her jeans out of her suitcase and pulled them on.

"He left me the money to fix it up too. Rose practically begged me to stay and make it livable."

"God damn Rose and Jackson!" Jane pounded her fists on her knees. "Just when I really thought you were going to get yourself out of this shit hole!"

The ferocity of Jane's reaction jolted Grace. "It should be a relief to you. You won't have to put up with me anymore. No worry that I'll come bouncing back to you."

Jane jumped up from the bed and stomped out of the room. In the hallway, she stopped and called over her shoulder. "All I can say is, those Dyers have tied a huge boulder around your neck. You're going to have to handle it by yourself. I won't let Prosperity reach its claws out and drag *me* back in."

Grace leaned against her doorframe. "Don't worry, I'm not asking you to stay." She hadn't expected Jane to jump for joy, but she didn't anticipate such a furious reaction. "What difference does it make to you where I go, as long as I'm out of your house?"

Jane looked her niece up and down. "This town is worse than a dead end. You've got talent. You could do something with yourself in the city."

Once again, hearing Jane insult Prosperity triggered a flare of resistance in Grace. She was suddenly grateful to Jackson.

"I can do something with myself right here." Grace wasn't exactly sure what she meant by this, but suddenly she began to feel excited. "All I was going to do in Seattle was get another waitressing job anyway. You said so yourself!"

"OK, Parrot. Nothin' I can do to change what you think. It's your life. You'd never listen to me anyway." She slapped the wall with the flat of her hand—a gesture that combined celebration and frustration. "Good enough, then. I'm outta here. Sherrie's ready to move in and I need the money. She just laughed at me when I offered to let her take over the Hoot Owl, so I'm cutting my losses and shutting it down."

Grace's thoughts started circling around the hole that had suddenly opened before her. If Jane closed the café, what was she going to do for money once Jackson's bequest was used up? Sure, she could paint, but she'd never be able to support herself that way. The Hoot Owl was the only place she'd ever worked. But she'd be damned if she'd let Jane see her panic.

"I'll only be here until I can get the cabin fixed up." Grace threw her words at her aunt, hoping they'd land with a sting. "Go ahead. Leave. Shut up the café. I'll be just fine. "

"You talk that over with Sherrie, but I know she's not going to want you here long. She needs a steady rent-paying roommate. You were supposed to be living in Seattle, remember? She's moving in on Monday. That's only two days away." Jane's hands were clenched into balls balanced on her hips, elbows sharp, feet apart. It was a position that didn't offer a hint of negotiating room.

Grace pushed past Jane and strode into the kitchen. She grabbed the telephone receiver and dialed Shauna's house.

"You guys are going to have to leave without me. No, I just can't, Shauna." She forced her words out, knowing Jane could hear, and knowing Shauna would be furious. "I'm still coming down to Seattle, but I've got to stay here awhile longer. Jackson left me the old cabin and I have to stay till I can fix up the place. I owe it to Rose."

Jane walked past, smirking and shaking her head.

"Look, I gotta go. I'll give you a call in a few days." She hung up the phone and walked out without a word more to her aunt.

Grace had never been inside the cabin. As a child, she dismissed the stories of ghosts, but now, holding the key in her hand, fear welled up. For a brief moment she wished Patrick were with her. Then, as if to chide herself for such weakening, she jammed the key into the lock and twisted, forcing the rusted mechanism to yield. She grabbed the metal body and yanked it down. The chain dropped away and before she could hesitate again, the door swung open.

In the moments it took for her eyes to adjust to the blackness, Grace recognized the odor of abandonment. In Prosperity's climate wet, rot, and mold saturated anything left standing for long, yet this cabin smelled of dryness, dust, and, most of all, of loneliness. Grace stepped back and took a gulp of the outside air and then turned on her flashlight. It was a gray afternoon and the cabin's small windows had long ago been boarded up. A thick tangle of cobwebs decorated the interior.

Grace pulled her father's tattered Peterbilt cap from her back pocket and tucked her hair under it. Then she pulled on gloves, just in case. As she stepped inside she felt like a spelunker, but one who owned the cave. This was hers—spiders, daunting darkness, disheartening smell, and all. Gingerly, she scanned the floor with the flashlight: a few sow bugs moving slowly out of the light beam, mouse droppings all along the baseboards, thick webs masking the corners. She lifted the light to inspect the log walls. Massive tree trunks stacked one on another, the lower ones smoothed, waxy looking. Silence. No ghosts, no monsters, no magical creatures. Only a home full of emptiness. Waiting.

Jake Oliver had built the original one-room cabin before the turn of the century. The walls were formed of the unmilled trees, raw cylinders pegged to rest securely on one another, insulated with crumbling mortar. More than ninety years later, the place felt solid. Surely someone had replaced the roof at one point, because if it leaked, there was no evidence of it.

Jake and his wife had lived there for nearly forty years. Grace could see the alterations he'd made to accommodate his family and those few items of modernity he deemed worthwhile. At the far end of the space, which appeared to Grace to be about the same size as the living room in Jane's small house, stood a stone fireplace. There were a couple of wires attached to the ceiling with small white porcelain tubes. She followed the length of this ancient electrical wiring till it disappeared where the ceiling and wall met. In the wall to her left, next to a small window, was an opening that led down a step to another door—the passage old Jake and his family had originally used to reach the outhouse, long since demolished.

Grace leaned against this door, tight in its frame. It didn't budge. She backed up and kicked at it with her booted foot. She pulled back and gave another, more ferocious kick, and with that it swung open to reveal a tiny space that brought the term "water closet" to mind. The room seemed embarrassed by its own necessity. There were a seatless toilet and tiny sink, both mottled with rust stains. Grace turned the tap. Nothing. Of course, the water must have been shut off long ago.

She turned back into the main room and cast her light around. What did they do for a kitchen? There were shelves next to the fireplace and a small wooden table with a surface that looked more like a chopping block than a place to eat. The floor, made of wide planks of thick pine, was smooth and rutted from use; dark scars, shadows of ghost furniture, marked where a chair and a bed had rested.

Grace stood in front of the fireplace. She slipped out of her boots, and slid her feet into two small depressions in the floor. An image filled her mind of a small, dark-skinned woman kneeling as she fed the fire. Jake's wife, rumored to have been a Snohomish Indian, probably used this fireplace for cooking. As Grace stood there, she was filled with a soft, sweet sensation. In all its barrenness, this shelter embraced and welcomed her. She shone the light on the walls—something in this old place was calling to her, something she'd never expected to find in Prosperity. This cabin offered itself as a canvas; it begged for color, for animation, for an artist's touch.

Grace swallowed hard. Her mind began to spin with images; her fingers itched to grab her paints. But there was so much to do. She couldn't just scrub it down and move in. She prided herself on being low-maintenance, as Pat had once said. But she did need a kitchen and a working bathroom if she were really going to live here.

She needed Walt deVore.

When he wasn't drinking, Walt could fix anything. Before Grace was born, Walt had been Jackson's right-hand man around the mill, working on engines and keeping the equipment and the log trucks in good shape. Jane still hired him whenever she had plumbing problems at the café and he'd take care of everything. He often worked off his bar bill by putting up shelves and helping keep the Bullhook in shape.

Walt liked to tease Grace, reminding her how he changed her diapers and rocked her to sleep. "I knew you when, kiddo," he'd say whenever she talked about moving to the city. "You're a Prosperity girl through and through." He did know her well.

She knew him, too. Her earliest memories of Walt were of a man slumped over on the bench outside of the tavern. She'd been about ten or so when her dad had told her Walt's story.

"You know, Parrot, each of us can only be responsible for so much in this world—things are going to happen that you just can't control."

Everyone in town knew what a great mechanic Walt was—he'd started fixing cars when he was in high school—so they were pleased when Jackson hired him to maintain the milling equipment and keep the trucks in good repair. Those giant haulers were built to withstand abuse, but as with any machines, things would go wrong. Walt could hear a noise in an engine or feel the resistance of a brake pedal and know just how to fix it. The drivers relied on him.

About the same time Jackson hired Walt, he also took on a guy to handle the books: Nathan Roberge. Warren spat whenever he said that name and there was a tone in his voice that scared Grace and warned her not to ask questions.

As Warren told it, Nathan didn't appreciate how essential Walt's work was. Things were pretty busy at the mill back then and there were days when Walt couldn't get to all the trucks as fast as he wanted to. When he went to Jackson and told him he needed to hire another mechanic, Jackson said it was a matter of affording it. He told Walt to talk with Nathan.

"I can just imagine how that bastard responded." Warren couldn't contain his bitterness, even in Grace's presence. "Bottom line was all that mattered to him. So, of course he said, 'no way.'"

That left Walt trying to keep up. And he did—until one day he couldn't.

According to Warren, Russell Thomas was a really good truck driver and a nice guy, liked by everybody. Like most of the drivers who worked for Jackson, Russ left his truck in the maintenance yard every few months for Walt to go over.

At the end of one long day, Warren had hitched a ride down the mountain with Russ. Tired, Warren closed his eyes, resting as Russ drove. When he woke up, they were in the maintenance yard and Russ was calling out to Walt, "Somethin's not right with the brakes. I was getting a bit of a pull to the right comin' down just now. Can you take a look at her before tomorrow?"

Walt came out and shook his head. "Don't know. I'm mighty busy with this skidder that broke down. You got to drive it tomorrow?"

"Yeah, well, she drives all right enough. They got some loads for me not too far up the mountain tomorrow. I think I can manage with her. Maybe you can take a look at the end of the week."

"You sure, Russ? Maybe someone else can handle your loads. I could get to her by tomorrow afternoon most likely."

"Naw, it's not a big deal. I just hit some good rocks the other day, might not even be the brakes. My luck it's probably the whole damn front end. But she'll make a few more runs. I'll keep her light. Don't worry about it. I'll bring her in on Friday."

As Warren told the story to Parrot, Walt even tried to talk Russ out of that plan. He'd grabbed the bar on the door of Russ's cab and hoisted himself up to look Russ in the eye. "I don't like the sound of anything wrong with the brakes," he said. "I'd put the skidder aside and take care of you, but Nathan has his eye on me. Wants that skidder back on the mountain soon as possible." Warren never forgot those words.

Or the fact that Russ's son, Jeremy, demanded to ride with his dad on this seventh birthday the next day.

Years later, long after her pain had become a chronic ache and the insurance money had dried up, Sherrie, Jeremy's mom, filled Parrot in on some details of the story when they both worked at the café.

One day after she'd taken a plate of food across the street to where Walt was lying on his bench, Sherrie had given Grace her version of the story: Russ had promised to let their son ride with him in the truck on his birthday, she said. Of course, Jeremy was all excited about it. He'd insisted Sherrie pack two extra-big lunches the night before.

"He was going to spend the day with his Dad and there was nothing in the world that could have made him happier." Sherrie smiled at the memory.

Russ had forgotten about his promise. But Sherrie wasn't about to let him disappoint their son. If the truck was in good enough shape for Russ to keep hauling, Jeremy deserved his ride. Russ relented. "The truck can handle light runs. I'll take him."

"I sent them off without a second thought," Sherrie said. "The kid was so proud and happy. I'll always remember that grin on his face." Sherrie sighed and sat down at the café counter next to Grace. "You know men by now, honey. Something gets in them when they're doing a job and they can't help themselves: they gotta keep up. Anyway, Russ must have decided to add a little more weight on that last run. Everything probably looked good."

"Your dad came to me after the accident," Sherrie told Grace. "He told me he and Henry had followed Russ's truck down the mountain. He saw the whole thing. Called it in." Sherrie stared down at the dingy countertop. "Took me a long time before I could ask him just what happened.

"For some reason, Russ took the first steep curve down from the landing a little too fast. Maybe it was those brakes. Who knows? His right front tire slipped and got caught in the ditch. Warren said he must have pulled the wheel a bit too hard to the left and overcorrected." Sherrie's voice took on a hypnotic quality, as if she were in a trance. "The truck rolled two-and-a-half times before it came to rest on its side down at the bottom of the mountain. I've got this thing in my head, like I was there or something—I can hear the awful sound of the truck turning over, the logs sliding out of the binders, the wheels bouncing off the boulders, the crash of metal as it landed. Jeremy bled to death before the aid car got there, you know. Russ never came to. He died a week later in the hospital. That was a blessing at least. He'd never have been able to live with himself."

Walt had trouble living with himself, too. After Russ and Jeremy died, he stopped going to work. His sister Marcia in Seattle came up and took him down to live with her and her son, Charlie.

"You remember that kid, Parrot? He used to hang around the café waiting for his dad. You were just a toddler and he was a teenager, but he put up with you." Grace had a faint memory of some boy who asked her if her name she meant could fly, but nothing more. She shook her head, impatient to hear what happened to Walt in Seattle. "Anyone could tell you Walt's not a city guy." Sherrie shrugged. "He was back in Prosperity a couple of years later, but he never held a steady job again."

By the time Grace was old enough to have a conversation with him, Walt spent most of his time keeping a barstool warm.

Now that she'd been inside the cabin, Grace decided the lock and chain were unnecessary, so she pocketed the key and headed to the café.

Kev was at his table by the window. When Grace walked in, he started bouncing on his seat and called out to her, "You didn't go to the city like you said. You're here!"

"Hey, Kev. Well, there's been a change of plans. Looks like I'll be staying for a while."

Ignoring her aunt's raised eyebrows, Grace reached across the counter and filled a cup with black coffee.

"Good morning," Jane offered.

Grace looked at her aunt without responding. They hadn't spoken since throwing verbal jabs in the hallway the day before and Grace didn't want to open the door to another round of the battle over staying or leaving Prosperity.

"Shauna called last night and left this number. She sounded pretty damn happy." Jane held out a scrap of paper.

"Thanks," Grace mumbled and pocketed the paper; even her friend's excitement about the city wasn't going to make her question her decision.

Walt was right where she knew he'd be—sitting on the sagging bench outside the Bullhook. Carrying the cup Grace headed for the door and stopped at Kev's table. "I gotta take this to Walt over there." She lifted her chin to indicate the man across the street. "I'll see you later."

"Ha!" Kev grinned, "I said 'maybe, maybe not!' Ha!"

"Yes, you did, Kev." Grace smiled at the boy.

She heard Jane's gruff, "humph," as she opened the door. At least Kev was happy she was staying. Walt would be too. And Jackson's money would keep her alive for a while.

Grace crossed the empty street and sat on the bench next to Walt. "Have you had your coffee yet?"

He squinted at her through tired eyes and reached out for the cup. "How's Rose? You takin' care of her?"

"Oh," Grace exhaled slowly. She'd nearly forgotten that the whole project with the cabin was tied to enormous loss. "She seems to be managing. Wants to be alone now, so I left her at the house."

"Yeah, she would," Walt sipped the dark brew and looked appraisingly at the young woman, who obviously had more on her mind. "You going to the big city soon, then?"

Grace leaned toward him. "No. Something amazing has happened. I'm staying, at least for a while." She watched him slowly drink his coffee and gather himself. "Guess what?"

"You're gonna get married after all, then? Well . . ." Just like Jane, Walt couldn't imagine any other reason for her to stay in Prosperity.

"No. No!" Grace was impatient now, and irritated. No one thought of her as capable of being truly independent—if she wasn't going to go to Seattle with her girlfriends, it *must* be because she was staying to live with Pat. Well, at least Jackson had given her more credit than that. This thought stabbed a knife into the shield separating her from her grief. She shivered and clenched her fist.

"I'm not getting married. I'm not living with Pat or with anyone else. Not even Jane." Walt's eyes widened. "I've got my own place! "

He looked down into the cup and tipped his head back to take a final swallow. Then he looked at her. "What are you saying?"

"Jackson . . ." Her throat tightened around his name. She forced a cough and continued. "He left me the old cabin by the mill." Grace reached in her pocket and produced the key; she held it up for him to see.

He tilted his head. "Really? That place livable?"

"Well, it needs a little work. I thought you might want to help me out. He left me some money, too, so I can pay you." She couldn't sit still any longer and started bouncing as if she were imitating Kev. She'd managed to tuck her grief away, and now excitement spilled from her.

"Well, isn't that the best yet?" Walt grinned. "Good ol' Jackson, figured out a way to keep you around and make you happy about it. That's just gotta be the best yet." He reached out and pounded her on the back.

"So, you want a job? There's a lot to do." Grace settled herself and tried to make her tone business-like: "You'd have to give up the booze for the duration." She knew how this went with Walt. When he had a chance to work, if the responsibility weren't too high, he'd throw himself into it and stay sober. Till the job was done.

He winked at her and gave a small nod. "I could probably manage."

"And you gotta promise me you won't let anybody see the inside till it's done. Especially Rose. I don't want her to see it till I'm finished."

"What you gonna do, Grace? Paint it pink and fill it with flying elephants?"

Walt, one of the few folks in town who liked to use her given name, was no art appreciator. Grace had learned early on not to expect any praise for her painting from this guy.

"Something like that. Right now, though, I just need a place to live."

"OK. I'll see what I can do." Walt put the cup down on the bench.

She grasped his slightly shaky hand in hers and shook it. "Are you ready?"

He wiped his other hand over his face and stretched his legs out in front of him. Then he shook himself and stood. "All right. Let's take a look at this place."

As Walt investigated, taking in the antique wiring, she explained her vision for a small galley kitchen just to the right of the front door—a simple stove, sink, refrigerator, and a few cupboards. She could do a lot with a little. Most of the space would stay a single open room where she'd have a table and maybe a couch or a couple of chairs in front of the fireplace. She'd need lights and a telephone.

"I'll sleep up there." She pointed to the narrow loft space that she hadn't actually seen yet. "I suppose I'll need a ladder."

Walt's eyebrows rose and he pursed his lips. "Guess so."

"The bathroom isn't bad," she said as she pushed open the door to the tiny space. "Needs new fixtures and a light. A shower would be nice."

"You got simple tastes if you call this 'not bad,' girl." Walt shook his head and gave a low whistle. "Jackson complained how his grandpa lived in this place. With nothing. Coulda afforded it fine, he was just a miser. Look at this wiring, Parrot. It's a miracle he didn't burn the place down. We gotta bring more power in here. You want a stove, a refrigerator? You'll need a two-twenty. I can do that, but it'll take a few bucks." He peered under the sink. "The plumbing's probably shot—you'll want to hook up to the town sewer; this thing was probably on an old septic somewheres." He stood up and faced her, "I can manage this. Take me awhile. Might need a bit of help. But if you got the money, there's plenty of guys who need the work."

"I'm leaving it up to you, Walt. But I plan to get this place cleaned up as soon as I can and start sleeping here. You'll have to work around me."

Grace had been stomping down the webs in the corners as they talked. Now she pulled a rag from her back pocket. She made a single swipe across one windowsill and the rag was black with thick dust.

"I've got to fill this bucket," she picked up a pail she'd found under the bathroom sink. "I'll be back."

The closest source of water was the outdoor spigot in the mill yard. While Walt continued with his inspection, she walked over and managed to fill the bucket before Patrick caught sight of her.

"What the hell, Parrot?" He stuck his head out of the office door. It was startling to see him there in shirtsleeves. It had never occurred to her that Pat might work in the office instead of out in the woods.

If she'd done what Prosperity expected, Grace would have married Pat as soon as they graduated and she'd be pregnant by now. But when he'd told her his big plan for keeping the mill going and demanded her help, everything had changed. She'd broken her promise to her father only once in her life when she'd told Pat about the owl's nest. But when he pushed her to show him where it was, Grace couldn't go that far; her refusal had meant the end of their relationship.

"Hey. I just need some water." Who was she kidding? She'd never be able to keep this project a secret. "I'm moving into the old cabin. Need to clean it up a bit first."

"Oh, yeah?" Pat stepped out of the office. Blinking in the sunlight, he stood looking at her. "Plannin' on sharin' it with the ghosts?"

"Hmm." She hoped she looked less rattled than she felt. She had to stop herself from thinking about all the things they'd promised each other and how much she'd loved him. He was a stubborn idiot. He was fighting to keep things from changing and that was just stupid. Everything changed.

"Thanks for the water. I'll need a bit more. Later." She lifted the bucket. "Oh, and I might need to use your Por-ta-Potty occasionally," and she walked out of the yard, leaving him staring after her.

Chapter 5

Once he got a good look at things, Walt realized he could handle the wiring by himself. He showed her where Jackson had begun the process, back when he thought he might use the place as part of the mill. That was before, when the mill was going strong.

Walt would need to disconnect the old fuse box, so the brittle knob and tube could be pulled. He could see where Jackson had planned to connect a circuit breaker box and pull in more power from the mill. He'd have to get some conduit to shield the wires, run them along the edges of the walls—wouldn't want to cut into those logs. The job had to be done right if Grace was going to live there.

The next morning he took a shot of whiskey to settle his hands, filled a thermos with coffee, and took his tools over to the cabin. Grace met him at her door with a bright smile. "Good morning! I didn't think you'd get here so early. This is great! You'll finish the job in no time at this rate."

The energy she emitted nearly bowled Walt over. He took a step back.

"Whoa. Hold your horses, there, kiddo. First things first." He stepped inside the cabin and put his tools down. Grace had taken a crowbar and pried the wooden boards off the windows.

The glass was undamaged and with a little scouring they let in a surprising amount of daylight.

"Can't do anything on the wiring until we get the power company to send a guy out. Once he gets here, we should be able to get you wired in a day or two."

"Can you work on the plumbing in the meantime?"

Grace's shoulders dropped and a whiny deflation crept into her voice. "Getting someone from Mountain Power to come up to Prosperity'll take forever."

"Oh, not necessarily. I know a guy. He owes me. Would probably work off the clock if I asked him to." Matter-of-fact. "Meanwhile, I gotta pull all these old wires anyway." Walt took in the changes that had happened since yesterday. "You sleep here last night?"

Grace's sleeping bag and camping pad were spread out under one of the windows. "No, but I think I will tonight. I'm gonna go pick up a chair from the secondhand store. I've got a lantern." She indicated a kerosene lamp she'd placed on the small table.

Walt nodded. "Yeah. Well, be careful with that thing indoors. And don't go using that fireplace until I've had a chance to check out the chimney." He began unpacking his tools.

"Yes, sir." She gave him a mock salute. "By the way, I'm not a complete idiot. I had enough sense to hire you, remember?" She picked up her purse and walked to the door. "I got things to do." And she left him to his work.

Knowing her aunt would be at the café by now, Grace headed back to the house to get the bags she'd packed for Seattle. She wrote a note and stuck it on Jane's bedroom door: *I'm gone. The room is vacant. Thanks for the loaning it to me. Grace.*

As soon as she'd cut herself off from the comforts of home, Grace began to realize she had a problem. It was going to be a few weeks at least until she had a stove and refrigerator. Even in winter when there was no logging and money was tightest, Grace had never wanted for a good meal. Now she didn't have the facilities to cook for herself and she was damned if she'd go to the Hoot Owl to eat.

"Don't be a ninny, girl. Jane'll feed you." Walt had laughed when she'd asked if she could use his kitchen. "Hell, your money is as good as anyone's!"

"Yeah. Well, maybe and maybe not, as Kev would say. She hates that I'm staying in town. She's been after me to leave Prosperity soon as I graduated, thinks I'm a fool for staying."

Walt looked like he was going to say something in Jane's defense, but Grace didn't want to hear it. She lifted her jacket from the hook she'd put up by the door. "I'll clean up your place and feed you. Just let me eat there and we'll be even." Grace didn't wait for a sign of agreement from Walt before she walked out of the cabin and headed for Sherman's store to stock up.

"Been awhile since I cleaned the fridge," Walt called after her. Then he went back to work.

For too long folks in town had little to gossip about that didn't bring their own desperation to mind. The idea that Grace wasn't leaving Prosperity offered a spark of hope, and talk jangled through town like a pocket full of change. Conversations at the post office, in the secondhand store, the tavern—any place but the café—were full of speculation about Grace and the cabin.

"Somethin's up between Jane and Parrot. Haven't seen Parrot at the Hoot Owl for days."

"I heard Jane kicked Parrot out."

"Did you hear Jackson left Parrot the old cabin? She's got some work to do if she's gonna live in that shack!"

"Well, the lock's off the door and I think I saw Walt deVore hanging around there."

A couple of days later Grace stepped out of the cabin and found Kev on the street looking up at her door.

"That's a haunted house. Not suppos'd to go in there. "

"Hi, Kev." She knew she'd have to deal with this eventually. "It's not really haunted. It belongs to me now. I'm painting it."

"You live here, not at your other house?" He shook his head. Change always troubled Kev.

"Yes. I'm not going to Seattle. I'm staying here. At least for a while longer."

"And now you have a different house, so you can't give me my pie?" Kev's effort to connect the dots brought Grace up short.

"Kinda. I guess that is kinda right."

"Maybe, maybe not?"

"No, Kev, not maybe. You're exactly right."

His grin was big enough to last the whole day. "Now Jane gives me pie. Right?"

"Right. She's got lots of pie, Kev." Grace wondered how long that would go on.

Walt finished up the wiring by Friday. Grace had spent the day looking for work in Cooper and a couple of the towns farther down the mountain. When she came home that evening a soft electric light was shining through the windows. She wondered how many chips he'd had to cash in to get the Mountain Power guy to put them on the fast track. He'd been pretty proud of his obvious pull, so she wasn't going to worry about it.

"Wow! You did it!" She pulled open the cabin door, but Walt had already gone home. He'd brought a small lamp and left it plugged into one of her new outlets. The camping lantern sat outside on the steps.

In the soft light of the lamp she looked around the room and her breath caught in her throat. There in the corner on the floor was a telephone. Walt had mentioned that he might be able to get her a phone hookup, but she'd expected that would take weeks. She ran over to the old black instrument. It must have been something Walt found in his attic, practically an antique. Grace lifted the receiver. A dial tone!

Without hesitation, she reached in her pocket for the piece of paper Jane had given her and dialed the number in Seattle.

"Hey!" She laughed when her girlfriends both picked up at once.

"You're not really living in that crappy shack are you? That's nuts." Jenn had never had patience with small talk.

"The city is even cooler than we thought, Grace!" Shauna rushed in. "When are you coming?"

Grace looked around her and tried to recapture the excitement she'd felt a moment before. "I got a phone! And lights!"

"What's wrong with you, Grace?" Shauna was fed up.

"Come on, get down here," Jenn demanded. "We can't keep your room empty much longer."

Now her own voice took on an irritated tone. "Yeah. Well, Rose asked me to get this place fixed up before I leave town. Should be done pretty soon." Why was she lying? The sour taste of regret filled her mouth, but she swallowed it down. "You know what? You should go ahead and find another roommate if you have to. I'll figure out something."

The city might be full of options and her friends might be happy there, but this cabin had been placed in the middle of Grace's path and she couldn't see her way around it. When she was inside the cabin—her home—the voices in the logs comforted her. And they called to her. The more time she'd spent there, the more her mind had filled with images. She couldn't leave until she'd made her vision real.

It had been well over a week since Jackson's funeral. The new phone allowed Grace to check in without disrespecting Rose's desire to be left alone.

"Hello." Rose sounded tired.

"How are you? Are you ready for a visit?" Grace missed their dinners together and didn't like the thought of Rose grieving all by herself.

"Hello, Grace. No, my dear. Thank you, but I need more time." Rose sighed deeply before she added, "Are you making any progress on that old cabin?"

"Yes! Walt's helping me. I'm calling you from the cabin. He got a phone line set up. It's great. I'm living here now."

"Oh, my! I thought it was such a crazy idea of Jackson's. Are you OK there?"

"Actually, I love it. I can hardly wait to show you what I'm doing. But not quite yet."

"Well, I'm not ready to go into town anyway. That's good you have a phone. I can call you if I need some groceries or something."

"Of course." Grace gave Rose her phone number. "I'm thinking of you every day."

Walt brought Tom Jameson's son, Ed, to help him get a ditch dug for the drains and pipes to connect the cabin to the sewer.

"We'll be at this for a couple of days, Parrot. You need to go pick out a shower stall and the fixtures. Here's a list of what we'll need." Walt handed her a brown strip of paper ripped from a grocery bag, his large scrawl running down the page. "They've got all that stuff down at the plumbing supply in Everett." He turned to get back to work, then stopped. "Oh, yeah, Clett's got a toilet and sink still in boxes in his garage from that remodel he never got around to. We could pay him a bit for it. But you need to go buy yourself some other stuff. I can put in a little kitchen, but I mean little. So go find a sink and something like an apartment-size stove and fridge. Might have to go to Seattle for all that."

"OK if I take your truck again?" Grace had been using Walt's old pickup over the last week. He'd given her the keys and not asked for them back.

He waved off her question. "Just go."

"OK. But hold off on that toilet and sink from Clett for a bit, ok?"

What Grace hadn't told anyone, though Walt might have suspected if he'd paid the least attention to her artistic efforts, was that she'd already picked out her appliances. Right after her first view of the inside of the cabin, Grace's painterly vision had taken over. She'd borrowed Walt's truck and after a frustrating job search in Cooper, she'd gone down to Everett. She wanted lots of color. Maybe her taste was connected to memories of sitting in Annie's lap looking at pictures of tropical birds in that old bird book. Maybe it was her effort to fight against the ubiquitous gray and green of the mountains. Whatever it was, with the money Jackson left her, Grace was able to feed her hunger.

She'd found a three-burner stove and a small refrigerator—the stove was deep red, the refrigerator fresh spring green. The kitchen sink was the most immediately rewarding find—the floor model was an eye-catching canary yellow and it was on sale. She'd grabbed it with glee, telling the salesman she didn't want anything delivered until she called him.

"Sure. Clett's not going to get rid of them any time soon; they're blue. Who ever heard of that?" Walt laughed.

Grace, headed back into the cabin, spun around. "Really?"

"Yeah. Bright blue. Must a been a close-out sale."

"On second thought, we should help Clett out." She was trying to sound thoughtful and hesitant, but her mouth was puckered with barely contained delight. "Go ahead, then. I can live with blue."

She ran errands for Walt and continued a halfhearted job hunt, but the whole time Grace was consumed with her ultimate vision for the cabin. Her head was filled with images, colors, techniques for getting the effect she was after. The walls of this old cabin were the canvas for her imagination, not just the frame for her shelter. When she went to Everett for plumbing supplies, she also stopped at the art supply store.

While the men worked outside, inside Grace began to paint. She started near the front door in the curved space between the two bottom logs. Studying the way the shadows fell in that space, she began mixing colors on her palette. It took awhile to create the perfect range of green tones for a creature she'd only seen in a book, but once she had the colors right, she stopped thinking. Her hands and her brushes knew how to shape the tiny frog; she trusted them. When she'd placed the minute dots of white in his eyes, bringing him to life, her whole scheme fell into place. This was what she'd dreamed of doing since she was able to hold a crayon. Her mother's spirit filled the cabin.

"Look, baby." Annie's voice rang in her daughter's head. "See his red eyes? And he has blue feet!" Her mother's hands holding the book, the warmth of Annie's body as Grace snuggled close: Grace's fingertips tingled as the memory filled her.

"I want to draw him, Mommy. I want my crayons."

Grace grinned.

Day by day, creature by creature, leaf by leaf, Grace began transforming the cabin into her fantasy. She told Walt to knock before coming inside, giving her time to drop the sheets she'd tacked to the tops of the walls. He knew she was painting, but she wouldn't be ready for him, or anyone, to see her work until the full effect was complete.

Kev had added a new phase to his morning routine. After eating his pie at the Hoot Owl, he would walk up to Grace's cabin and knock on the door.

"Are you finished painting?" he'd shout.

"Not yet, Kev." Grace would answer.

She had offered to show him what she was doing, but Kevin had shaken his head and said, "When it's all done, it will be ready."

And Grace certainly couldn't argue with that.

For the last week, as Grace crafted a tropical jungle inside her cabin, Prosperity had been drenched in a near constant downpour. Even with his determination to get the cabin comfortable for Grace, Walt was temporarily defeated by the persistent rain.

But Walt's slowed progress, even the constant showers, barely registered with Grace. When she opened the door and stepped outside to get water or breathe the forested air, Grace often felt a shiver of surprise that the outer world still existed—the smells of early summer, diesel exhaust and moist earth sighing in the slowly accumulating warmth, frog song and the hollow rumble of big trucks. And the rain.

All the living, shadow-casting trees had long since been taken from the area surrounding the cabin. Even under the veil of the unbroken storm, anyone entering or leaving Grace's new home was visible from the mill, the school and the few houses across the street. The shelter of the forest was a short walk up the road and Grace couldn't avoid being seen as she headed up toward the hiking trails.

But Grace Tillman walking in the forest, rain or shine, had long been a common sight. Pat could have just waited for her to step out, he could have pretended a casual, accidental meeting. It took a clearer intention for him to choose a moment when he knew she was inside to approach the cabin.

It was later, after she'd calmed down, when it occurred to her that she'd been thinking about him with real fondness when he showed up. In fact, Patrick had been constantly on her mind in the last couple of days as she conjured a jaguar sitting high on the wall above the fireplace. That large cat, especially his eyes, had brought back a sweet memory of Pat at age ten, when he'd rushed at her from across the playground to tell her he'd seen a lynx, a real one! His dark eyes were full of amazement, and tiny drops of sweat outlined his forehead. He smelled like he'd slept on a bed of cedar boughs, which, it turned out, he had. He grabbed her arm and pulled her into the shadow of the school building where no one could hear them.

"I didn't tell anyone, not even Dad. I'm just telling you."

"What are you talking about?" Grace remembered being more annoyed than curious at that moment. He'd pulled her away from a game of kickball and Shauna was staring at them, her fists on her hips, furious.

"The lynx. A real, live lynx. I saw it last night when we were camping up over Hancock Ridge." Like all the guys in their class, Pat was in the Boy Scouts and they got to do lots of cool stuff like backpacking up in the mountains for over a week in the summer. Grace only got to do that with her father and Jane. "It was so cool. It had yellow eyes, Parrot. I saw its eyes. It was slinking over a boulder just ahead of me. I almost didn't believe it was real, 'cause it disappeared so fast. But it was. If I told my dad or the guys, they'd want to go hunt for it. But I couldn't kill it. I just couldn't."

Grace realized, as she was painting that jaguar, that that had been the moment when she first fell in love with Pat. She just hadn't known it then.

At the sound of his knock, she wiped her paint-spotted hands on her jeans. The rain had tapered to a fine mist, but the air still held a chill that rushed in as she opened the door. Pat stood on the bottom step, placing them eye-to-eye. His feet were planted in a wide, firm stance and his arms were folded across his chest. His face was dead sober. Water dripped from the beak of his cap.

Grace's first impulse was to grab hold of him and pull him inside and show him her creation. But the anger he emitted stopped her. She positioned herself in the doorway so he couldn't see inside. She tried a timid smile. "It's nice to see you."

"I just need to know something." He looked down and dug his hands deep into his pockets as if they might betray him. "You here for good?"

She poked her head out and looked from side to side. No obvious witnesses, but this was Prosperity; somebody was always watching. "Let's take a walk."

He stepped back. "It's a simple question, Grace."

She reached behind her and grabbed her rain jacket, then stepped out and pulled the door closed behind her. "I need to get some fresh air anyway." She took a deep breath.

"You've got yourself pretty close to the action for someone who isn't on our side, so I need to know if you're staying."

"What action? You mean the mill?" They were walking up the road toward the back of the mill yard. Without talking about it, both of them headed instinctively toward the woods where they'd have some privacy.

Pat looked over his shoulder toward the office as they passed. Grace noticed his body stiffen. He walked faster and motioned for her to keep up.

"Afraid you'll be caught fraternizing with the enemy?" Grace stopped. Pat was several strides ahead by the time he turned to look at her. "I'm not picking sides, Patrick. I don't want any part of this war; there's not going to be a winner. Things are never going to be like they were. You're an owner now, you've got to see what's coming isn't going to be stopped by scaring that owl away."

He stepped up to her and put his hand under her chin. He gently turned her face to look at his. "You want to know what I see? I see a girl who is as tied to this town and logging as I am. She's just too stubborn to admit it." He let his hand drop from her face as his eyes locked onto hers and held them. Then he took her hand and led her slowly toward the trailhead. "What are you going to do, anyway? I hear you and Jane aren't even talking. She's gonna lose the café, you know."

"She doesn't care if she loses the café. She's leaving town anyway." A familiar warmth started to flow from his hand through Grace's body. "She's renting the house to Sherrie Thomas." Grace hated the whiney and bitter sound of her own voice. "I don't want to talk about my aunt."

"Yeah, well, at least everyone knows where they stand with Jane." Pat looked at Grace. He waited for a long moment, his eyebrows raised. The question of her loyalty hung between them.

She pulled her hand away and spoke out to the trees. "For the first time in my life I have a home of my very own and I'm not going to walk away from that. I don't know what's next." Then she looked back at him. "I don't even know how I'm going to survive, but I would like us to be friends again."

Pat stared over Grace's head, back toward the mill. "I don't have time for this." His voice was firm, but the sadness in his eyes was unmistakable. "We have to grow up, Grace. Maybe no one is going to win this battle, but when it's over people will remember what side folks were on and that'll tell 'em who their real friends are." He walked back to the mill, leaving her there at the beginning of the trail.

Chapter 6

The sun broke out, warming and misting the air with thin clouds of evaporation. The water that had collected on every surface trickled in sparkling beads from branches and roofs. The town glowed like a bearded hermit stepping from his annual bath.

As Jane approached the cabin, she looked up and down the muddy street, wondering how many folks were standing behind their curtains watching her. Everyone was well aware that Grace and Jane weren't speaking—it was the loudest silent argument in town. Jane had few supporters in Prosperity these days and nobody liked the idea that Grace might be hurting.

Walt and Ed stood looking down into a sloppy trench that ran from the side of the cabin out to the street. "Is that where you're going to bury the next kid who shows up to save the trees?" Jane couldn't stop herself.

Walt looked up, ignoring her question. "'Bout time you showed up."

"Is she home?"

He shook his head. "She took my truck and headed down to Cooper. Said she was going to see if anybody was hiring waitresses." He stepped back from the ditch and walked up to Jane. "Why'd she have to do that, I wonder?"

"You can keep your wondering to yourself. Just tell her I was by, I want to talk to her." Jane might have to eat some crow for her niece, but she didn't have to add a lecture from Walt deVore to her list of humiliations.

She turned around slowly, giving any hidden observers an opportunity to see how she'd made the first effort. Then she ducked her head and hurried away.

That evening Jane sat at the counter in the café. Before her was the inventory she'd begun: cutlery, mostly still usable; plates, bowls, cups—all white, most chipped; huge, dented pots, most with lids; metal mixing bowls, no matched sets; salt and pepper pairs (how many?); sugar dispensers (how many?); one nearly empty cash register; one jukebox. Only three people had responded to the ad she'd placed ("restaurant closing, everything for sale"), but when they showed up they just shook their heads.

She'd called the phone company earlier in the day to disconnect the phone, so she was surprised when it rang.

"Jane here."

"Walt said you came by." When Walt first told her, Grace just nodded and returned to her painting. Half an hour later she opened the cabin door and asked Walt what Jane had wanted. He shrugged his shoulders.

The more her painting grew, the more attached Grace was getting to the cabin. But it was becoming clear that Jackson's money would barely cover the costs of all the renovations. Grace still hadn't found a job, and if something didn't turn up she'd have to leave town soon. On her trips Sherman's or walking down Main, Grace was having trouble keeping her eyes from turning toward the Hoot Owl.

"Right." Jane paused. "I'm leaving a week from today. No one is going to step up and buy this café from me. No big surprise there. Thought I might sell some of the fixtures and stuff, but didn't. So, that's it. Didn't make any sense to leave without telling you."

A long pause on the other end, then, "Aunt Jane?"

"I'm still here."

"What if I . . .?"

"What?"

"Never mind. Forget it. I'll find something else."

"Right. That's what I thought. I'll let you know my phone number. When you come to your senses and realize you need to get out of this dump, call me."

Grace hung up the phone. So, that was it. No Jane. No Hoot Owl.

She found her brush and returned to painting the head of a snake that poked out from under a large palm leaf on the frame of the bathroom door. She'd finished the walls and ceiling in the main living area and she had to admit, the effect was pretty spectacular. There were a few areas that needed work—that one corner where the perspective was off, and the jaguar looked like he was sitting in midair—but it wasn't bad. Last week she'd been ready to give up and throw a coat of white all over it. But then she'd hit on a way to scale her sketches that allowed for the irregularities in the sizes of the logs and that had helped a lot.

She couldn't keep this whole thing a secret much longer. Walt needed to get inside and install those appliances. And she had to get some kind of a job.

Cooper hadn't yielded a single possibility and Grace couldn't imagine traveling farther down the mountain every day for work. How would she do it anyway? She couldn't borrow Walt's truck indefinitely.

Was taking over the Hoot Owl really such a bad idea?

The Hoot Owl had once been Annie's Pies—her mother and Jane had been co-owners. At three, little Parrot had sat on the counter in the café kitchen while her mother rolled out dough. At thirteen, she'd begun working there herself. She'd done every job in the place except paying the bills. She could learn that pretty quick.

It was clear that Jane's crazy anti-logging politics had driven a lot of folks away from the café. If Jane were out of the picture, things would be different.

But would she ever consider turning the Hoot Owl over to Grace?

Grace dropped her brush into a jar of murky water, wiped her hands, and picked up the phone.

"Jane? Look, what do you have to lose? If things don't work out, I'll shut it down myself. I could see if Lyle would come back and help me out for a few hours a week. I don't think he's found anything else since you let him go."

"Oh, Jesus, Parrot. That cabin's not enough of an albatross around your neck? You want to take on a failing café too?"

Grace knew better than to respond to this.

"And what are you going to do about the bills? Even if you don't have customers, those bills are still there. I'm getting ready to declare bankruptcy and let the bank have it."

"Give me a few months. What difference will it make? If I can't turn it around, you can still do that."

Grace held her breath while she listened to sounds of Jane fumbling for a cigarette, lighting it and inhaling. She looked around her. With her own hands she had created a tropical jungle in the middle of the Cascade Mountains. How hard could it be to run a café?

"OK, Parrot. I guess you need one more dose of reality to smack you in the face before you're going to understand." Jane took another drag on her cigarette. "OK. Six months. You run it and I'm putting your name on everything right along with mine. I'm not sitting back and letting you put me deeper in debt than I already am without you carrying your share of that load."

"Really? You mean I'd be half owner?"

"Goddammit, Parrot! When are you gonna take off those fuckin' rose-colored glasses? Yes, I mean it. You want to take on the café, you're gonna have to pay the bills!"

"Thanks, Jane. I never thought . . ."

"I know you never thought., But you'd better start thinking now, little girl. Go ahead, see if you can butter the town up, remind 'em who your daddy was, and maybe they'll forget about you being my niece. Six months. Then I'm pulling out of my half of the business—it'll be all yours or we're bankrupt together. Come by tomorrow and I'll go over things with you."

And she hung up.

Grace continued to hold the receiver to her ear and let the dial tone buzz through her head. What just happened? She'd never experienced a tornado, but she imagined this was what it felt like after you'd been picked up by a wild wind and landed in a new reality. In a daze she lowered the receiver and looked at the monkey climbing over a log near the ceiling, at the toucan in the corner looking down its long bill, at the red-and-black snake whose body appeared to slither between the logs—her roommates. "Wow." She sat on the floor and spread her legs out in front of her. Leaning back on her hands, she started to laugh.

It was a long night. Wearing a headlamp and getting up from her work now and then to reposition the lamps, Grace painted.

A focused energy drove her; she didn't pause to question a single stroke. Her hands moved in direct response to her vision, each brushstroke, each color knew its place. When finally her hands could no longer guide a steady brush, she lay back and took it all in. A jungle, a tropical tangle of greenery populated with exotic birds, flowers of brilliant contrast, creatures she'd seen only in her dreams. This world breathed its humid breath on her and she was calmed.

The morning had aged toward noon by the time Grace roused herself. She pulled the sheets off the walls, raised the narrow windows, and opened the front door to invite the fresh air and sunlight inside. Kev may have come by, but she'd slept through his knocking. Too bad. It was time to show this place off and if it wasn't going to be Kev, Walt deserved to be her first visitor.

She'd expected to find him working outside on the stubborn drainage ditch, knee-deep in mud as he had been for the last several days, but he was sitting in his truck, head back, asleep.

Grace knocked on the truck window. "Hey, you OK?"

Walt sat up, startled, and rubbed his hands over his grizzled face. "Whew. Just sat here for a minute to catch my breath. We finished that damn ditch and I'm ready to get things hooked up inside."

"OK then. Come on in."

Grace stood back, allowing him to take his time climbing out of the truck, walking up the steps. She didn't want him to see her biting her lips, pinching the sides of her jeans with her nervous fingers, but she followed close behind as he entered the cabin.

He took a couple of steps inside and stopped. She held her breath. Slowly he turned left to right, then gradually he tilted his head back, back, back. His jaw hung open as he turned, inch by inch, till he'd made a complete circle. Then he made a snorting noise through his nose, straightened up, and looked at Grace. "You've been busy."

She let out her long-held breath as she nodded. "What do you think?"

"Oh, it's something your momma would love all right."

"Huh."

"Yep. It'd make her downright happy, I'm sure. So, tell me when the stove and all will be delivered. Let's get this thing wrapped up. I could sure use a beer."

"Right. I'll call them today. Should have it by tomorrow or the next day."

"Good deal. Give me a call when they get here then." And he walked back to his truck, climbed in and drove off.

Grace stood on her front step, her hands on her hips watching him. OK. *My mother would have loved it. Not too bad, coming from Walt.*

After arranging to have the rainbow of appliances delivered the next day, Grace considered Kev. She wanted to show him what she had done as she'd promised, but she expected once he saw it, her cabin would be all he would talk about for days or maybe weeks. She had loved the hours by herself crafting this jungle, turning her imagination inside out and inhabiting that vibrant space as it developed before her. A walk in the forest alone had always been her favorite activity, and living in this exotic space by herself brought her that same joy. Once Kev broadcast her accomplishment to the town, she could forget about being alone. But maybe that was just as well. If she were going to start running the café, she was going to need all the friends she could get.

The next morning Kev arrived at her doorstep before the delivery truck.

"Are you finished painting?" he shouted.

Grace opened the door. "Yep. I'm done. Come on in."

Kev's eyes widened as he climbed the steps and entered the cabin.

Grace stood behind him and softly closed the door.

Kev's mouth hung open and he backed up into her, grabbing at her shoulder. She could sense his fear and cursed herself for failing to anticipate this.

"It's OK, Kev. They aren't real. I painted them."

"Why?" he asked, gripping her hand now, but staring at the ceiling.

"Well, I think it's kind of fun. These birds and animals are pretty, don't you think?" She hoped he'd like the color and fantasy of it: the ceiling covered in shades of green like a jungle canopy with shafts of sunlight shooting through it; hiding in the corners and tucked among the curving logs of the walls were creatures, birds with fanciful plumage, frogs and snakes in brilliant colors.

"Ummm. Maybe, maybe not." His voice was low and she could sense him trying to overcome his own fright. "Why did you paint snakes?" Kev pointed with his free hand to a large, dark serpent coiling in the corner.

"Snakes live in the jungle too, Kev. In some countries far away from here, there are real jungles where animals and snakes and birds like these all live together."

"But not in here. Right?"

"That's right. None of these guys live here. I just made them up."

At that, Kev relaxed. "Oh." He turned and looked closely at her face. Then he stepped away from her into the center of the room. He looked from wall to wall—everywhere there was jungle greenery and lush, tropical flowers. In one corner a long-tailed monkey dangled from a vine, and peering from another corner were the golden eyes of a tropical cat.

Finally, Kev smiled. "You're a good maker-upper, Parrot."

Grace breathed her own sigh of relief. "Thanks, Kev. I'm glad you think so."

Kev stayed to watch the appliances get unloaded and as Walt began to work he said, "Don't be scared of the snakes, Mister Walter, Grace made them up. They won't bite you." Then he looked at Parrot. "I can come back here. I'm not scared."

"Great, Kev. Come back on Saturday. Everything should be done by then."

"Maybe, maybe not," he called as he shuffled out to the street.

By the end of the week Jane had taken Grace to the bank and put her niece's name on the café account. This was tantamount to a public announcement and they both knew it.

"OK. Monday morning I'm gone. Sherrie's gotta move out of her place, so I'm hitting the road. Found a room in one of those big boarding houses in Seattle. It'll do till I get a job. Here's the phone number."

Grace took the paper Jane held out to her. "Gonna wish me luck?"

"It's gonna take a hell of a lot more than luck, kiddo. Honestly," Jane shook her head, "I just wish you'd come to your senses."

Over the weekend Grace spent hours at the café, washing the windows, cleaning the neglected corners, and making a few pies, though there were still no customers. The town was waiting for Jane to leave and no one pretended otherwise.

On her way out Monday morning Jane parked her truck in front of the Hoot Owl. She got out, stood by the open door and called to Grace, "One piece of advice, Parrot—and I'm not setting foot in that place again—don't order in bulk if you can help it. It only saves you money if you use it all up. And, believe me, you won't."

Grace put down the mop and stepped to the door, "Goodbye, Jane. I might have a few more questions."

"Look, anything you don't know by now can't be that important." She stuck her head in the door and looked over at the jukebox. "That's the only thing I'll miss, and it won't be for long, I'm sure. Oh, yeah, I left a chocolate cream pie in the freezer for Kev. After that's gone, you're on your own." She slapped her hands together and climbed back into her truck. "Good riddance, Prosperity!" she shouted out her window as she drove away.

From the doorway Grace stared at the truck till it turned off Main Street and was lost in the trees.

Earlier in the week Grace had gone by Lyle's trailer and asked for his help. "I don't think there'll be much money for a while, but I know I can't handle the place alone. Would you consider it?"

"Are you kidding? I'm there in a heartbeat." At five foot four with the broad shoulders of a wrestler, Lyle looked Grace in the eye as he stood at the door, barefoot and unshaven, but eager. Lyle had bounced from job to job since his tour in Vietnam. He was now approaching his fortieth birthday and had weaned himself from the drug habit he picked up along with the medal that hung from his bathroom mirror and the jagged scar that ran from his right foot to his groin. He'd come to Prosperity thinking he could hide out till he got clean, then he'd move on. Now, three years later, he was straight and stuck—trapped by a disability check, empty days, and his fear of the temptations that lay outside Prosperity.

"Hell, once Jane's out of town, and not rubbing her environmentalist nose in everyone's face, they'll come back for the food."

They agreed there was nothing to lose by keeping the place closed for a while after Jane was gone.

"It'll take more than a couple of days for folks to believe she's really left, you know. We might as well do it right and clean up in the meantime. Maybe a few new items on the menu would help."

Grace hoped she could convince folks she wasn't on Jane's side in their battle. It was going to be tough. Maybe they ought to make a big splash, a "Grand Reopening!"

Lyle rolled his eyes at this idea. "People around here like to figure things out for themselves, you know that. They don't like to be hit over the head with stuff. They'd just laugh and walk away."

Hearing this, Grace knew it was the truth. When Jarvis closed up the hardware store and Sherman's started selling all his inventory, you would never have known except for a small piece of notebook paper pinned to the front door of Jarvis Hardware. If you got up close enough you could read the clumsy pencil lettering that said, *Get it at Sherman's*. It was the gossip tree, the Prosperity telegraph, that spread its sturdy boughs across the community and filled everyone in on Tim and Norma Jarvis's divorce, and the bills that had been piling up. Sherman handled the extra business without so much as a wider grin.

So, instead of planning some grand party, Lyle and Grace spent the first week after Jane's departure giving the Hoot Owl the deepest cleaning it had ever had. When Kev showed up first thing Tuesday morning, Grace let him in and gave him a piece of the pie Jane had left for him. Then she tried to explain.

"I'm in charge of the café now, Kev. Jane's moved to Seattle."

"Maybe, maybe not!" He opened his mouth, full of pie, and laughed hard, spraying the table with chocolate cream. "You and Jane are playing a game." He grinned at her as he crumpled his napkin in his awkward fist and rubbed it over his face. Then he became serious. "Did you make it up, like the snakes?"

"No, Kev. It's real. I'm staying here. I'll give you your pie in the morning." Grace stopped herself from wiping off the table—she could do that after he was gone. Instead she sat down opposite him. "The café is going to be closed for a couple of days, but I'll be here cleaning. We'll open up on Monday and I'll expect you to be my best customer."

"You'll go to the post office like every morning?"

"Yes, Kev. Like every morning." Grace looked at the boy's wrinkled forehead. Only a few weeks ago she'd been ready to abandon Kev, thinking he was stuck but she didn't have to be.

"But, you know, it's OK if things aren't the same every morning. Maybe one day you'll try a different kind of pie."

"Ha! Maybe, maybe not!" The cloud that had troubled his face cleared and his eyes sparkled. Then he pushed himself out of the booth. "I'm going home."

Lyle put a bit of fresh paint on the woodwork and Grace cleaned out the window boxes, dumping the cigarette butts and filling them with soil. Mrs. G had come by one morning and, seeing the efforts Grace was making to spruce the place up, she'd offered a couple of pots of daffodils that had just begun to bud. "You can transplant the whole lot into those window boxes. They'll bloom in a few days."

"This is why I couldn't leave," Grace said as she gave Mrs. G a hug.

The menu needed a redesign and Grace threw herself into the task, illustrating it with drawings of the forest. They decided to add a Reuben sandwich and a daily special to give themselves a little room for creativity with the leftovers. Rather than spend money to get the new menu printed, Lyle took the new menu up to the post office and used the copy machine. Grace colored each one by hand.

In the still-dark of Monday morning, Grace walked up the street and heard some kind of animal scurry around in front of her. As she got close to the café door, the neon sign in the window of the Bullhook cast enough light for her to identify the tail of a rat disappearing behind the building. A whiff of sulfur hit her nose.

Before Grace could grasp what was going on, the sound of slow-moving tires crunching down the street startled her. She spun around. Henry Martin pulled his pickup into the spot in front of the café door. His headlights illuminated on the whole scene. Egg yolk ran down the front door. Brown shells littered the sidewalk. Grace's keys slipped from her hand and landed in the gooey mess on the sidewalk. Something dark dripped onto her newly planted daffodils. She traced the dark drips up the window to a cartoonish painting of a burly guy sitting at a table holding a fork in one hand and knife in the other. In a bubble over his head were the words "We want Spotted Owl Omelets!"

Henry leaned his head out of the window and said, "Don't let it get to you. It's nothing."

Henry wore a dirty green cap with a Mariner's blue trident embroidered on the front. Beneath it his long hair was pulled back in a ponytail. He gave Grace one of his rare smiles and his gold eyetooth gleamed in the streetlight. Henry had been one of Jane's most loyal customers. In spite of what the rest of the town did, he had always stopped at the Hoot Owl first thing in the morning for his coffee.

"They meant it for Jane. She's been getting stuff like this for a while." His voice was soft, almost a whisper.

"She has?" Grace breathed out slowly. Pulling her eyes away from the caricatured face painted on her freshly scrubbed window, she turned to Henry. "She never said anything."

"Well, she wouldn't, would she?" By now he'd turned off his engine and gotten out, closing the door carefully as if trying to preserve a bit of the early morning quiet. He took a clean handkerchief from his pocket and handed it to her. He may have meant her to use his offering to wipe up the mess, but as soon as she took it the tears started to flow and she blew her nose.

"Your aunt isn't a bad person. She just gets too passionate about things. You know what I mean?"

"But she's gone now. Don't people know that?"

"Well, I'd say not everyone got the message yet."

Grace looked back at the cartoon figure. "Unless this was meant for me."

"Why? Who would want to get to you, Parr...er...Grace?"

She stooped to pick her keys out of the goo.

"Let's go in. I'll start the coffee." She stuffed the handkerchief in her pocket. "I'll wash it and get it back to you."

"That's OK, you keep it."

She unlocked the door, stepped in and switched on the lights. The café sparkled from its recent cleaning. An image flashed across Grace's mind's eye of herself bouncing on tiptoe in her new clothes as she waited for her father to walk her to school on her first day. On that day and on all the other special days—her first lost tooth, the day she first drove, her first date—there had been this emptiness, this hollow place inside her. The place her mother should have filled. And on those days when the tooth fairy didn't show, or Daddy forgot to read to her like he promised, or he seemed to not even know she was there, and today when the grand reopening she'd hoped for was ruined, the empty space was big enough to lose herself in.

"Damn it." Grace fussed with the coffeemaker. Thoughts of her mother had been hovering around as she spiffed up the café. Seeing the mess outside was like having someone you love come close up behind you and instead of embracing you in a warm hug, give you a kick in the rear.

Henry slid onto his customary stool. "Looks nice in here."

Grace grunted and began filling a bucket of water and gathering rags.

Lyle pushed through the café door. "What the fuck? Those idiots!" He checked the bottoms of his shoes and then intercepted Grace.

"Here, give me that. I'll clean it up. Jesus, they're doing this all over the state. Couldn't they be a little original at least? It's not like they're going to get any publicity up here." He carried the cleaning supplies out to the sidewalk. The door slammed behind him.

Chapter 7

July 11, 1991

   Walt got everything done yesterday. I stood in the middle of the cabin and cried. It is so cool! Every time I come in the door I get this eerie feeling, like just the second before I entered the whole jungle was alive with birds singing and creatures scurrying between the logs and bugs flying around. Everything freezes and goes silent when I enter. Then I can feel my mother. It's so weird. Like she's right here with me and she's happy. I want to show it to Pat so much. He'd love it! But he just wants to fight. If I'm not willing to help him destroy that nest, I'm the enemy. I know those were his stupid cartoons on the window. I'm not going to play this game. I just wish I didn't miss him so much.

   (here several sketches of various jungle birds and animals.)

   Grace woke to the sound of pickups pulling into the mill, bumping across the gravel lot, cab doors slamming. The air was full of men's rumbling voices and the smell of exhaust. For nearly a month, the mill had been mostly quiet—two or three log trucks leaving the yard in the morning coming back loaded on a single run in the afternoon. All Grace had heard was that the men were reorganizing, trying to figure out how they were going to fulfill the contracts Jackson had signed. More and more restrictions were coming down from the government.

But this morning something had animated everyone.

Grace looked out her window and saw a group of familiar faces. When these guys got together in the morning that used to mean business at the Hoot Owl. Since she'd taken over, Grace hadn't seen one of them.

OK, then. Grace thought. *You won't come to me. I'll bring my mountain to you.* She dressed and ran over to the café. She'd made a few pies and stuck them in the freezer so she'd always have something in case some hiker wandered in. Now she pulled them out, cut them, and laid the pieces on a tray. She took a deep breath, picked up the tray, and walked back over to the mill. She couldn't really afford to give away food, but then, it was all going to go to waste if no one bought it.

She stepped onto the gravel of the parking lot, holding the tray in front of her like a peace offering.

"What's this?" Terry Childers had been a regular at the Hoot Owl back before what Grace had begun to think of as the big rift. He hadn't had as much as a cup of coffee at the café in weeks. "Your favorite, Terry, apple crumble."

"Jesus, Parrot. How am I supposed to resist this?"

"You're not. What's up, anyway?" Grace hoped that a taste of her pie and some casual conversation might remind him what he'd been missing. But Terry grabbed a slice off the tray and turned away from her to talk with Burt Samson.

"You got the light rigging ready? Looks like we'll be needing it."

"Yeah. It's all stored in the shed behind the office." Burt had his broad back to Grace. She stared at the slight stoop of his shoulders and the worn elbows of his flannel shirt. The tray felt heavy in her hands and she started to back away.

"We got some guys here never worked nights. We'll have to take it easy." Burt's deep voice stood out from the general din around her. He'd turned in her direction. "Hey, Parrot, what you got there?"

Grace looked up and took a step toward him.

Instantly she was surrounded; hands, thick-fingered and black-nailed, reached out for the free food. A few mumbled "thanks Parrots" but the men clearly had more urgent business on their minds. It was like she'd entered a corral full of hungry horses ready to bolt. She held her ground, kept the tray out in front of her and listened to the swirling talk.

Some new government regulation meant that time was getting short to cut the wood in the national forest outside of town. The mill had a contract that was going to expire and everyone feared it wouldn't be renewed. It was now or never.

When the tray was empty, Grace backed out of the throng. As she walked away from the yard, she passed the mill office. The door was open and she caught a glimpse of Pat standing in the shadows.

"What happened here?" Lyle stood in the café kitchen looking at the mess of empty pie plates she'd left behind. "We get an early morning rush?"

"Yeah, in a manner of speaking, only we didn't make any money." Grace told him what she'd done and what she'd overheard.

"You're in charge, but I can't see givin' away free food when you're wondering if you can pay the phone bill." Lyle picked up the pie plates, carried them to the sink, and turned on the water.

"I know. Just thought it might be a way to prime the pump. If they're gonna be working, they'll need food." Grace didn't expect an immediate melting of the ice shrouding the Hoot Owl, but seeing those guys scarfing down her food had created a warm breeze of hope.

"Yeah? By the time those guys get a paycheck, you better pray they still remember your generosity." Lyle pulled a soapy pan out of the sink and raked it with the scouring pad.

"You know what's going on at the mill? They were talking about cutting at night." Grace pushed open the swinging door and headed to the front of the café. She spoke to Lyle through the pass-through as she poured water into the coffeemaker and flipped the switch.

"Well, all I hear is that they've got a deal to cut on national forest land, but not much time to do it." Lyle dried the pans and stacked them on the overhead racks. "The new regs are not making anybody happy. Guess we can hope a few of the guys will be so angry at the government they'll forget about Jane and drift back in here."

The next evening Sherrie Thomas knocked on the door of Grace's cabin.

When her husband and child were killed in the truck accident, the whole devastated town had rallied around Sherrie. Grace had been just starting kindergarten. She'd offered Sherrie her childish condolences: "Jeremy is an angel with my mommy now. She'll take care of him." A look of distress had contorted Sherrie's face and Jane had sent the little girl outside to play.

In fifth grade, Grace began spending more time at the café after school. Those were good days for Prosperity, and the café was always busy. Jane was able to hire Sherrie to help out. But when things started slowing down and the tables were more often empty, Jane told Grace that Sherrie wouldn't be working at the Hoot Owl anymore.

Sherrie didn't disappear, though. Jane insisted she come to the house for dinner at least once a week. Grace watched Sherrie gather a cloud of discouragement around her as she reported leaving one job after another. She helped out in the mill office, but that brought up too many memories and she had to quit; she tried doing daycare in her home, but folks couldn't afford to pay her enough; the stint at Sherman's lasted a bit longer and it looked like she'd finally landed in a spot where she could stay, but when the mill started cutting back and all the regulations made everyone in town jittery, that job dissolved too.

After Warren was killed and Jane started talking like an anti-logging fanatic, Sherrie stopped coming over and rarely showed her face at the café. Grace missed her, but she understood how Sherrie felt. The battle that had forced the split between Grace and Pat had wedged apart lots of relationships in Prosperity.

Just before Jane finally left, Sherrie's financial plight had reached desperate proportions. In the last year, she'd been driving down to Cooper and working as an aide in the elementary school. Being around kids who reminded her of Jeremy gave her comfort and made her look forward to getting up in the morning, but it wasn't enough to pay her mortgage. The bank was merciless.

The unexpected timing of Warren's death, had left Jane with a mortgage-free home and no buyers, allowing her to do one more kindness for Sherrie. The irony of the town pariah throwing lifelines to the drowning as she exited was not lost on Sherrie.

Now Sherrie stood in front of Grace biting her lip, and looking more worried than angry. Grace invited her in, but she shook her head and looked back over her shoulder as if expecting someone to speak for her. When she turned back, Grace caught a whiff of desperation from her.

"We need your help." She looked up at Grace, and the thin smile she offered tugged at Grace's heart.

"Whatever you need."

Sherrie's withdrawal had spoken loudly of the bitterness Jane created. Her aunt had made herself a target for the town's fear and anger. It had crossed Grace's mind more than once that Jane had done an awfully good job of diverting everyone's attention away from the actual activists who were making their voices heard in Olympia and DC and effectively slowing logging to a near standstill.

"We need to feed the men, Grace. They've got to meet this contract—it's the last big one Jackson signed. The regulators are breathing down their necks. There's no time for them to set up a kitchen on the mountain. We need to use the café."

"Of course we do." Grace didn't hesitate. Pulling together in tough times was what Prosperity did. Most of the men who cut the trees and ran the equipment that turned those trees into lumber, were unmarried or without families to send them off with the kind of hearty food they'd need to keep going. This town was what they had.

Early the next morning Grace began creating grocery lists and packable menus. Wives and daughters of the loggers, women she'd known all her life but hadn't seen in weeks, started showing up at the café in pairs and small groups, bringing produce from their gardens and helping hands. Lyle jumped in and organized the brigade of cooks.

It took only a few hours to get them working like a well-rehearsed team. They cooked hardy soups, baked bread, set up a sandwich assembly station, and kept the coffee urns going. The café kitchen was overflowing with cooks who nudged one another like cattle heading to the barn.

Before pulling a tray of cookies out of the oven, Grace yelled over her shoulder, "Here comes something hot and sweet, watch out!" Mrs. G cried, "Ooo-whee! Make way for that hottie, Parrot Tillman."

Ruth Nordeen took over the soup pot like the mother of seven that she was: "Get me more salt over here, Parrot. Who's chopping those tomatoes? I need them in here now."

Someone turned on the music and before long the women's voices, singing, "Help! I need Somebody!" echoed off the metal counters.

The intense effort continued through the week. They spelled each other over the days and nights. More than once Grace prepared to leave the café at one or two in the morning, exhausted, as Marilee Sharp or Dorianne Travers came across the street from the Bullhook where they'd been tending bar to help out in the kitchen.

The mothers among the group rounded up all the teenagers who were too young to be cutting timber and organized them into a delivery squad. They hitched rides in the log trucks up to the landing and brought the food four times a day.

At night, the men worked by lights they'd strung from spars across the mountainside. The shadows cast by those unnatural beams, combined with the men's fatigue, made the night work treacherous. Robbie Travers nearly lost a finger when it got caught under a choke chain, and Todd Sharp was hauled down the mountain on a stretcher after misjudging the angle of a falling hemlock.

A week of trying to keep up the pace around the clock, and the number of near accidents was too high to be ignored. The crew boss finally told them to stop cutting at night and just keep the landings lighted, so the trucks could be loaded and runs down the mountain could continue. The women managed to keep the food production going for ten days, but there was still a lot of standing timber to cut. Mrs. G showed up for her shift on the second Thursday morning saying, "If they can keep this pace, they'll get it done. They're getting their second wind up there."

Grace looked at the calendar, "The government isn't going to enforce the regulations on the stroke of midnight, anyway. Right?"

No one answered this. They put their heads down and got their hands moving.

"Let's just keep it up, gals." Mrs. G was a cheerleader at heart. "We can do this!" All that day, they pumped one another up, believing the men still had time. Their shared hope was like an epidemic of blindness. They were all caught off guard when Henry stumbled through the door of the café that evening carrying a load of reality and dropped it right in front of them.

"Time to quit, gals. The Feds sent an inspector. They're pulling the plug on us."

Once the big push in the woods was halted, the town deflated. No one was willing to say so out loud, but everyone knew that if they couldn't fulfill the last contract, the mill wasn't going to survive. Folks began to consider their options.

"You don't know nothing about that mess someone left in front of the café a few weeks back, do you, son?" Burt Samson asked Patrick the day after they'd shut down the operation.

"What the hell are you talking about?" Pat laughed.

"There's been some talk about how there was a cartoon painted on the café door or something. Rotten eggs. Mean stuff." Burt tried to look into his son's eyes, but Pat kept his gaze down.

"So what if it was me? I'm not sayin' it was, but so what? Those Tillmans are a bunch of tree huggers and everyone in town knows it."

"Yeah? And you let Parrot work her butt off to feed us all through that push? I don't know what's going on between you and that girl, but you need to remember how people talk around here. We can't afford to look like a bunch of ignorant roughnecks who gotta thing for killin' owls. Who knows but some reporter could get wind of what's happening here. What do you think they'd do with that?"

"You think the federal government is going to care what one reporter says about a town too small to even show up on those maps they got in DC?" Pat sat down hard on the desk, spraying papers all over the floor.

"Human interest."

Burt stooped and picked up an invoice that had floated behind the desk.

"It's what sells papers and it's what gets folks paying attention. Right now those hippy kids are getting all the attention, cryin' about how ugly the clear-cuts are. But for my money they look like a bunch of lunatics. We gotta stay out of the limelight. We do not want any inspectors poking their noses in our woods, do we?" Burt pointed his finger at Pat's chest. "You got a responsibility now, son. You're the face of the mill now, so don't go adding fuel to the damn fire."

"I'm going nuts in this office, Dad." The men had had a meeting, back when Jackson had first presented his plan for turning the mill over to them. They'd agreed to keep the most experienced woodsmen in the woods. Let the younger guys rotate through the office, the mill, and finally the woods. Give them the bigger picture. Pat was put in the office to start. "I'm no good at this."

"You're a fresh face, son. Not rough and scaly around the edges like the rest of us. You could make us all look good if you had the right attitude." Burt lifted his cap off his head and ran his hand over his thinning gray hair. "You've got history here. You know what me and your uncles feel about the forest. You're the future. That's what people need to understand." He handed the invoice to Pat.

"And what are we doing with this?" He swept his hand around, taking in all the paperwork scattered across the floor. "Do I need to bring your momma in here to get this place organized?"

Pat raised his eyebrows. "Would she do it? That would be great!"

Burt laughed. "Are you kidding? She'd love to get her hands on this place. She'll organize the life out of this place if we let her."

After the intensity of working day and night to keep the crew fed, Grace felt more comfortable around folks in town. Business wasn't any better at the café, but at least now she knew it wasn't because they thought she had picked the other side. Who could afford to spend money when no one could be sure if they'd have work next month or even next week?

Grace's bills wouldn't wait, though. She'd bought a lot of food for the mill on Sherrie's promise that once they got the wood cut and shipped, the mill would be able to pay her. But the men hadn't cut enough to fill the whole order and Pat managed to be somewhere else whenever Grace stopped by the mill office. She suspected the money wasn't coming any time soon.

She cut way back on her food orders and kept the lights on for the few wayward tourists or hikers who stumbled in for directions or to buy a cup of coffee or a burger. Lyle was a pretty low-maintenance guy, but he had to buy gas for his truck and pay his insurance. They talked about him moving on, finding another job where he actually got paid, but he was willing to hang in there living on his government check for a bit longer.

"Prosperity is kind of hard to leave," he told her. "Even in bad times, it grows on you."

She laughed. "Don't I know it? Sounds like you have the same disease as I do."

Grace had shelter and plenty of wood to keep her warm, but the situation wasn't good. There were a couple hundred dollars left from Jackson's bequest and she used that pretty quickly paying the most urgent bills at the Hoot Owl.

She began having dreams about repo men coming to take the stove out of the café and crows picking the red vinyl seats apart to make nests out of the stuffing. Usually when she was anxious she could calm herself by painting, but even that had stopped working. She couldn't think of a way out. Early one morning, unable to sleep, she stood in front of the pile of bills stacked on the café counter. There was nothing left but to call Jane down in Seattle.

"It's really bad, Jane. We can't even pay the phone bill. I thought I'd better call before they cut us off. I don't see any alternative. I'm going to have to shut down." Grace could feel her jaw starting to quiver. She clamped her mouth shut. Couldn't expect any comfort from Jane. Just give her the facts.

"Jesus, Parrot, it's barely been a month. I seem to remember you bragging that you could make it pay in six months."

"Yeah. That was before the mill lost this last contract."

"So, you come to your senses then? Well, hallelujah! You lock up that cabin and come on down to the city. I'll find you a room and we can start the bankruptcy thing."

"That's not why I'm calling." Once again, Jane's bitter dismissal of Prosperity brought out a stubborn resistance in Grace. What came out of her mouth next surprised her more than it did Jane. "I'm not ready to give up, damn it. There's got to be something else I can do. I'm not going to the city."

Grace heard her aunt breathing into the phone. She pictured the scowl on Jane's face. "OK, Miss Head-in-the-Sand, how about this? There's some hungry people with a bit of change in their pockets camping out in the woods and trying to save the trees."

"Oh, thanks. That's a great way to get our windows shot out." Grace would have hung up if she weren't so desperate. "Why don't I just hang out a sign saying 'town traitor'? I can't feed those protestors. This town is just getting over you. That's all they need."

"Sorry, sweetheart, but as I see it this is about the only option left that doesn't involve insurance fraud. Unless you want to start going topless and offering other services behind the counter, you're not going to pay the damn bills. Your name is on that bank account too. So either figure a way out of this, or I'm doing the decent thing and filing for bankruptcy."

If she did what Jane was suggesting she might end up losing the very thing that made her want to stay in Prosperity in the first place. She belonged here, it was the only place she'd ever lived and the town was her family—these folks loved her and their love had gotten her through the loss of both her parents. Jane might be her biological family, but it was Prosperity's enfolding arms that had always given Grace comfort.

"I just can't," she said. "There's got to be another way."

"Look, Parrot, those kids in the forest are there because they believe that cutting all the trees is ruining our planet. And I believe it too. We gotta change what we're doing." Jane could make it all sound righteous and brave. "Those damn loggers have got to get their heads out of their asses and start looking around. The industry is doomed. If they can't see that . . . hell. Anyway, those kids need to eat, and you can feed them, and you just might be able to survive in the bargain. You know your way around in those woods well enough to get to the camp without anyone seeing you. Lyle's certainly not going to go blabbing."

"Shit."

"They'll keep it up with or without your food. It's on you now. Six months." Then the phone went dead.

That was all she could hope for from Jane. Grace was on her own. Clearly if she didn't find a way to keep the café running, she'd have to leave town anyway and she'd be carrying a bundle of debt besides.

When she heard Lyle come in the back door, Grace picked up the pile of bills and walked into the kitchen. "We're in a bad place. I talked to Jane and she had an idea."

"Good morning, Grace." Lyle hung his jacket on the coat rack by the door and grabbed an apron. "From the look on your face, I got a feeling I'm not going to like this idea."

"Yeah. Well, I don't like it either, but it might be our only hope." She waited for him to stop acting like it was a normal work day and look at her. "Feeding the protestors." She watched his eyebrows rise, his eyes get big. "We could hike up to their camp and bring them food. Like a catering service for hippies." She laughed in spite of the miserable tangle in her stomach.

"Wow." Lyle leaned back against the pantry door and folded his arms across his chest, and took this in. "You think it would work?" He grinned at her. "I mean, I don't like it any more than you do, but those kids probably have money. And if we can stay alive here for a while, something just might change." He nodded his head, dropped his arms, and pushed himself upright. "OK, Parrot. If it doesn't work, leaving is always an option. That's my motto."

First, they had to make contact.

Lyle agreed that Grace presented less of a threat to a group of hippies expecting trouble in the woods than he did. Plus, it wasn't unusual for her to put on a backpack and take a hike; people in Prosperity had seen her do that all her life. Lyle stayed out of the woods whenever possible.

The next morning, she packed up a bunch of sandwiches and cookies and headed up what the locals called "the middle trail." This was one of the three hiking trails that led from Prosperity up through Jake's preserve and into Mount Oren National Forest.

Everyone knew where the group of tree huggers had set up camp; it was a couple of miles from town on the edge of some old growth, just inside the park border. When the guys had set up their last-ditch operation, they'd been careful to keep well away from that spot.

Grace always enjoyed a chance to hike in the forest. Even with the sense of betrayal she was carrying with her that morning, she was still cheered by the calls of flickers and the shafts of sunlight that shot through the green. The first half mile or so was a gradual slope, but after the trails converged and she took the fork leading up toward the camp, the trail began switchbacking steeply. If she got this gig, she was going to get plenty of exercise. As she got close to the camp, she heard laughter and the strains of a guitar. She rounded the last switchback in the trail and found them. Dotting the forest floor were a few orange tents, covered with dark rainflies. They'd hung a large blue tarp among three trees; beneath it a few sleeping bags were laid out over another tarp on the ground; three or four people were dozing or reading in this shelter. The guitar player was sitting on a boulder near the tarp, he faced into the forest, his back to Grace.

Warren had taught his daughter how to hike quietly and it was her habit. She made no noise as she approached the camp. No one noticed her until she was standing in their midst.

"Hi."

Nervous as she was, Grace hoped she appeared friendly.

The music stopped, books dropped. Then nothing. No one moved or even smiled.

"I'm Grace."

"Hi, Grace." A woman's voice. Grace turned to see dark dreadlocks framing a bright round face peering out of one of the tents. The young woman stepped forward; she appeared to be about Grace's age. Like Grace, she wore mud-splattered jeans and a dirty down jacket. Her smile beamed welcome. "Hi. I'm Chelsea."

"Hey. I was just wondering if you guys would like some food. I mean, to buy some food." Grace started shifting her backpack off of her shoulders.

"Yeah? You delivering?"

"What is this, you sent by the enemy to poison us?"

All this from the direction of the large tarp. Grace turned toward the voices. She hadn't registered this group in detail before: a gray-haired man in khaki trousers and a fisherman's knit sweater leaning back in a camping chair. He nodded somberly at her.

"We're fine. Don't need a thing." The other two were younger, maybe high school age, in jeans and sweatshirts. The thought flashed across Grace's mind that this was a father and his sons, all fighting for their cause together. Against her town. Suddenly she felt surrounded and vulnerable. She looked back at Chelsea, whose smile had faded.

"You want to sell us food?"

"Yep. I run the café down in Prosperity and I thought . . . You know, since you're here and you don't appear to be leaving any time soon." She rested her pack on the ground and opened the top flap. She pulled out a few sandwiches wrapped in plastic and held them out toward Chelsea. "I thought you might be getting hungry."

"You're from that logging town?" Chelsea eyed the thick slices of what looked like homemade bread. "Why would you do this?" "

"Well, honestly? I'm desperate." Grace knew she was no good at lying. All she could do was lay out her situation and pray. "My business has dried up. No one can afford to come to the café for meals anymore. So, I figured . . ."

"Who knows you're doing this?" Grace was startled by a voice behind her. She swung around to see the guitar player— the only guy whose face wasn't hidden by whiskers. He was tall and wiry. Grace felt a momentary urge to give him a sandwich whether he paid for it or not.

"Well, it's just an idea me and Lyle—the guy who works with me at the café—we just talked about trying it. So, I came up here to see. Nobody else knows anything about it. That's the deal. I could bring you food, but nobody in town can know."

"Right." Chelsea nodded. She put her hands on her hips, shook her head and started to turn away. Then she stopped and looked over at Grace's pack. "Got anything in there for a vegan?"

SECTION 2: CHARLIE

Chapter 8

"Now the goddamned government says it a crime to cut trees."

"Yeah, we're criminals. Fuckin' criminals with chain saws."

Charlie Roberge was headed north from the California border pushing through Oregon when he heard the talk over the CB. More jobs shutting down. More lumbermen racing against time. The cloud-masked sky was falling.

He began counting the mile markers on I-5 when he crossed the Washington State line.

He'd just glimpsed the gilded dome of the capital building poking through the top of the fog as he passed Olympia, when he saw the nose of a southbound Kenworth ramming through the low-lying cloud. Behind that one came a mile-long line of logging trucks with their empty beds collapsed. Charlie reached into the pocket of his work shirt and pulled out a cigarette. He held it between his lips, unlit.

The southbound log trucks breathed like dragons roused from their caves, smoke streaming from their vertical exhaust pipes, their binder chains rattling in frustration. Designed to haul the weight of big timber, all they carried now was weightless hope. The caravan curved around the interchange, winding off the freeway and turning west. It was no secret where they were headed. The loggers' plan was to block Highway 101, stopping traffic across the Hoquiam River and grabbing the attention of the world.

Charlie bit off the filter of his cigarette, spit it out the open window, and reached for the Bic on his dash. He'd made it a hundred and forty miles without a smoke; that was good enough for today.

The cab of his Peterbilt was as close to a home as any Charlie had had since he was eighteen. He conscientiously swept wood debris and mud from the floorboards every day; he wiped dirt from the seats and dash and emptied the ashtray with the care of a compulsive housewife.

Holding his foot on the gas, he forged north. He wished those southbound truckers well, but their fury was infectious and he couldn't afford to catch it.

The phone call had come in the early morning over a month ago. Charlie had been asleep in room seventeen of the Siskiyou Motor Lodge. He always slept in seventeen when he worked southern Oregon. It was tucked behind the main strip of rooms that faced the highway. It was almost quiet and he could park his Peterbilt in the shadows.

The sound had pierced its irritating way down through the thick dark of his dream. Charlie rolled onto his side to avoid it, but as he reached out to grab a scaly tree branch and pull himself deeper into the woods, he found instead a tangle of sheets, the softness of a mattress beneath him. Still the insistent noise.

Finally the phone dragged him up through the forest of his nightmare. Coughing, he grabbed the receiver.

"Yeah?" Sleep cottoned his voice unmistakably.

"Charlie? That you? Get up, boy!"

"Who is th—Dad?"

"Charlie, times' wastin'. You got to get movin'!"

Charlie held the receiver out in front of his face, put his feet on the thin carpet, and shook his head. This had to be a dream. He hung up the phone and walked into the bathroom. In the few moments before the phone rang again, Charlie had pissed, splashed a few handfuls of cold water on his face, and considered the possibility that his father had actually called him.

He grabbed the receiver after the first ring.

"Dad? Jesus, I thought I was still dreaming. How did you find me?"

"Dispatcher. What the hell? You think you can't be found, boy? You done with that piddlin' job in the Siskiyous yet?"

"Yeah, Dad, I'm done."

"You got another job lined up?"

Charlie hesitated. He didn't want to give his father the advantage of knowing how desperate he was for work, but, hell, he was a log truck driver. Desperation was part of the job these days. The initial adrenalin the ringing phone had shot through him was wearing off and the old disappointment was surfacing.

"What is this, another great job offer from the reputable Nathan Roberge?"

"Listen, Charlie, I may not always play by government rules, but I ain't no criminal and I take care of my family. So, you shut your mouth and listen to me!"

"OK, Dad."

"You got truck payments, don't ya?"

"Yeah, Dad, I have truck payments. You know I do. That's not why you woke me up. Get on with it."

"Well, as a matter of fact, that's exactly why I woke you up, Charlie. 'Cause I got a way for you to make those damn payments."

Charlie reached out for the pack of Marlboros on the bedside table. His father had been trying to entice him into one of his schemes for years, but Charlie had been determined to make it on his own without resorting to the quasi-legal behavior Nathan was so skilled at.

He sighed and lit up, inhaling long and slow before answering.

"I'm sure you do, Dad." Holding the receiver, Charlie walked over to the window and looked out at his truck. Why couldn't he just to do honest, necessary work and not have to sit in some stale office pushing paper around? All he'd wanted was to work in the woods and be proud of his job. When he was a kid, loggers had the best job in the world. Hell, being a logger was all Charlie dreamed about until Uncle Walt let him crawl behind the wheel of one of the gigantic Macks he was working on; from then on Charlie was hooked on log trucks. He'd set his sights on owning his own rig. Being his own boss, he believed he'd always have work. But that was before all this crap with the fucking owl. Now nobody could count on having any kind of job in the woods unless they were some sort of goddamned owl inspector.

"You got to promise me you're not going to back me into a corner here, Dad. This isn't like the last time, when you tried to give me a kickback on your scaling bullshit, is it? 'Cause I ain't that desperate." Not yet, anyway.

Three years before when Charlie had gotten the bank to loan him the money for the truck, he'd called Nathan to tell him the great news. Nathan had been even more delighted than Charlie had expected. This, it seemed, was going to work right into his plans. Back then Nathan was working as a scaler at a small mill in Fog Valley, Oregon. He was in a position, he told his son, to help a driver make a nice bit of extra change.

All Charlie had to do was look the other way and Nathan would do the work.

As a scaler, Nathan measured and graded the logs brought into the mill; he was the guy who determined how good the wood was and how much of it a log was going to yield. It took an expert eye to see the flaws in a log, to know, before it was milled, how much of it was going to be wasted by splits and knots. Nathan was good at his job and he knew how to make it pay just a bit more than any other scaler around. He'd offered to split the take with his son, and Charlie didn't have to do a thing—that was the important part. Instead of double-checking the scaler, as was Charlie's habit, he would have had to accept his father's judgment without question. Charlie knew himself—back then such guilt-freighted passivity was out of the question. He'd work for a fair dollar and take his chances. Back then there were better options.

But what Charlie saw out that window now was a hulking burden of debt, a far cry from his ticket to the good life.

"You listen here, Charlie Roberge, I'd never tried to get you into somethin' that would send you to jail. Hell, you're my goddamned son! I wouldn't do that. I just want you to be aware of opportunities. There are opportunities that come my way you wouldn't know about 'cept if I told you. So that's what I'm doing. Telling you."

"Yeah, Dad. So tell me about this opportunity." Charlie took another long drag and turned away from the window.

"Well, Charlie," Nathan's voice took on a gleeful giddiness that set Charlie's stomach churning. "What's so sweet about this particular opportunity is that you'll get to go home again."

"Home?"

"Yes, son, back to Prosperity."

Now, as the miles rolled under his wheels, bringing Charlie closer to the town where he was born, anxiety flooded through him. His last view of Prosperity had been out the rear window of his mother's Chevy station wagon as she drove the two of them away from his wooded childhood and down to the city where he would endure his adolescence. That car had been weighed down with mountains of his mother's bitterness. He was twelve years old the last time he saw Prosperity, and the name still tasted of confusion and grief.

Who would remember him? Surely his Uncle Walt, even in a drunken haze, would know his nephew. But there could not be many others. The guys he'd learned his way through the woods with, they must have all scattered by now.

Nathan had given him one parting warning: "Stay away from Parrot, Charlie. She's probably still there. Don't go riling things up with that girl. It won't do nobody any good."

Parrot. He hadn't thought of that name in years. Now, seeing the exit sign ahead, Mt. Oren National Forest/Prosperity, he was suddenly twelve years old again, his back pressed against the red vinyl of a booth in the Hoot Owl Café.

"What are you doin'? Are you writing?" Her sticky hands poked at his math sheets, getting crumbs all over them.

"Go away. I have to do my homework." He sat up and leaned over the table, using his arm to shield his paper.

"Why is it homework, if you're doing it here? This is my mommy's café. She bakes pies. You want some pie? I like the cherry. And the rhubub. What do you like?"

"It's rhubarb, not rhubub. Now go away."

Strange how the details came back to him—the jukebox was playing Johnny Cash: "She'll go sailing off on any old wind that blows." Across the café Nathan was talking in a low murmur and Charlie could hear Annie's nervous giggle.

Parrot climbed up onto the bench on the opposite side of the table from where he tried to focus on math problems. She scooted over to the window and pressed her head against the glass.

"My daddy is sad."

In her voice, innocent and raw, these words sounded prophetic. Charlie looked up. He wondered if she were going to start crying. Instead, she slid down on the red bench and stretched her little body out along its worn surface, disappearing from his view.

Everyone in town knew Parrot's dad, Warren. He was the best logger Jackson had; even Charlie revered him. It was hard to imagine Warren sad, but Charlie suspected his daughter was right.

Charlie glanced over his shoulder; his father's back was to him, but Charlie could see Annie's face clearly. She was smiling and there were tears in her eyes. She leaned across the counter and reached a hand out to brush Nathan's hair off his forehead.

Charlie dropped his pencil; it rolled under the table and he crawled down, into the dark space. He sat on the floor and looked over at the little girl sleeping with her legs pulled up under her and her thumb in her mouth. He felt bad he'd brushed her off. *Poor kid*, he'd thought.

He scooted out from under the table. "Dad," he called to Nathan. "Can we go home now?"

What would she be now, twenty or so? Still in Prosperity. *Of course my father wants me to keep away from her; seeing me is*

only going to remind her of him and that won't be good. Not for him and not for me, Charlie thought. And he geared the truck down as he began to climb into the mountains.

It was after midnight by the time Charlie pulled into Prosperity. He hadn't been sure he'd remember the way, but as he drove down the main street, it all came back to him. These streets were used to the weight of trucks like his: the ruts were smooth, and Charlie could feel the give of his tires easing into them. It was like driving an old horse to the barn. In the glow of his headlights, the mill looked smaller than the picture he carried in his mind—the one created by a boy who knew no other lumber mills. Charlie was momentarily confused by a gravel parking area behind the mill office and what looked like a couple of new houses down the street. He remembered a ragged space, blackberry bushes humped among a few scrawny maples separating the mill from the town. How often had his mother sent him down across that tangled space, that no-man's land where Jake's old cabin stood, to hurry his father home for dinner? He had hated the trek, feared the stories of ghosts and monsters that haunted the abandoned cabin.

They'd surely torn that place down by now.

Charlie drove around the back of the mill and found a spot behind a pile of raw logs. He'd leave his truck there for the night till he checked in with Walt and got the lay of the land.

He turned off the engine and looked around the inside of the cab, sticking his Bic in his pocket and brushing the dust from the seat. He opened the door and stepped down, stretching his long legs. He stood to his full six foot three and leaned his shoulder against the door of his rig to shut it. Charlie rubbed a hand over his face, his chin darkened by a three-day growth. Taking a deep breath, he pulled a cigarette from his pocket and held it between his fingers as he surveyed the territory. From this vantage point things made more sense. The new houses and the parking lot had disoriented him; he'd been looking in the wrong spot. There was the old cabin. And it looked like someone was living there—there were lights shining out of the windows. Hell, there were windows.

Things had changed.

Charlie and his mother, Marcia, had only been living in Seattle for a few months when she went back to Prosperity to find her brother and gather him up after the accident. She offered him the same cure she'd provided for herself.

"You are not responsible, Walt. Stop beating yourself up. You need to get away from that stinking, inbred town. You can find a decent-paying job in the city and put that all behind you." As she drove him out of the mountains, she harped on him with a sisterly impatience.

"If anyone's to blame, it's Nathan. You told him you had more work than you could handle. He didn't care about anything but his own damn cheating self." She played that note so often that both her son and her brother soon became deaf to it.

Walt stayed with Marcia and Charlie for a couple of years, giving his nephew a hint of what a father could be, and initiating him into the clanging magic of engines. But Walt never made peace with the city.

But by the time Charlie had worked his way up to star forward on his high school basketball team, Marcia's roof was feeling too low for her brother. Against her pleas, Walt made his way back to Prosperity—to drink himself to death, Marcia said. To take care of the old house, he said.

"The kid doesn't need anything I can give him." Charlie's assimilation into urban life freed Walt from any sense of responsibility to his nephew. "He's found his place."

But what Walt saw in Charlie's aggression on the basketball court wasn't so much an assimilation to urban life as the accommodation of a young man at war with mounting internal demons. The landscape of Charlie's dreams had remained the mountains and the towering trees of Prosperity. The city jangled him and set his nerves on edge, filling him with fears he couldn't explain. On the basketball court, he ran that frenetic energy down to a place where he could breathe and sleep.

Marcia pushed Charlie into college, harping on it as the only way to a decent life. But once he got there, his mother's predictions about his future faded, as the demons of anxiety blossomed. Charlie knew he couldn't go on sitting in a classroom taking notes on American history and sociology. He needed to be doing something. The intimacy of a dorm room made him claustrophobic.

At the end of the first week of his sophomore year, he was standing on the porch while his mother spat at him, "All the sacrifices I made to get that money together! You're a damn fool, Charlie. You'll end up a con man like your father. Or worse—chopping logs. Everybody knows that's a dead end."

Then she turned her back on him and slammed the front door. That was the last image Charlie carried of her—the fury of her red face, the tremble of that slam shuddering through his body.

He'd almost shouted back at her, reminded her that his father had a college education, well, a couple of years in college anyway, and look at where that led. But he knew it wouldn't do any good. His mother was a stubborn woman. He assumed she'd calm down in time, but meanwhile he had to find a way to support himself.

There was lots of work in the woods that year—forest managers around Washington were setting the limits as high as they could—but Charlie didn't have the kind of connections that he needed to get a logging job. He couldn't trade on his father's name, that was certain. Aside from his parents, his only other living relative was his uncle Walt.

"What do you mean you left school? Are you a damn fool?" Had his uncle spoken with his mother? Charlie was blindsided by Walt's reaction.

"But you know what it's like, Walt. You told me yourself, you couldn't stomach classrooms."

"Yeah, well, that was me and I'm nobody you want for a role model. What do you plan for your next round, becomin' a drunk?"

"I thought . . . Well, I just want to work in the woods. You know guys. I thought you could maybe . . ."

"You really think the guys I know are gonna want somebody with my blood cutting trees next to them? Wake up, Charlie! You got a couple of big strikes against you around here—me and your dad. You'll have to go down to Oregon or California, where nobody knows you or your family. Good luck with that."

Without any family connections, Charlie knew he'd have to have a lot more skill than he did to get any logging company to hire him. If Walt couldn't help, he was really on his own.

So, he'd taken the only other path he knew anything about and started driving an eighteen-wheeler. He'd learned the basics from a truck-driving course advertised in the classifieds of the *Seattle P-I*. And soon his home was the cab of a truck.

Charlie drove over-the-road for few years. The constant movement kept his demons at bay and the money wasn't bad. Not a lot by most standards, but Charlie had virtually no expenses. He had no wife, no family to support; he had no house, not even a car. All he bought was his daily food, an occasional night in a hotel when he couldn't stand the truck for another minute, a rare change of clothes, and his union dues. Everything else he earned went into the bank. His goal was the down payment on a log truck. Being an independent log truck driver sounded like heaven back then.

During those over-the-road years a white plastic alarm clock with its glowing numbers oriented him when he woke in the dark. He would rise from his narrow bunk in the back of the cab, dress quickly in the jeans and T-shirt he had folded on the seat the night before. Breakfast was bad coffee in a Styrofoam cup and a donut with hard icing, usually white, that shocked his teeth.

To keep the demons appeased, Charlie followed a careful ritual as he prepared to roll out onto the highway. First, he circled the truck checking for any signs of tampering in the night. He'd test the tires, the lights, the turn signals, the mirrors. If he stumbled at any point or the order of his routine was interrupted, he would be haunted all day by images of lacerated cars with their doors ripped off and their smoking, bloody innards exposed. He coped with this constant shadow of anxiety by building elaborate, detailed stories that filled the void of his what-if worries.

Compulsively he grasped small details in his daily life and divined their potential for trauma, their possibility for disaster. And then he rehearsed. If he noticed a young woman pull into a truck stop to fill up, as she headed toward the mini-mart to pay, he might conjure exploding tanks blowing her car across the lot, shooting her body through the plate glass storefront. Seeing a stray dog wandering along the street near the freeway, he pictured it running into traffic and being flattened by his tires.

He placed his faith in this belief: if he could imagine it, make it vivid in his mind, it would never happen. His life had taught him that having dreams and wishing for positive outcomes led to disappointment, so he turned that lesson on its head. He believed that by picturing disasters he could prevent them.

One disaster Charlie had never imagined was his mother's death.

Marcia had a heart attack while Charlie was on his first job trucking. He was twenty-one and they hadn't spoken in a year.

Walt's phone call had found him down near Sacramento, hauling a load of something useless under a short deadline, keeping an eye out for cops.

"Charlie, you need to pull that rig over. I got some bad news."

The suddenness of a heart attack seemed the right way for her to go, once he considered it. She was a black-and-white woman, all or nothing, love or hate. And she would have hated a drawn-out dying. But they'd never had the reconciliation Charlie had expected.

Walt said he could see to the arrangements if Charlie wanted. Even as much as she railed against it, she'd have wanted to be buried with her kin in Prosperity. Didn't Charlie agree? Sure. She'd never gone to church after they moved to the city. Never talked about things like that. Whatever Walt did was fine.

Charlie didn't tell his boss or the dispatcher, the few folks he spoke with regularly, about his mother's death. He never took any time off, wasn't there when she was buried. She'd shut him out and hadn't tried to reconnect; he didn't feel entitled to open grieving.

His dropping out of college had infuriated her, but it didn't explain her complete rejection. Charlie suspected the real reason—the one that had always hung between them: He reminded her of Nathan, the man who had betrayed her. There was nothing Charlie could ever have done to fix that.

Chapter 9

As Charlie walked the few blocks from the mill to the house where he grew up and where his uncle lived, the moist mountain air calmed him, welcomed him home. Some things had changed in this town, but the Bullhook was still there, the school, even the café.

Walt's front door was worn, the paint peeling, and Charlie felt his age as he knocked.

"Jesus, Charlie, get in here," Walt pulled his nephew through the front door, then stuck his head out, looking up and down the street.

"Guess it's late enough no one saw you. We can do without Dorianne Travers announcing your arrival and reminding the whole town who I'm related to."

"Hey, Uncle Walt, good to see you, too. It's been a long time." Charlie grinned and patted his grizzled uncle on the back. The two men shared curly hair—though Walt's had gone pale and thin—and the cleft in Charlie's chin was mirrored in his uncle's face. Charlie had often been told he looked more like his mom's side of the family than Nathan's. He'd counted that as a positive.

Looking around at the unkempt space, the house where he'd spent his first twelve years, Charlie's memories were bombarded by this altered present.

A wooden hat rack had stood to the right of the door, its brass hooks laden with worn jackets that marked his moves through soccer, baseball, and Boy Scouts; his mother's red raincoat with the frayed cuffs; his father's hard hat and orange vest; at its base a pair of tall black rubber boots caked with mud—the ones he'd slid his six-year-old feet into to follow his dad to work one morning, the ones that had caused him to trip and fall down the steps, chipping his front tooth. Charlie's tongue found the rough edge now, though the boots, the jackets, and the hat rack were gone. There had been a braided rug, oval and slightly lumpy, seasoned with rain, mud, snow, dead leaves, bits of fir cones and pine needles—the debris that trailed anyone who walked through the door. The floor where he stood was bare weathered wood now. In front of him the staircase was the same, though the carpet, once a deep rose, was worn flat and colorless.

And on the third step there was the stain from the cup of coffee his father had thrown as he'd stormed out, yelling, "Marcia, just shut up for once and leave me alone!"

His mother had made a point of leaving the coffee puddle to sink into the carpet. Charlie remembered picking up the pieces of broken cup, blood blossoming on the pad of his thumb.

"You've made a few changes to the place, eh, Walt?"

"Shit, Charlie, it's been fifteen years, hasn't it? Not like I had any money to keep it up proper, but I do my best."

"Actually, it's been seventeen years since Mom and I left." Charlie dropped his duffel at the base of the stairs and faced his uncle. The disorientation he'd felt driving into town rocked him again. He remembered his uncle's thick black hair—folks laughingly accused him of slicking it back with axle grease. What grew on Walt's head now was thin and nearly white. The once robust, alcohol-reddened face was ragged, the eyes sunken. Charlie could smell the whiskey on him. That, at least, was familiar.

"How are you, Walt? How are things going around here?"

Walt walked down the hall and into the kitchen, leaving Charlie to trail behind. An open bottle of whiskey sat on the battered wood table in the center of the room.

"Want a drink?" Walt poured brown liquid into a glass and held it out to his nephew, then he took a swig from the bottle. "Listen, Charlie, I know your daddy sent you here with some idea that you could make him a few bucks and find yourself some work, but I'm not for it."

Charlie took the glass and looked at the smudged rim. He put it down on the table and sat on one of the ladder-back chairs that looked vaguely familiar.

"Yeah? You got a better idea?"

Walt took another swig and leaned back against the countertop. "They could use a decent mechanic in this town."

"Walt, I'm a truck driver, not a mechanic. And I've got truck payments." He wished he could get some of that whiskey down his throat without putting his lips to the filthy glass. "Jackson still got guys cutting wood that needs hauling or not?"

Walt shook his head slowly. "Boy, you don't know nothing. Jackson Dyer ain't got any work for you. He's dead and buried."

Charlie leaned forward and slapped his hands flat on the table. "What are you saying? Jackson's dead? When? Jesus. Is the mill shut down then? Goddamn, Nathan!"

Walt was silent for a while.

"No, mill's not shut and they got some kinda wood to haul." He sat down and looked at his nephew through rheumy eyes.

"How much of your father you got in you, Charlie?" He leaned forward and with great care laid his head on the table and closed his eyes.

Charlie sat there for several minutes considering the question his uncle had asked. When he heard Walt snoring he rose and made his way upstairs to his childhood bedroom. A single bed with a thin chenille bedspread, yellowed with age, was all that remained to testify to his years of residence.

He walked over to the window next to the bed. His footsteps echoed off the empty walls and dust coated the windowsill, but the night view made him catch his breath. As a boy he had stared out at the sky on the cloudless nights of summer, dreaming of space travel, wishing on a million, billion stars. When he moved to the city, the loss of dark sky had been as painful as the absence of his father; yet, over the years he'd forgotten. Now he lifted the window and leaned against the sill, remembering.

The next morning Charlie was groggy as he dragged himself from bed. When he slept in a bed he hadn't prepared himself, he never slept well. At dawn he stumbled downstairs and found that Walt had made it from the kitchen chair to the sofa in the living room before passing out again. Charlie searched the cupboards for cleaning products; he needed to scour the bathroom before he'd be able to get himself ready for the day.

Beneath the sink he found some old, rusted containers of Bon Ami and a bottle of ammonia. He wondered if these could possibly be the same containers his mother had used. Didn't appear that Walt had put them to much use, but the place wasn't quite the wreck Charlie had expected. He pulled a roll of paper towels, some dishwashing soap and the scouring powder out of the cabinet and lugged them upstairs to the bathroom.

He'd finished the sink and tub and was just beginning on the toilet when Walt banged on the bathroom door.

"What the hell, Charlie?"

"Morning, Walt. It's not half as bad as I expected, you know. You had a woman living here?"

Walt grunted and turned away.

"I'll go piss in the yard. "

"No, no, Walt. Here, I'll get out. You go ahead."

"Goddamn, Charlie, your mother got herself all inside your head, didn't she? Thanks for lettin' me use my own goddamned shitter." Walt pushed past his nephew and slammed the door behind him.

Charlie leaned against the door.

"Seriously, Walt, you got a girlfriend or something? I don't want to get in the way of anything. I can go sleep in my truck or, hell, I can grab a tent and sleep in the woods."

"Shut your mouth, boy. You just got here, you ain't going nowhere." The sound of Walt's peeing was loud enough to make Charlie step back from the door.

"You can do my cleaning if you want. Grace used to handle that but now she's runnin' the café, she don't have time for me."

"Grace?"

Walt pulled open the bathroom door and looked at Charlie.

"You just keep your distance from Grace, Charlie. She don't know nothin' about your no-good dad and all that and you're not the one to be tellin' her. You got that?"

"Who the hell is Grace? What are you talking about, Walt?"

"Listen to me, Charlie," Walt grabbed the front of Charlie's work shirt and pulled his nephew's face close to his own. His breath made Charlie pull his head back so forcefully he nearly dragged both of them off their feet. Walt let go and grabbed the doorjamb to steady himself.

"She's none of your business and you are going to stay clear of her. You hear me?" Walt's command was so unexpected that Charlie could only nod, bewildered.

Walt found his footing and started for the stairs, "All right then. I'm going down to the café for my coffee. You can get yourself something at the gas station. Then, if you're stuck on doing what your daddy tells you, you go to the mill and ask for Pat."

After he heard the front door close behind his uncle, Charlie began to wonder how soon he could get over to the Hoot Owl and have a look at this Grace.

"Name's Charlie. You Pat?" Charlie stuck out his hand to the young guy standing near the pile of logs at the back of the mill. "That's my truck. I hear you guys could use a hauler."

"Where'd you hear that from?" This guy wore a brown Carhartt jacket that had seen better days. There was a gash in the right elbow that revealed the filthy lining; his pants might once have been blue jeans but now were mostly dirt. He kept his head turned to the side as he spoke to Charlie, his eyes trained on the logs in front of him. He used his hands to guide the driver of the log lifter working in front of where they stood. As Charlie waited, one log after another was raised off the pile in the jaws of the lift and deposited on the nearby scale.

"Walt deVore's my mother's brother. He and I are kinda close."

"Yeah? You a drunk too?" Now Pat folded his arms across his chest and looked straight at Charlie. His expression said he believed he knew what he was dealing with.

"No, sir. I am not. What I am is a damn good log hauler and I understand you might need one." This was one cocky punk, but if there was any chance of work Charlie was willing to pretend respect.

Pat looked over at the log truck Charlie had pointed to and raised his hand to the lift driver, signaling him to stop. "Hey, Henry, come down here. Check this guy out."

Charlie looked up into the lift and grinned. "I'll be damned! Henry Martin. It's Charlie Roberge." Henry was a bit bulkier, but otherwise looked as if the seventeen years had skimmed right over him. Charlie would have recognized him anywhere. The orange safety vest and ear protectors had initially rendered him invisible, but now Charlie could see his old friend's dark eyes and the familiar open grin.

"Jesus," was all he said as he slowly climbed down. "Jesus." He looked at Charlie with that old mixture of tolerance and condescension. "What the fuck you doin' here, man? Jesus."

"You know him?" Pat took a step toward Henry, caught his eye.

"I guess so. Only grew up together, but it's been a while."

"Yeah, well, I had a few things to do." Charlie reached out his right hand and took Henry's.

"That your truck over there? You a hauler? All right, man. We can use a good one." Henry stepped back a pace and looked his old friend up and down.

"He's OK then?" There was a hint of relief in Pat's voice. Charlie sensed this kid was fighting hard to look like he knew what he was doing.

"Yeah, I'd say so, Pat. He's OK. And I'd bet he's just as hungry as we are." He gave Charlie a questioning look.

"Hungry ain't the word for it, man. That truck is eatin' me alive."

Henry put an arm around his old friend and pulled him out of Pat's hearing. "Listen, Charlie, you know what we're doing here, right? It's no fuckin' daylight hauling job. You're ready to risk it, right?"

"Like I said, Henry, I need work bad. So don't tell me anything I don't have to know and we'll be fine."

Henry nodded and with a slap to Charlie's back, he turned and climbed up into the cab of the lifter, muttering to himself, "Charlie Roberge. Jesus."

Pat told Charlie to be back at the mill at 5 p.m. He'd tell him where the site was then and not before.

"Henry trusts you and that's fine, but the way things are going—fuckin tree huggers hanging out at the bar, for shit's sake. You slip up and we're the ones who'll pay for it. Once you've hauled some logs for us and you're in it too, then I can trust you to watch your mouth."

Now that he was back in Prosperity with old memories muddling his thoughts, a sense of regret wearing the disguise of duty directed Charlie's steps. When he turned away from the mill yard, Charlie headed toward the cemetery. He took the gravel path that ran behind the mill. His boots crunched under the arbor of old cedars. Yellow dandelion heads shone all along the trail. The familiar smell of the scant sun on wet trees calmed and softened something inside him, something that hadn't been calm for a long time.

He followed this unmarked path as it wound around the houses on the far side of town and headed down toward the church. At the top of a rise in the road, he stood looking down at the small cemetery on his left. As a kid, he'd come here on Halloween nights once or twice on a dare, and there were the times his Cub Scout troop had picked up trash and pulled weeds around the place. This was his first view of it through adult eyes.

He stepped through the archway and took a deep breath. As he walked among the gravestones, he recognized a few names: his third-grade teacher, Erma Thatcher; his Cub Scout pack leader, Daniel Boylton. The older graves, Jake Oliver's for one, were at the back. One of the tallest markers, white granite with bits of mica that caught the sun, had the name Warren Tillman carved into its face. A clear memory, like a whisper directly in his ear—his mother's voice, "Warren Tillman was such a fool. He just let it go on right under his nose." Then her sobbing. "Almost as much a fool as I was."

Charlie didn't see a deVore on any of the prominent headstones. But there were a number of flat markers, some so worn they were hard to read. He took his time.

When he finally found her, she was off to the side near the hedge of arborvitae, next to a pair of older markers for Minnie and Alton, grandparents who had died before Charlie formed a memory of them.

At her grave Charlie bent to pull the tall blades of crabgrass and gray dandelion puffs. From his lowered position he glanced back at Warren's grave. There, on the weedless rectangle of grass, a vase filled with white roses recently cut and a small American flag spoke of loyal care.

Charlie turned back to his mother and let the weight of difference rest in a guilty fog about his shoulders. He had not been loyal, he had not remembered, he had not taken care. And now he was only here because the man she'd called "that no-good, cheating SOB" had sent him back here, back home.

"Anybody see you?" Pat was taking his lines from some old gangster movie.

Charlie gave him an are-you-kidding-me look. "Uh . . . a few deer. Otherwise, I managed to get here undetected."

"Look, this is no game. We don't know who we can trust anymore."

"OK. Nobody saw me. Just tell me where to go." As he spoke, Charlie walked slowly around his truck, looking carefully at the tires, testing the chains, checking the lay of the back end.

"I'll show you." Pat pulled open the passenger side door of Charlie's cab. "Holy shit. You ever use this thing? Looks brand new."

"I like to keep it clean." Charlie climbed into the driver's seat. He went through the rest of his routine, checking the gauges, the lights, setting and resetting the mirrors. Finally, he turned to Pat. "OK, where to?"

Pat guided him out of town and up a logging road that Charlie knew hadn't been there when he was a kid. This part of the forest ran right along the border between the national forest and Jake Oliver's woods. Back then, nobody would have considered driving a truck up through these trees.

The headlights shone on the muddy ruts, large rocks casting shadows. Along the right side of the road, branches of hemlock and cedar like dense fur brushed dark and soft on the side-view mirror. On the left, the forest had been thinned; there were open patches and Charlie caught glimpses of a ragged carpet of splintered wood, discarded limbs, and bark that shone red in the moonlight.

"You guys been working up here for a while?" His hands were vibrating on the steering wheel, reading the road like tire-cushioned Braille. His booted feet worked the pedals, the engine roaring at him. But he wasn't finding the calm that usually came with feeling the power moving up a mountain. Charlie didn't like riders when he worked.

"Yeah, well, we were working that north slope there," Pat jerked his head to the left, not taking his eyes off the road ahead, "when they fucking shut us down. Still had lots of equipment up here. Couldn't see a need to bring it all down."

"Yeah." Charlie's stomach tightened. His father would hit it off good with this kid. "So, you kept going. At night?"

"We ain't stupid, man. Just keep driving, you'll see."

Charlie shifted down and let the engine's growl act as his response. Hunger can make any man stupid, he thought. So stupid he can mistake dangerous for righteous and end up driving blind.

This thought triggered the old anxiety. A litany of all the things that could go wrong played in his mind: a log would slip sideways out of the grasp of the lifter as he was loading his truck, crushing someone; his brakes would lock up, or he'd lose his lights; or most likely, he'd end up in jail, probably sharing a cell with this idiot, Pat. The only way Charlie knew to get control when this started was to let it play out, to imagine a full-blown disaster.

Pat wouldn't shut up. "You grew up around here, huh? Go to Cooper?"

Charlie took his time answering. His father was hooked into this job probably through one of the older guys. Best not to play on that connection. Nathan had left way too much bitterness in his wake.

"Moved down to Seattle when I was in seventh grade. This my first time back." Static on the CB broke into their conversation. Pat grabbed the radio before Charlie could reach over to where it hung from the rearview mirror.

"Empty mile three, heading for the curve." Pat spoke into the radio.

A voice crackling with static: "Roger that. I'm loaded at the landing."

"Roger that." Pat released the button and let go of radio. It swung back on its cord and dangled above the dash.

Charlie looked at his odometer as he asked Pat. "How far's the landing?"

"Mile seven. There's a siding at six."

Charlie nodded. Before Pat could start up with the personal questions again, Charlie had a few of his own. "How long you think Dyer's can hold on? I've seen a lot of bigger mills go under in the last year."

"You know it's our mill now, right?" Pat leaned forward and turned toward Charlie. "Before Jackson Dyer died, he turned the mill over to us to manage." He poked his chest with his index finger. "We got a contract overseas and we're gonna to fill it."

Charlie took this in. "Who's us?"

"The crew." Again the finger on his chest. "Guys worked at the mill and in the woods, the sawyers, cutters, choke setters, everybody. Not a lot of us left by then, but Jackson knew who would stay loyal." He grabbed the radio again. "Empty mile five. We'll pull into the siding at six."

"Copy. Loaded mile seven. Heading down."

Charlie scanned the road ahead looking for the siding, but his headlights only exposed the thickness of trees on his left and an open expanse on his right. They were climbing steeply now. His right wheels hugging the edge.

"Right up there, hard to see, a flat spot on the right. It'll hold you." Pat pointed into the darkness.

"Jesus. Isn't there a spot to the left?" Charlie geared down. The engine announced itself, the jake brakes drumming.

Pat's hand continued to point, Charlie could hear the downhill-bound truck now; he still couldn't see the siding, just open blackness.

"Pull over, now. Turn her soft." Pat gestured with the radio squeezed in his hand.

Charlie braked down again. Still nothing visible on his right.

"Now, asshole!" Pat yelled at him and started to reach for the wheel.

"I got it." Charlie steered the Peterbilt off the road onto a flat outcropping that hung over the valley. His headlights shone out into the void.

Pat spoke into the radio. "Empty at the siding, mile six."

"Loaded mile six." And here she came, growling, more than eighty thousand pounds barreling toward them as she pulled out of a blind curve ahead.

Images raced through Charlie's head now. The downhill truck losing control as she straightened out from the curve, heading right for them, knocking them both over the edge. Charlie gripped the wheel and let them come. The shattering sound of metal and glass, the sensation of being thrown against the door, tumbling into the darkness. Adrenalin pumped through him just as if it were happening.

"Hey. He's passed us. What you waiting for, the green light?" Pat pounded the dashboard.

Charlie looked over at his passenger. If Henry weren't on this job, Charlie just might have turned around right then. But where would he go? What else could he do?

Pat went silent once they were on the road again. Charlie's breathing slowed.

Dense tangles of living trees crowded on either side and caught the edges of spray from the truck's headlights as they climbed inland. Charlie began to get the picture. The cut was selective, precise. This wasn't national forest anymore. This was private land.

Henry was operating the lifter. When Charlie got out of his truck to watch him place the logs in her bed, Henry called down to him. "Hey, Charlie. That siding's a bitch at night, isn't it?"

"No shit. Where the hell are we?"

"You don't want to know, buddy." Henry pulled his head back into the cab and got back to work.

Charlie ran half a dozen loads over the course of the night. When he headed down the last time, Henry jumped in the cab. "Take me home, man."

"Yeah? Don't want a beer? It's been a long night." Charlie pulled out from the landing and headed down the mountain.

"Yeah, well. Tavern's closed now, Charlie. Anyway, we don't show up in town after a night like this, man. We don't need anybody seeing us dog-tired at five o'clock in the morning."

"Right." Neither man said anything more till they'd traveled halfway down to the mill.

"You figure it out?" Henry's slow voice in the darkness.

"Huh?"

"Shit, Charlie. You know where we're at here."

Charlie shook his head and hit the palm of his right hand hard against the steering wheel. "Does Rose know about this?"

Henry sighed. "That something you need to know or are you just asking?"

"Yeah. Forget it."

Chapter 10

Charlie fell into a routine over the next week. He'd drive the muddy road up the mountain through Jake Oliver's preserve and down to the mill several times each night, finally hauling his last load somewhere around four a.m. Then he'd crawl into bed as the sun was coming up and wake in the afternoon. He'd fix himself a meal that would carry him through the evening, then go to the mill yard and wash his truck before the night's work began again.

The late summer days were beginning to whisper hints of fall and there were hikers and hunters driving through town looking for trailheads, hoisting ridiculous packs on their backs and charging up logging trails.

On Sunday morning after Charlie had fallen asleep just three hours before, pounding on the front door woke him. Walt stayed locked deep in an alcoholic slumber, snoring like an out-of-tune diesel engine. But the pounding jolted through Charlie's system and he jumped up, terrified.

He leaned his head against the window next to his bed and he looked down at the front of the house.

"Charlie. Get up!" Charlie could see the ragged cuff of Pat's jean-clad leg and the back of his fist as he raised it, preparing to pound the door again.

Charlie threw open the window and leaned out. "Shut the fuck up! What the hell?"

Pat stepped back off the porch and looked up. "We need to get out in the woods."

"Jesus, man, I just got to bed."

"Yeah, well, I didn't. Come down here. I need to talk to you."

Charlie pulled his head back inside and shut the window. This job was getting out of control. And Pat—the kid was more than a little crazy. He really believed they'd be able to keep the mill open and save their jobs by stealing trees from Jake Oliver's preserve. Charlie knew it wouldn't work; the whole thing was plain wrong. But right now the money was coming and he wasn't ready to walk away from the woods. His body vibrated as the adrenalin continued to course through him. *Shit.*

He pulled on the filthy jeans that he'd laid carefully across the chair the night before. He grabbed the pack of Marlboros off the bedside table and headed downstairs.

As he pulled open the door, he growled, "I don't drive without sleep." Then he turned his back and walked into the kitchen. Pat followed. The stuttering bass of Walt's snoring rumbled through the house.

"We gotta head off those damn tourists. I saw a car pull onto the turnoff for the road we're using." Pat pulled out a chair but didn't sit.

"Well, what the hell do you think we can do?" Shit. Here it comes, Charlie thought. If not today, soon. This can't go on. "You sure they're just hikers, not those protesters?"

"No. Hell. No, I'm not sure." Pat began to pace around the small kitchen. "We gotta do something. They're going to see new tire tracks. They'll smell something."

"OK, look. Those kids set up a camp on the other side of Oliver's woods, right?"

"Yeah. Next to the park boundary, near the top of the ridge."

"Right. So how'd they get there? Closest way?"

Pat took his time. Charlie knew any born-and-raised Prosperity kid could picture all the trails through the woods in his head. "OK, probably start above the mill and at the junction, I'd take that one steep trail that switchbacks across the face of the mountain. There's other ways, but they'd be a lot longer."

"If these guys are joining them, that's where they're going, then. They aren't headed up where we are. Maybe you ought to follow them, make sure."

But it was just a matter of time; Charlie could see that Pat knew this too.

"Me? Charlie, you gotta do this. No one around here knows you. Those assholes all know me and know I run the mill. They'd put it together."

"Oh, you run the mill? Didn't know that." Charlie wasn't smiling.

"Fuck. That's what they think, anyway. We only need another week and we'll have enough wood to fill the order. We can't let them stop us now. You gotta go."

"Yeah. Well, I don't gotta do anything, but looks like I'm not getting any sleep." Charlie turned on the kitchen faucet and pulled out the Mr. Coffee and the can of Folgers he'd bought the first week after he'd moved in. "You add a few hours to my pay and I'll take a walk up the mountain. See what I see."

Pat nodded. "Good." He turned away from Charlie and let himself out. Walt kept insisting Charlie had to stay away from the café and he hadn't had time or energy to fight him on it. He started the coffee and headed upstairs to dress. He might not be able to prevent the inevitable, but he could at least enjoy a beautiful day in the woods.

He should have asked Pat for a few more details. The trail map in his head had been drawn by a boy who used fallen branches and deer tracks as landmarks. Over seventeen years a growing forest struggling against greedy loggers erased such delicate signs. Didn't really matter, though. What made the most sense was to head up toward the operation, so he could see if anyone was checking them out.

When he saw the first Private Land No Logging sign, Charlie pushed his way right past it. He looked around him at the huge, mossy trunks and up at the thick canopy of interwoven green. *Yeah, Jake, I know,* Charlie thought. *This is a hell of a lot prettier than a clear-cut—that's obvious. But they're just trees, they'll grow back. That's the beautiful thing about it. We can cut 'em down and use 'em, build the things we need, replant, and in a few years the place is green again.*

Charlie took his time, relishing the cool, rich air on his skin and in his lungs. He'd left his cigarettes at home. A slight breathlessness as the trail got steeper slowed him. *Gotta quit that shit. Get out here more.* He was lost in his own thoughts, in the feel of his feet finding stability among the stones and roots that crossed the narrow trail, in the effort of his legs as he climbed. The sound of someone headed down the trail startled him—the soft clang of metal on metal, the slight quiver in the earth with each nearing footfall, and a faint humming of a female voice. He stopped abruptly and listened. Yes, definitely a female voice, coming closer. He looked up the trail, but it wound through thick undergrowth with trees so close to its edges that he couldn't see far ahead. *OK, he thought, I'm just a hiker, there's no problem.*

He continued ahead a few paces and saw a red knit cap emerge from behind a tree, then a curtain of black hair that caught a glimmer of sunlight. She was looking away from him and he realized she'd stepped off the trail. Then he heard a distinct sound of trickling water. He coughed loudly.

"Ooops. Never fails. If you get lonely in the woods, just step behind a tree and pull your pants down. Someone will show up right away." She laughed.

Charlie responded with a loud chuckle. "Guess I'm right on cue, then." But he didn't move.

"Come on ahead. I'm done," she called to him.

"You're coming down awfully early. Camp nearby?" He asked as he walked a few steps up the hill and came up next to the young woman who sported the red cap. She was looking down, away from him; her hair reminded him of crows' wings, blue-black, draped across the back of her neck.

With little effort she lifted a large pack onto her shoulders. An aluminum water bottle swung from a tie near the top. As she reached up to pull her cap down over her hair, the water bottle clanged against what looked like the handle of a large knife sticking out of the top of the pack. She turned toward him, squinting her eyes against the few rays of sun that had managed to work their way through the veil of fir and hemlock, and gave him such a startlingly beautiful smile it felt like a gift.

"Umm. Enjoy your walk."

She nodded, stepped back onto the trail, and began walking down the mountain.

"Hey, wait," Charlie called to her. "You couldn't tell me where, um, where there's . . . I mean I'm looking for . . ." She stopped and turned to look back at him. She put her hands on the shoulder straps of her pack and tilted her head.

"What?"

"I, um, I heard there's a camp of tree huggers around here. You know where they're at?" Charlie knew he'd be lousy at this subterfuge shit.

She shrugged her shoulders, and the water bottle clanged against the knife in her pack.

"Nope." She began to turn away again but stopped. "It's easy to get lost around here if you don't know these woods. I'd stay on the lower trails if I were you. They'll get you back to town sooner or later."

"Thanks." He said, but he didn't want to let her go just yet. "I thought everyone would know where those protesters were."

She shrugged again. "Looks like you thought wrong. Sorry." And she took a few steps down the trail.

"Wait. Wait." What was he doing?

She stopped her forward motion and planted her feet. Without turning around, she said, "Yeah?"

"Look, I'm not . . . I mean, I don't know what you think, but I'm just taking a hike here. I have no intention of getting involved in anything." This was weird, what was he saying? Why didn't he just shut up?

"OK." She looked over her shoulder and studied his face for a moment longer. "Bye then."

"You live in Prosperity?" He called after her.

She laughed and picked up her pace.

Charlie started to follow her but realized that would only make matters worse. "Name's Charlie," he called after her. Then mumbled to himself, "in case we run into each other again."

As he stood on the trail watching her descend, she nodded and raised her hand in acknowledgment, "I'm Grace," he heard her say, though she didn't pause or turn around. Charlie wondered for a moment if he'd really heard her, or if his imagination was taking over and creating a disaster he hoped to avoid. He stood watching the red cap peek in and out of the trees till it finally disappeared where the trail bent back toward town. Had she said Grace? Maybe he'd misheard Stacy or Tracy. Could this be the girl Walt had warned him to stay away from? Charlie turned and headed on up through the smoking dew that rose toward the ridgetop. It had been too long since he'd had a woman in his life. Not a decision as much as a consequence of other choices. Being alone suited him, mostly. And yet.

And what had happened to Parrot? Nathan's adamant instructions and Walt's drunken anger began to churn in Charlie's imagination. Nathan had selfish interest in mind when he demanded his son to keep away from Parrot, but who was Walt protecting, him or Grace? Would she turn them all in? Expose the tree theft? Being back in Prosperity was spooking him. This job was no good. And now a girl—two of them, actually—who might be dangerous.

Charlie kept trudging up the trail. He breathed in the green air and coughed. The craving for a smoke threatened to overtake him, but he pushed on. He wasn't doing this for Pat; he didn't care if some hiker stumbled upon their setup. If the operation were shut down he'd have to scramble, but there would be a lot of relief. One way or another this thing was going to end. As long as he got out before the whole rotten job exploded around him.

Visions of doom blossomed in Charlie's mind. Images of cops and handcuffs, of a witness box where he had to decide: cover for Nathan or expose him? He let the scene spin itself out. The cell door sliding shut on him and Nathan walking away, leaving Charlie to rot. But the anticipated relief didn't come. There were too many ways this could go wrong. Too many bad endings. Charlie feared he couldn't imagine them all.

Best-case scenario? Maybe he'd make the next few payments on his truck.

The trail turned sharply to the left and Charlie stopped. He caught his breath and looked around him. These were old trees. Doug firs, hemlock, spruce, and even giant cedar. At his eye level the trunks, gray and pleated, were branchless, some dangling delicate drapes of Spanish moss, others scarred black by ancient lightning strikes. Many harbored birds and rodents in cavities made by woodpeckers, or hollows formed where their roots arched out of the duff. He tipped his head back. The green started high—twenty-five, thirty feet up—and then formed a mass, hiding the tops of these behemoths far out of sight.

And he? He was a speck, an insect—no, insects belonged in this world, provided a necessary benefit. He was more like a virus, a microscopic enemy with the power to kill. Charlie began to calculate. Valuable timber, but you'd have to be picky. Many of these trees were probably eaten away inside, their cores feeding a turbulence of wild, unseen life. Each night he was hauling out the best of their kind. Specimens that had held their places for a hundred-fifty, two hundred, three hundred years. They were here long before Jake Oliver sought to preserve them. Charlie was looking at time.

He had never doubted the rightness of logging. The need for it, the directness of it. He'd hauled ton after ton of lumber from clear-cuts. Logging was a harvest and when it was done crews went in and replanted. In time, the forest would reform.

The scarcity of this old wood made Nathan's mouth water, Charlie knew. "Rarer means more expensive. You keep your nose to the ground, son. Let them put limits on the big boys. A little independent outfit can maneuver, get around where the big operations can't go."

The familiar tug: *the old man's no dummy, he can pull it off. Step up, be a son. Don't be a fool, Charlie*—the same part of his brain that whispered, *those cigs'll kill you.*

But if not this, what? Go back to long distance hauling? Shit. That would kill him faster than anything.

Maybe he'd head up to Canada. Henry said something about an operation needing log trucks up there. That might be far enough away from Nathan.

Charlie pushed on. The white sky wedged itself between the trees, forcing the green aside as he reached the ridge. A large boulder marked the trail's edge and offered a seat from which to take in the forested valley. Charlie sat, his hands leaning hard on his knees. There was no mistaking the scars from the clear-cuts that blotched the hillsides, massive squares of orange—the color of tree blood, the debris from a messy harvest—a few patches speckled with green where saplings were beginning to stake their claim. His farther gaze took in layers of mountains massed with green, the ever-replenishing resource, treasure for the taking.

And he had been its servant. Without him, the trees died where they stood, unmoving, unavailable. In spite of what those hippies said, the old trees died, killed in a way by their own gifts—fuel for the hunger of wildfire, eaten from the inside by bugs, infection, fungus.

And yet. It wasn't an honest living anymore. Not this way. Guys like Nathan could still make money, but nobody who just kept his head down and did what he knew how to do. *So what's that make me?*

Charlie stayed there until his craving for a smoke made him jumpy. He took a long look across the valley, then turned his back and headed down the trail toward Prosperity.

When he reached the junction of four trails, just above the spot where he had met the girl, Charlie stopped and looked across the trail to his right in among the giant trees. The familiarity of this spot startled him; the shadows, the contour of the duff-covered space between the trees, and a sharp scent of pine carried to him by the morning breeze—he hadn't thought of that childish adventure in years but it was all there before him now.

As a nine-year-old, Charlie had spent a long dark night in a hole in the ground and now, as he stood in his thirty-year-old body, his nervous system crying out for a cigarette and his lungs rebelling against the unaccustomed exertion, he remembered the view from that hole and guessed he was near the spot.

Charlie had been a devout Cub Scout. The leader of his small troop, Mr. Boylton, used the story of the 1935 kidnapping of George Weyerhaeuser to get the boys' attention and add some drama to their practice of woodsmen skills. Like the boys in Charlie's troop, George had been a fourth-grader when strangers whisked him off the street as he made his way home from school. (Unlike Charlie and the rest of his Cub Scout troop, George was normally driven to and from school, but this day he chose to walk home. Charlie recalled being dumbfounded by this choice.) The young CEO-to-be was held for eight days by kidnappers who put him in a hole in the ground. Mr. Boylton read to his boys from an FBI report that was still vivid in Charlie's mind. The hole was about four-foot square covered with a board. The boy had been chained hand and foot. When the kidnappers released him, he'd made his way alone through the woods to a stranger's house.

This story had been like jet fuel to Charlie's fear-propelled imagination. His mother had tried to dissuade him, but he would not be stopped from dragging his father's pick and shovel off to the woods and digging his own hole of captivity. There was an inconsolable desperation about his need to test himself; he hoped for more spiders, more mice and lizards, more terror and threats to his health than George Weyerhaeuser ever contemplated. Charlie needed to know that he was a survivor and that nothing the evil world of kidnappers could throw at him would cause him to succumb. The hole he dug had perfectly square edges and a flat bottom.

Nathan, Charlie now recalled, had barely looked up from his paper when his son announced his intention to spend the night in a hole in the ground. "Nobody's going to pay a ransom for you, kid," he'd said.

Now Charlie stepped off the trail and bent down, keeping his eye focused uphill, searching for the perspective that matched his memory. He felt the ground gingerly.

Then he laughed.

Did he really expect the hole to be there twenty-one years later? How many snowfalls, windstorms, not to mention tons of rainwater, had washed through here in all that time? He stood upright again and smiled at himself. What a hard night that had been. Cold and damp and full of scary sounds. He hadn't dared close his eyes. But he'd survived. As soon as there was enough light to make out the trail, he'd raced home. But when he reached the front porch he'd felt a need to hold out a bit longer before giving in to the safety of his own bed.

Charlie was slumped against the porch railing asleep when his father stepped out the door. Nathan never believed he'd done it. Accused his son of hiding in the backyard all night. Nothing Charlie ever said about that night would change Nathan's belief.

"OK, Walt." Charlie set a mug of black coffee in front of his uncle. "I need some answers."

"And I need a little nip in here." Walt's finger shook as he pointed to the mug.

Charlie rummaged in the kitchen cupboard.

"No, no. Under the couch." Walt tipped his head toward the living room.

A half-full pint of rum lay on its side among the tufts of dust like a sloshed knight defeated by a pack of bunnies. Charlie spiked Walt's coffee and poured himself an unadulterated cup, pulled out a chair and sat opposite his uncle.

"What's the deal with this Grace? Who the hell is she?"

"Shit. What's wrong with you, boy? You can't be losing your memory already." Walt took a gulp of his coffee and leaned back in his chair. Shook his head. "You don't remember Annie's little girl? She's all grown up now."

"Annie's little girl? Wasn't her name Parrot?"

"Hah!" Walt nodded and pushed himself up from the table. He tipped the rest of his coffee into the sink and grabbed the bottle of rum. Then he turned back to his nephew. "Yeah, Parrot. She wants to be called Grace now—it's her real name." Walt took a swig from the bottle and then slapped his hand on the counter. "I told you to stay away from her. Dammit Charlie!"

Charlie held his hands up in surrender. "Look, I ran into her in the woods. I was hiking up and she was coming down. Early. Anyway, what's the deal? I get why Nathan doesn't want me to remind her of him, but why do you care?"

Walt shook his head and let out a rum-tainted sigh. "That girl has been through enough and reminding her about Nathan is only going to upset her. You need to talk to your father about it. I never wanted to be part of the whole thing in the first place. Now that Warren's gone, there's no reason." He put both hands on the table next to his nephew and leaned forward on his stiff arms. He bit his lips and swallowed hard, blinking the fog from his eyes. "But you listen to me, son. Your father's going to try and make out how he was an innocent bystander in all this. When he gives you his version of the story, then you come to me and I'll tell you the truth. Your goddamned father is responsible for a hell of a lot he don't take any credit for." He pushed himself away from the table and grabbed his jacket off the back of his chair. "Hell, if it weren't for that son-of-a-bitch, Russ and Jeremy would still be alive!"

Charlie shook his head as if that might make all this fall into place. "What the hell are you talking about?"

Walt waved a dismissive hand and walked out of the kitchen and out of the house.

Fatigue was catching up with Charlie. His body needed to go back to bed, but there was no way his mind would settle into sleep now. He took his wallet from his back pocket. The last number Nathan gave him was printed neatly on an index card that Charlie had trimmed down to fit in one of the slots next to his single credit card. He stared at it for a long moment and then tucked it back in its place. It was ridiculous to waste his time getting a crooked, self-justifying story from his father.

"Walt! Goddammit!" Charlie let the front door slam behind him as he raced out after his uncle. But Walt waved a dismissive hand behind him and continued to walk toward Main Street.

Charlie matched his steps with his uncle's. "I'm going to the café and find out what's going on for myself, then. This is ridiculous."

This bought Walt up short. He stopped and turned to his nephew. "OK, look, Grace doesn't know a thing about your father or any of it. And, believe me, you don't want to be the one to tell her. So if you're going to the Hoot Owl, keep your mouth shut and drink your coffee. Too many folks in this town care about that girl and you aren't going to be the one to blow this whole thing wide open after all these years."

Charlie put a less-than-patient hand on his uncle's shoulder. "If you just tell me what the hell's going on ..."

"Hey, Henry." Walt's greeting was louder than it needed to be to reach down the street to where Henry Martin had just exited the café. "Hold up." Then Walt shrugged Charlie's hand off and said to him, "Go ask Henry. He's as involved as the rest of us."

"Really?" Before Charlie could absorb what this might mean, the three men converged in front of the Post Office.

"Mornin' Henry. How's it goin'?" Charlie reached out to shake his friend's hand; Walt nodded and continued across the street.

"Why you up so early?" Henry grinned.

"So I could take a goddamned walk in the woods. Pat came pounding on my door before dawn and sent me off to go track some hikers he thought were in the wrong part of the woods." As Charlie recounted the start of his day, fatigue hit him hard. "I need some coffee, man. Come with me to the café. I got some questions I need to ask you."

"I bet you do. Heard you ran into Grace this morning."

Maybe this wasn't going to be as hard as Walt made out. "Yeah. So, what's the deal? Some big secret I'm not supposed to tell her, Walt says."

"Shit, man." Henry tipped his head and stared at Charlie. "That's right, you left just when all the crazy stuff happened. You don't know what's gone on here since. . . ." Henry took a few steps up the street toward Walt's house. "You got some Folgers or something at the house, don't you?"

Charlie sighed. "Yeah."

"Let's go have a talk, man. We don't want to do this at the Hoot Owl."

SECTION 3: SECRETS

Chapter 11

August 3, 1991

This is how a traitor lives: Wake at five a.m., down to the café to prepare food for Chelsea and her crew, hike two miles up the mountain to deliver the day's order, back down the trail to the café where Lyle has the coffee going and is, hopefully, fixing a few breakfast orders. Work the front of the house feeding the people I've known all my life whose lives depend on Chelsea and her crew failing. Do that till noon and then trade places with Lyle in the kitchen if there are any lunch customers. Close up at four--no one is going to come in for dinner—home, collapse. The hardest part of it all is keeping the secret—and hating myself half the time.

This whole thing is insane, but I am learning a lot: ways to cut corners on the food ordering, how to skimp on serving sizes without anyone noticing, and how to feed a vegan. Plus, instead of a tip, I usually get a lecture from Jason, the guitar player who always looks so hungry.

He says "It's all about the money, Grace. That's all that matters to those loggers. They see trees as just a commodity, but without the forest the entire ecosystem is in jeopardy. We'll lose the salmon. There'll be no oxygen."

I want to tell him it's not so simple. Try raising your family without a job. And try living without lumber. These are good people you're talking about; they breathe the same air you do, and they love the woods, too. But I can't afford to argue. The money I'm taking in on this strange catering job is keeping the café's doors open.

All I can get out is "there's more than one side to everything."

The morning Grace met Charlie in the woods, she got back to the café as Henry was finishing up his coffee.

"You been doing a lot of early morning hiking there, Parrot. In training for something?"

"Morning, Henry. It's nice and quiet in the woods in the morning. You ought to try it."

"I been up there plenty. Usually not so quiet where I'm at, though."

"Hey, I met a guy this morning. He was going up the trail as I was coming down. Coulda been a government inspector or something." Grace poured herself a cup and sat down on a stool next to him. "Any reason there'd be someone like that around now?"

"What makes you say that?" Henry was suddenly serious, paying complete attention.

"Oh, I don't know, just a feeling really. He didn't have a pack or anything with him. Said his name was Charlie."

Henry sat back and smiled. "Tall guy, dark hair, mustache?"

"Yeah. Kinda cute."

"That's Charlie." Henry reached over and patted her shoulder. "He's no inspector. Kinda grew up here, actually."

"In Prosperity? When? How come I don't know him?"

Henry downed the last of his coffee and got up, "Oh, it was a while back, you were just a little kid when he left." He pulled a couple of bucks from his pants pocket and put them on the counter. "Have a nice day, Parrot." And he left Grace sitting there with a full cup of coffee that hadn't even cooled yet.

Jackson had been dead for two months and Rose had survived the loss by withdrawing from everyone in town except for Grace. After that initial phone call, Grace had filled a grocery bag with milk and eggs and fresh vegetables and headed up to Rose's.

The widow met her at the door in her robe.

"I was going to call you, but honestly I just haven't been eating." Rose stepped back to let Grace in.

"Well, I've been missing cooking in your kitchen, so I thought I could just come up once a week and fix you a little something." Grace began putting the groceries in the refrigerator. "How are you?"

"Oh, Grace." Clearly Rose had no energy to protest. "I don't really know." She stepped up to Grace and wrapped her arms around her. "I've been drifting through the days. But I'm slowly getting used to him being gone. It is good to see you."

Grace hugged Rose back, struck by how much she had missed her. "You need fresh food. And you need some company."

"I suppose." Rose stepped away and lowered herself into a chair. "I'll leave the door unlocked and you can let yourself in. I'm not very good company. I may not want to chat, but if you don't mind . . ."

So, Grace had returned to her old pattern of cooking dinner at the Dyer place once a week. Usually when she arrived,

Rose would be in her bedroom and there would be a note on the kitchen counter. "Grace, no need to stay, just leave the food on the stove. Thank you." Next to the note was always more money than Grace would ever have charged.

One afternoon in the middle of July, Grace arrived at the front gate to find Rose on her knees, digging in a flowerbed.

"'I'm afraid I've ignored this too long." Rose chided herself lightly. "The garden just keeps growing."

The women smiled at one another and that evening Rose and Grace ate together at the dining room table. After that Grace watched as Rose slowly embraced life again. The older woman talked to Grace about her flowers, about how beauty grows so eagerly from dirt.

Before Jackson's death in the spring, Rose had planted her vegetable garden. When she withdrew from the world, the beans and kale, potatoes and peas grew untended. With her renewed energy, Rose harvested what the birds and slugs had ignored. Each time Grace visited, Rose showed her something from the garden to add to her menu.

Still, Rose had not ventured off the property; Grace remained her link to the town, delivering news and supplies.

It was early August when Rose walked into the café for the first time since her husband's death. Grace raced to give her a hug with the delight and awe of one who has witnessed a miracle.

"Rose! Wow. How wonderful to see you."

"Thank you, Grace. I decided it was time."

"Come, let me get you something. Sit down here, by the window. See what I've done? I planted those window boxes. They used to be just weeds and cigarette butts, but don't they look nice with the geraniums? Mrs. G gave me some daffodils when we first fixed the place up in the spring, but after they faded, I thought, "now, what would Rose plant?" Those geraniums are all your doing."

"Is that so?" Rose tilted her chin to look up at Grace with a twinkling smile.

"I mean, I thought about you when I planted them and I really hoped you would get to see them."

"Grace." Rose's tone was now serious. "You didn't think I'd stay in that house forever, did you?"

"Well . . . I don't know. I worried about it."

Grace sat down next to her friend. Rose put her hand on Grace's.

"My dear, grief can seem like a bandit, can't it?" Rose spoke softly. "You feel robbed of your grip on life—you live for a while as if you were on the edge of a deep well and you just want to fall in and never come out. You have no explanation for why you're still breathing or why you're able to move your limbs. But somehow, life eventually reminds you that you are still part of things." She squeezed Grace's hand. "And if you're as lucky as I am and you have someone who cares about you, you begin to remember how sweet life can be." Rose looked out the window. "The geraniums are lovely, dear."

They sat together and watched the sun play on the red petals and the curled edges of the leaves. On the electrical wires that crossed the street overhead, a crow alighted and began cawing. The door of the Bullhook opened and Walt stumbled out.

"Oh, my, Walt deVore." Rose shook her head. "He's still drinking I see. Too bad . . . such a waste. I remember when he was the only mechanic Jackson would allow to touch his car." She turned and looked at Grace, "I believe I'd like a cup of coffee, if it's not too much trouble. And maybe a piece of pie."

Grace jumped up, beaming "You bet—good idea. How about apple? I got some of those tart green apples from Darlene's tree. You'll love it."

As Grace ran off to get Rose's order, the older woman turned back to the window and tapped the glass. The crow flew off and Walt looked across at the café. He raised his eyebrows and his mouth gaped open.

"Rose Dyer! Hot damn!" he shouted as he sat down hard on the bench, staring at her. She smiled and gave a small wave.

"Do you want to talk to Walt, Rose? I'll go get him . . ." Grace put the coffee and pie in front of her. "He was amazing working on the cabin. Stayed sober the whole time and as soon as the job was done—well, you know Walt."

"No, no need, dear. We've seen each other and that's enough for now." Rose took a bite of her pie. "Oh, my. This tastes just like the apple pie your mother used to make." She took another bite and closed her eyes, savoring the taste. "Oh, Grace, how marvelous. I never realized, but Annie must have used those apples of Darlene's too. They're some old variety. Can't get those in the stores."

Grace smiled and slid into the bench opposite Rose. "Jane left a bunch of old recipes. I found this one I thought might be in Momma's handwriting. That's cool." The young woman paused, letting a comfortable silence sit between them.

Rose handed her fork to Grace, "Take a bite. It shouldn't go to waste and I still don't have my full appetite back."

Grace took the fork. "I always wished I knew more about my mom. Dad never talked about her." She looked back across the table. "No one did."

"Isn't it interesting how we cope with our losses? I didn't think I could ever talk about Jackson again—and you know I didn't for a long time—but I came into town today knowing that I'd find someone who knew him, so I could talk about him."

Grace picked up this offering gratefully.

"You know how special he was to me. I want to take you to my house, so you can see what I've done to it. What a gift that was! No one has ever . . . well, you know."

"I'm going to go by the sawmill today, so I'm sure I'll see it."

"Oh, the outside is OK, but I really fixed up the inside. You have to come by after I close up here. OK?"

"I think I've got quite enough to do today. I want to see how they're getting on without Jackson." Rose sighed. "But I'd love to come to dinner at your place another time. Maybe next week?"

"OK, you've got a deal. Next Monday instead of me coming to you, you come down here and I'll cook for you at my place."

A couple of hikers walked into the café and looked around.

"Can I help you?" Grace said. She gave Rose a squeeze on the shoulder and walked over to them.

They turned out to be hungry, paying customers and Grace was busy for a while. Rose finished her pie and stood by the register.

"No, no, that's on me—a celebration of your coming out." Grace told her.

"Grace, that's not right. I know you're struggling. Don't be silly." And the older woman put a five-dollar bill on the counter.

Grace sighed and picked it up. "By the way, Rose, do you know a guy named Charlie Roberge?"

Rose's eyebrows rose as she inhaled as if preparing to say something. Then she bit her lip and looked down. "That's a long time ago."

"You knew him a long time ago? When he was a kid?"

Rose's face had changed when looked up at Grace. She looked older, tired. "Why are you asking me about Charlie?"

"Oh, just something Henry said. I met this guy when I was hiking one morning. Henry knew him and said he was from around here, but I'd never seen him before."

Rose nodded slowly. "Maybe we can talk about this another time. I need to get on to the mill. Bye-bye, Gracie."

"See you Monday."

"Yes, yes, my dear," and Rose hurried out of the café and crossed the street.

Twenty minutes later, as Grace was clearing one of the window tables, she looked up and saw Rose sitting on the bench engrossed in conversation with Walt.

When Grace stepped out onto Main Street and locked the café door that afternoon, she was caught off guard by the sharp wind that had picked up during the day. Fall was unmistakably gathering energy.

"Hey, Parrot! Come on over here. Have a drink with me." It was Walt. She'd seen him, but thought he was too soused to notice her.

She walked across the street to where he was sitting. "Hi, Walt. I'm bushed. Not in the mood for a drink. You OK?"

"Sure am, sugar, and I got cash, thanks to you! What kind of talk is that? A drink'll do you good." He was close enough that Grace was surprised she couldn't smell him. Normally, she'd have been able to catch the odor of stale alcohol seeping through unwashed skin. But it wasn't there.

She looked closely at his face. "Walt. Is that you?"

"You better believe it, darlin'. And I certainly hope you wouldn't stop to chat with just any old scruffy bum on the street."

"But what happened to you?"

"You mean how come I look so beeeeutiiiiful?" He stretched the word out as he lifted his chin, showing off what she realized was a set of clean clothes.

"Wow! You *are* beautiful, Walt. You got some new clothes. Good for you."

"And I didn't spend a bit of my own money, neither . . ." He was being coy and having fun playing with her. She had little patience for it, but her curiosity got the better of her.

"All right, Walt. You win. I'll go have a drink with you and you can tell me how you got new clothes without paying for them. I just need to sit down."

"You got it, babe. We'll get you the best seat in the house." He moved in next to her and offered his crooked arm. Grace slid her arm through his; he beamed as they walked to the door. With a flourish he pulled it open and ushered her in.

"Walt," she couldn't get the guy in the woods off her mind. "Do you know a guy named Charlie Roberge?"

"Charlie? Why? You seen him?" He narrowed his eyes and Grace detected something like anger. "Hold on, sit down here." He directed her toward a booth behind the pool table. "I'm drinkin' whiskey, I'll get you one."

"No, no, wait. What's the deal? Can't you just tell me who he is?"

"Sure thing, just got to keep my whistle wet. Hold your horses." Grace knew if she were going to learn anything from Walt she had to get the story before he got too drunk to tell it.

He came back to the table with a couple of beers, which was a good sign. When Walt shifted from whiskey to beer it was his way of trying to stay sober—it gave Grace hope that he wanted to tell her the story as much as she wanted to hear it.

"Charlie's always been good to me, you know. Give me a little bit when he could spare it, usually sent a check in the mail, but havin' him around's been nice. He's the one got me new togs."

"Hold on, back up a step there. How long's he been in town? How come I never . . ."

"Oh, Lordy." Walt took a big gulp of his beer and shook his head. "I never said that, did I? No, I didn't . . ." Another gulp. "You just forget about him." Walt turned his head away to look over his shoulder. There were a few guys at the bar, guys who used to come to the café but now spent their limited funds on alcohol, their backs hunched against the future. When he turned back toward Grace, Walt put his finger to his lips. "We can't say nothing about Charlie. So, shhhh." He picked up his beer and took a long drink.

Now she was downright irritated. "Walt." Grace reached across the table and put her hand over his beer before could bring it to his lips again. "Just tell me who he is."

He stared at her with pleading eyes. Grace thought he might actually be on the verge of tears. Then he slowly brought the first finger of his right hand to his lips and drew a line, zipping them tight.

She was shocked. When had Walt deVore ever refused her anything she'd asked?

"What's the matter with you tonight, Walt?"

"Oh, hell, don't mind me. I'm just an old souse."

Grace could tell she wasn't going to get anything out of him. She stood up. "I'm tired. I'm leaving."

"Get me another whiskey on your way, will ya, hon? I think I'll just sit here awhile."

"Walt, I'm goin' home. I'm done waiting on folks for today." Grace didn't care if she sounded upset. He wouldn't remember any of this in the morning anyway. It bugged her not to know who this Charlie was. She was going to find someone to fill her in. She pulled open the thick, wooden door of the Bullhook and let it slam shut behind her.

Aside from Rose's visit, the day had been nerve-racking enough; she didn't need Walt's drunken nonsense. Loggers had begun to straggle back into the café and that felt good; but her mind kept going back to that first morning, the cartoon on the window, the rotten egg smell—and that was before she'd actually betrayed the whole town! If anyone found out about her feeding the protesters . . . The tension was wearing on her. As she stepped over cracks and bulging roots that poked up through the sidewalk, she tried to calculate how much longer she'd need to keep making deliveries up the mountain.

Chapter 12

August 8, 1991

   Strange dream last night. I have this weird feeling that I've had the same dream before. I was in my old bed and Momma was sitting on the bed next to me. I could smell this sweet warm scent and I heard her soft voice. She said "You'll be fine. It won't be for long." She hugged me. I could feel her arms around me. It was so real.

   This place I've created, this jungle, maybe it's calling my mother back to me.

   Rose is coming to dinner tonight! Can't wait to show her what I've done.

   (sketch of a table set with elaborate plates of food)

   It was five p.m. and mountain shadows ate away at the daylight with merciless greed. Most folks wouldn't notice it yet, but by the end of August Grace began to feel robbed when the light died a few moments earlier every day. It took an extra effort to keep her spirits up this time of year.

   In Grace's clearest memories of her mother, it was dark outside and the rain was falling. The two of them cuddled under an old blue blanket by the fireplace, Annie reading to her from the bird guide that she kept by the kitchen window. There were pictures of jays and robins and towhees, birds that even four-year-old Grace could identify. Then Annie opened Grace's favorite book, the one with pictures of parrots and toucans, honeycreepers and macaws—magical, bright birds whose pictures made her own Parrot giggle with delight. Mother and child, snug and warm while the heavy rain muddied the paths through the woods and overflowed the rivers, made up stories about the lives of red and yellow crowned cranes, iridescent green and blue hummingbirds.

Just as Grace pulled her chef's knife from its holder to begin chopping the vegetables for dinner, the phone rang.

"Grace dear," Rose's voice sounded hesitant. "I don't think I should come to dinner."

"Rose, no! What's wrong?"

"It's nothing, really. I'm feeling tired. I don't like the idea of driving back up to the house in the dark. I'm just not ready. We'll do it another time." Her words ran together in a rush, gaining conviction as she spoke. "I'll see you soon. Bye."

Stunned, Grace put the phone down slowly. This wasn't like Rose at all. What was going on? She grabbed the phone and quickly dialed the Dyers' number.

"Hello?"

"What's really going on, Rose? Are you sure you're OK?"

"Oh, I'm fine, Grace. I told you. I'm just not ready for an evening out."

"OK. Well then, let's chat for a bit." Grace had more than dinner on her agenda; she might have to put off showing the cabin to Rose, but she wasn't about to pass up this chance to find out more about Charlie. "I visited the cemetery the other day."

"Go to see your father, did you, dear? I went to Jackson's grave too. It's kept up pretty well, don't you think?"

"Yes, mostly. But I didn't go just to visit my dad and Jackson."

"Oh?"

"You remember the other day, when you came into the café? I asked you if you knew Charlie Roberge? I was hoping you could tell me more about him. I just can't understand how I didn't know about his family."

"Yes, well, they moved away a long time ago, honey. I think . . . let's see . . . you were probably four or five. You had other things to focus on then and you probably weren't paying too much attention to what was going on with other people. They just moved away—I think they went to Seattle."

"How old was he then, when they moved away?"

"Oh, let's see . . . I guess he was around thirteen or fourteen, you know that was such a long time ago, wasn't it, Grace? My memory is a bit hazy going back that far."

"That's fine, Rose, you have already told me more than I knew. But now I'm really curious. If he got out of here at thirteen, why on earth would he come back here now? Does he have any other family around here, a brother or sister or something?"

Rose didn't respond for several seconds. "I don't . . . Oh, my memory is just terrible . . . it's been a long time."

"Well, it's strange, don't you think? Why come back to Prosperity now? It's not as if he's going to find a job around here. I asked Walt about him the other day and he acted so weird, like there was some big secret about this guy or something."

"I'm sorry, Grace. I am getting tired now." An unfamiliar tone of irritation had crept into Rose's voice. "I'll come down to the café in a day or two."

"OK, I'll stop talking. Just answer one last question: why would Charlie give Walt money and buy him a new set of clothes?"

"I don't know!" There was no mistaking her anger now. "I can't keep track of everybody. Good night, Grace." Click.

Grace was stunned. She couldn't remember Rose ever treating her so rudely. As she took stock of the vegetables lying half-chopped on her cutting board, she tried to sort out the last few days. Ever since she'd started asking about that guy, Charlie, people had been acting strangely. She scrapped the onions and celery into a container, stored them in the refrigerator, and climbed the ladder to her loft. Often, she could sort things out when she wrote in her journal. This time, though, her head spun with questions and she couldn't imagine where she'd find the answers.

What is going on? Why would Rose lie to me and get so angry when I asked about Charlie? If there is one person who keeps closer tabs on people in this town than I do, it's Rose. And what's Walt hiding? If I weren't keeping my own secret from them, if my conscience were clean, I'd be pissed. I don't know the rules in this new world. Are traitors allowed to get mad at the folks they're betraying?

And now I've got another problem. Kev. He's seen me in the mornings walking past his house on my way to the trailhead. People think Kev is stupid, but if anyone is going to figure out what I'm doing, it'll be him.

"What do you think, Kev? Is my chocolate pie as good as Jane's?" The piece of pie Grace put in front of the boy was smothered in whipped cream.

"Too much white," Kev said flatly. "Why do you take a walk for exercise every morning? Mommy said you don't want to get fat, but I said 'maybe, maybe not'!"

"Well, your mom is right about that one. I do not want to get fat, Kev. So, I'll hold off on the whipped cream on your pie, and on mine."

Grace knew how this would go. When something changed in Kev's world, he'd talk about it obsessively until he made some sense of it. His questions would call too much attention to her treks.

Grace slept fitfully that night. The only thing she'd resolved was that her morning routine had to change. Rising an hour earlier than usual, she went down to the Hoot Owl and packed up the protestors' order. Then she circled around the back of the mill to stay off Kev's street, adding an extra half mile to her hike.

"I'll just be coming up once a week," Grace told Chelsea the next day. "Folks are starting to talk."

"Too bad. We'll miss your fresh cinnamon rolls!"

Jason stepped forward. "Just tell them what you're doing. They're bound to find out anyway. Aren't you tired of lying?"

Grace wanted to scream, but she pinched her lips tight, pulled on her pack and stomped out of the campsite. The wind was gusting through the high branches—the gods gossiping about her foolishness.

Jason was right about one thing—she was making herself sick keeping this secret. The thought of the town finding out made her hands shake and her stomach clench. But if Grace could hold on for just one more month, there was a chance she could get on top of the bills. It wasn't clear why, but business had started to pick up. Some folks had a bit of money in their pockets.

And something else was happening: a shift, too subtle to name and so welcome Grace feared looking too closely might jinx it. A quiet sense of purpose was crawling back onto the shoulders of a few of the men—it was as if they'd shaken off that coating of doom everyone had been sinking under. Their boot steps sounded firmer on the Hoot Owl's wood floors, they settled into their seats with the fatigue of working men— their legs stretched out in front of them, their hands swollen and veined from labor. They dropped crumbs of conversation with their crumpled napkins and the few coins they left tucked under their empty plates. She picked these up and rolled them slowly between her fingers. Grace didn't want to press, ask anything directly, the wounds of lost work were still tender and hot. And worse, she feared being lied to. All her life she had trusted these men—most had been close friends of her father, had had his back in the woods, and had grieved his loss by her side. But the shifting ground she'd felt when Rose had refused to give her an honest answer about Charlie had unsettled even these bonds.

Deceit was passing through Prosperity like a virus. Sitting back and watching the epidemic spread was driving Grace batty. She needed some straight answers. If she could untangle the secrets around who Charlie was, Grace had a feeling everything else would start to come clear. She would start with Henry. She'd drag the story out of him. She'd withhold his coffee if she had to.

Grace made her way down the mountain and slipped past the mill and her unlit cabin. She entered the café through the back door, greeted Lyle, and barged into the dining room. A few early morning hikers were sitting in the corner booth, mumbling over their bacon and eggs, but no one sat at the counter. None of the other tables was occupied. For the first time in years, Henry Martin hadn't shown up at the Hoot Owl for breakfast. This could not be a coincidence.

Now Grace was on a mission.

She picked up the phone and called Jane in Seattle.

When Grace capitulated and made a deal with the protestors, she nearly choked on the bitterness. She had told Jane it was not something she ever wanted to talk about again, and if her aunt even hinted that she was pleased about it, Grace would never talk to her about anything. Their conversations had been brief financial reports and little else since. Until this morning.

"You know, people who don't manage bankrupt cafés in backward logging towns don't all have to get up before dawn, Parrot." Jane woke with sarcasm on her lips. Always had.

"This is important and it's driving me nuts. You're the only one who can tell me what's going on."

"OK." Grace could hear her aunt rustling around, probably looking for a cigarette. "Shoot."

"Who is Charlie Roberge?" The sound of a match striking, an inhale, and a long silence.

"Jane?"

Nothing.

"Jane? Who the hell is he?"

"Where did you hear that name?"

"He's here. I met him when I was hiking down from . . ." Grace glanced over at the group in the corner. "You know. He was going up and I was going down. Early. Real early. I thought maybe he was a state inspector or something, no pack. But Henry said no, he's 'one of us.'" She made air quotes with her right hand. "But he wouldn't tell me anything else about him. Neither will Walt or Rose. Everybody seems to know him, but they won't talk to me about him. What's the big secret?"

"Well, I don't know why he's there, but I suppose it's time." A weariness crept into Jane's voice. "You get yourself down here—let Lyle take over things for the day. This isn't a conversation for the phone. Let me know which bus you're on and I'll meet you at the station."

"Wait. What's the big deal?" Grace gripped the receiver with both hands. She tried to keep her voice down. The backpackers in the corner were looking at her. "Just tell me now. I don't want to go to Seattle."

"Listen, this is a long conversation and I'm not going into it on the phone. If you really want to know who he is, come down here. A day in the city won't kill you. Call me back when you know which bus you'll be on." And Jane hung up.

Chapter 13

The bus wheezed to a stop, and Grace peered through the grubby window. The bus had traveled a convoluted path to cover a crow's thirty miles from Everett to Seattle; in the course of the trip the sky had cleared, and the gray had given way to a strong, defiant blue.

"Damn," she muttered under her breath. Her early morning hike had been cold and wet. Now, when the afternoon weather was perfect for a hike in the mountains, she was stuck in Seattle.

Only a few months ago she'd been eager to live in the city. During the last months in Prosperity, the draw of this place had dulled, and its harsh energy now set her nerves on edge. Her body stiffened with city-armor as she grabbed the straps of her backpack, pulled them tight, and stepped off the bus. Wariness widened her peripheral vision, turning every stranger into a potential threat.

Jane stood huddled against the building, a cigarette dangling from her hand. Grace relaxed a little as she caught her aunt's eye.

"Well, you got me to the city."

Grace was stunned by how exhausted her aunt looked. Jane's eyes were swollen and there was no sign of her sassy grin.

"What the hell is going on? Are you OK?"

Jane pushed herself off the wall and groaned softly.

"Let's go get some food." The two women started down the crowded sidewalk. Pigeons scuttled and bobbed in the gutters, their iridescent feathers flashing among the garbage and stink. Crumpled in a dim doorway a person whose gender was unidentifiable under the caked dirt and tattered clothes sat cross-legged holding a cardboard sign. Whatever you can spare. God Bless. Grace stuck her hand in her pocket and pulled out a couple of quarters. She dropped them in the upturned cap.

Jane looked over at her niece and rolled her eyes.

"I know, I know." Grace mumbled into her aunt's ear. "I just can't stand the thought of living on these streets." Looking around she asked, "God, don't you miss the woods?"

"There are lots of trees around, Parrot. Ask me if I miss Prosperity."

Grace knew better.

Jane steered her niece toward a restaurant. She paused a second to toss her cigarette onto the sidewalk and then pulled open the thick wooden door and walked in. They were greeted with a pungent mix of spices and stale air and the sounds of clinking glass and low voices.

At a long, polished wood bar a few men in shirtsleeves hunched over their drinks. Jane, nodding to the bartender, headed to a corner table toward the back and pushed her purse across the bench before she sat. Grace followed slowly, her eyes gradually adjusting to the dark.

When she reached the booth, Grace dropped her pack, kicked it under the table and slid into the seat across from her aunt.

"I don't know how you can live in the city, Jane. I've only walked a few blocks and I already feel beaten up. I know it isn't healthy for you."

Jane shrugged.

Again, Grace noticed the weariness on Jane's face. Was it just that Jane was getting old? Grace wondered about her aunt's health, but knew better than to question her. Jane had always hated talking about her body almost as much as she hated the confines of Prosperity.

"You look good, Parrot. The café must not be getting you down yet."

"Everything's fine, hunky-dory, great. Now tell me who this Charlie is. I could almost believe there was some kind of conspiracy between you and everyone else in Prosperity, except that you don't speak to anyone else in town."

Jane check her watch, waved a waiter over and ordered a beer. She looked at Grace. "It's after two. You hungry?"

Grace shook her head impatiently. Her eyes were wide and her lips set in a tight line.

"Ok, I'll take that for a no, then." Jane looked up at the waiter, "that's it for now."

She took a pack of cigarettes out of her purse and put them on the table and made a ceremony of reaching for the tin ashtray, sliding it across the table, tapping a cigarette out of her pack and lighting it. Grace began drumming her fingers on the table.

Finally, Jane spoke.

"Honey, first thing I need you to know is that I love you and I loved your dad and your mom."

Whoa. Grace was stunned. She'd never heard anything like this from her aunt.

"People don't always make perfect decisions when they love people," Jane continued, then looked away. Grace got the distinct impression this was all rehearsed. Jane sighed and turned back to Grace.

"Oh, hell, you were just a little girl and you couldn't have understood; we had to protect you."

"Well, I'm not a little girl now and your protection is about to drive me insane."

"Yeah, well. If you want to sleep with Charlie Roberge, if that is what this is all about, go ahead. No harm in that. He's probably a pretty good-looking man if he takes after his father at all."

"What the hell? No, I don't want to sleep with him! Damn it, Jane—are you going to tell me who he is or am I going to have to beat it out of you?"

The waiter showed up with Jane's beer at this point.

"Thanks," she said. "I think you better bring me a whiskey too." She turned back to her niece.

"Your mother ran off with Charlie's dad. There, is that clear enough for you?"

"*What?* 'Ran off?' I was four when she died. When did she have time to 'run off' with anyone?"

Jane shook her head and sipped her beer, "You really wanted to believe that, so we figured it was the best thing."

"'We?'"

"Warren and me."

Grace stared at her aunt, wondering if she'd gone completely nuts since she moved to the city. "Wait a minute. What are you saying?"

Jane leaned forward and looked into Grace's eyes. "You heard me."

"My mother didn't die? She just left me and ran off with some guy?" Grace's mouth formed the words, but her mind couldn't comprehend them.

"Left your dad. You were sort of collateral damage, as they say. She was in a bind, honey. She and Nathan, Charlie's dad, well . . . she was pregnant."

Grace sat back. She felt the blood draining from her face.

"Let me get this straight. My mother was sleeping with this guy and got pregnant by him while she was still living with Dad and me. And then she just went away with him and left us?"

"There wasn't any 'just' about it. But yeah, that's what happened."

How could she believe this?

"So what, everyone in town knew what she'd done and they all kept it a secret from me all my life? How is that possible?"

"Well, you know, your dad was a pretty special man, and nobody in that town was about to cause him any more hurt than he'd already had. What with Annie, and the war and all." The waiter came over with the whiskey. Jane took it from his hand before he could put it down and took a swallow. "He couldn't talk about her; he was too hurt and too angry. He couldn't tell you what she'd done. So when you started saying she was dead, we all went along." She threw the rest of the whiskey back and set the glass down in front of her. She looked into Grace's eyes now.

"We saw you working it out, finding a way to be OK with it and we thought if you were OK . . ."—her voice was almost a whisper now— ". . . maybe then he'd be OK. And, you know, it worked, more or less."

Grace didn't know what to say or do; she put her hands flat on the bench on either side of her to keep from falling over. The whole world was tipping out of balance. A minute, or maybe a century, passed in silence and then Jane looked down and reached for her coat.

"What happened to her?" Grace demanded.

"Your mom?" Jane sighed and pushed her coat back into the corner. "Well, I'm not really sure. We lost touch."

"She's still alive?"

"I suppose she is."

"She wouldn't even know me. My own mother. I could walk right by her on the street and she wouldn't even recognize me. I wouldn't . . ." Tears were streaming down her face, but Grace seemed not to notice.

"Why? Why did she leave me?"

Jane pursed her lips, leaned forward and looked hard into Grace's eyes.

"It wasn't that easy, honey. Believe me, she loved you more than her own heart. It was just a bad situation and I . . . well, from where I stood, it seemed like the best solution."

"From where *you* stood? What did you have to do with it?"

"We were best friends, don't forget. Annie told me everything. And Warren, well he wasn't talking much in those days, but he was my brother. I knew him, and I knew he just couldn't live without you."

It was like some sort of awful, hideous soap opera. Grace wanted to laugh out loud, but the tears wouldn't stop.

Jane took another long drag on her cigarette.

"I did what I thought was best for everyone involved. It was a hard time. I told your mother to go. I told her to leave you with Warren and I'd help him take care of you. I told her . . ."

"You told my mother to leave me?" Now Grace's voice had dropped to a whisper, an incredulous gasp. Everything was upside down; what had been the floor was now the ceiling, the inside, now outside. The only explanation was that somehow the rules of physics were no longer in effect.

Jane wasn't making eye contact with her niece anymore; her voice flat as she reported what had happened.

"I told her that once your father had gotten over her leaving and had calmed down, I would bring you to her. I thought it would only be a few weeks or something."

Jane brought her eyes up and sighed.

"Oh, hell I don't know what I thought. I was just worried about Warren." Then she shrank back against the booth and seemed to wither into an old woman as Grace stared at her.

"But you never did it." This woman, her aunt, was a monster. A hateful, horrible thing. "You never took me to her."

"No. How could I? Warren needed you. You made him happy." Tears formed in the corners of Jane's eyes. She looked down and began to sob.

The anger and hatred Grace recognized a moment before dissolved into numbness. She looked across the table at her aunt's tear-streaked face and wondered, *Who is that woman and why is she crying? I am supposed to be crying, not her.*

But Grace's eyes were suddenly dry and wide, wide open. She had to let as much light in as she could. A darkness was approaching. For now, a flimsy, opaque membrane was keeping the reality of Jane's words at a slight remove. Grace heard—her ears were working as they always had. The words were English—a language she still recognized as familiar and meaningful. But it was all still in her head, in the concrete, cold, thinking realm.

There must be a barrier, Grace thought, *somewhere in my neck, because my guts and my heart feel fine. Everything will settle down here in a minute and I'll be able to walk out of here just like I walked in—normal. Everything will be normal. As long as the barrier holds.*

But she couldn't take her eyes off Jane's face. She couldn't push herself out of the booth, stand up, and walk away. She couldn't figure out how to get her body to move.

What she wanted was to lie down on the floor, right there, right on the cold tile of the restaurant where she could rest her head alongside the spilled peas, abandoned crusts of bread, and dropped cutlery. She imagined how good it would feel to have the blood return to her head, to regain the strength to stand. But she knew that once that happened, once the world was upright and she was on her own feet, nothing would ever be the same. If she could just hold herself in suspension like this, maybe the barrier would not break; maybe she would never have to feel it.

Aunt Jane, Dad's biggest supporter. People talked about how Jane loved her brother so much no other guy had a chance with her. And it was true. Grace could see that now as she looked at the pleading face across from her.

"Parrot? I know you have to hate me. I just hope . . ." Jane seemed so much smaller now.

"I don't think hate is quite the right word."

Grace couldn't let her go on; she didn't want to hear what Jane hoped for.

"I'm not exactly sure what this is called. I've never felt it before. Numb. Empty. No feeling at all. That's it. I have no feeling for you at all." With that, Grace was finally able to command her feet. She stood, picked up her pack, and walked out of the restaurant.

Once outside, the glare of daylight and the blast of car horns knocked Grace back against the building; she leaned there as strangers swarmed around her. She closed her eyes, breathed in the diesel fumes, and let the cacophony of the city engulf her.

"Hey, baby, got any spare change?" Her eyes popped open to see a dirty hand, palm open in front of her. The stench of stale alcohol. A fleeting image of Walt deVore flashed across her mind. He knew the truth. Rose Dyer knew the truth. Even

Mrs. G knew the truth. The whole damn, stinking, lying town knew the truth and *no one* had the guts to tell her. All these years! Grace pushed herself away from the wall. Shrugging off the begging hand, she stepped into the flow of people.

Her mind boiled, heated by shock and confusion. Was everything she'd believed about her mother a lie? Had her mother even loved her at all? Why hadn't she come back to get her? What had Jane told her? What kind of woman keeps a child from her mother?

Even as these questions formed in Grace's mind, she was aware of an aura of unreality about the whole situation. It was like something she'd read in a book, a story about someone else, some whimpering, pitiful child. A story too cruel to believe.

Smells of urine and garbage blew out from the alleyways. Loose pages from old newspapers, discarded cigarette butts, candy wrappers, and clumps of gum decorated the sidewalk. Her feet moved swiftly over concrete; they carried her toward the water, down the steep hill toward Puget Sound.

At the bottom of the hill a man stood on the corner playing a flute. His yellow hair was a mass of dusty curls, his eyes were closed, and his thin body swayed with his music. A narrow instrument case, lined with bright red velvet stood open on the ground in front of him and a scattering of coins and a few pale green bills lay inside. People pushed past, tourists with cameras held up to their eyes, groups of women sipping lattes from paper cups, strollers with crying babies in front and sacks of vegetables in back forged through the crowd, propelled by young women with harried expressions.

With no thought of a destination, Grace had wandered into Pike Place Market. Assaulted by the noise and the smells, she stood frozen. Coffee fumes mixed with the odors of the glistening fish; piles of summer fruits and tables of green; strains of flute music from her right, amplified drums on her left. Hawkers called, children laughed, venders shouted greetings over the heads of their customers.

An arguing couple jostled Grace as they passed, momentarily rousing her. Food. Maybe she could think if she ate something, if she could find a quiet place to sit. She wandered through the warren of stalls and shops and found herself in a small walled garden. Shiny metal tables and folding chairs were scattered over an uneven brick patio. Along one side was a chowder joint; a ragged fishing net knotted with clamshells was draped above the doorway. Tourists were lined up cafeteria-style with yellow plastic trays.

She turned to leave and passed a spiral stairway that climbed to the street above. Tucked behind the stairs, she saw a sign that read "Hummus, Falafel, Spanakopita." Feeling a bit like Alice tumbling into wonderland, she walked toward the sign with no idea what its words meant. Something about their foreignness and their vaguely organic quality drew her.

"May I help you, miss?" It was a female voice, lightly accented and musical.

Grace peered behind the staircase and found a counter with glass cases displaying foods she couldn't identify. "Ummm, what's good?"

"If you're hungry, miss, everything is good."

"OK, well, yes, I guess I am hungry. What do you recommend?" She didn't trust herself to make a choice.

"How about a sample plate, miss? A little bit of everything, eh?"

"OK, good idea."

"All right then." The woman, who looked about Grace's age, turned and called to a little girl who sat on a stool in the back of the tiny kitchen, "Nuket, come. Help me."

The little girl jumped down and grabbed the top plate from the stack on the shelf behind her. "Here, Mommy. Should I get a fork?"

"Yes, my sweet, a fork and a napkin. And put them on the tray. Are your hands clean, Nuket?"

"Oh," she looked down at her palms and pulled her stool over to the sink and held her hands under the running water.

"She needs to learn. It is good for a daughter to learn from her mother in the kitchen. She is a big help to me." The woman spoke with clear pride.

"She is a lucky girl." Grace stood paralyzed by the pain. She had been even younger than this child when she last stood in the gleaming kitchen, watching Annie's hands rolling pie dough. Her vision blurred with tears.

"Are you OK, miss?" The woman held out a napkin. "Here, you go have a seat. Nuket will bring your food to you."

Grace spent the rest of the afternoon sitting on a metal chair in that garden. Crowds came and left: families with squirming kids who threw their crackers on the ground; old men who sipped their chowder with their jackets zipped up to their chins and their woolen hats pulled down over their ears; gaggles of teenagers who clomped down the staircase and ran across the courtyard tossing cigarette butts and "fuck-off-assholes" in their wake. Men in suits and ties ordered wraps from Nuket's mother and walked out of the garden checking their watches.

As the brick wall brightened with the sunset, Nuket began to pull the shutters across the counter of her mother's stand. She leaned out, surveying the courtyard, and saw Grace still sitting in the corner. "Did you like it, miss?"

Grace had fallen into a trance, tracking memories of her childhood, bits of conversation with Rose and Jackson, even casual comments made by people like Mrs. G and Sherrie.

Measuring her experiences of these people who'd become her family against the new reality Jane had exposed, she was unsure of everything. With effort, she roused herself.

"Oh, it was delicious. Thank you."

It was getting late. Where could she go? Shauna and Jen lived somewhere in the city. But the thought of explaining it all to them made her weak. And what if *they* knew it all already? What if they'd kept the secret too? No, she couldn't face it.

Nuket's mother stepped out from behind her counter carrying a plastic bag of garbage. Grace stood and picked up her pack. "Um, excuse me, but do you know where I could get a room around here? A cheap room?"

"How the hell did that work? The whole town?" Charlie sat at the table in Walt's kitchen trying to absorb what Henry had just told him.

"What can I tell you, man? It's a small town. People are loyal around here."

"Loyal. Right. A bunch of liars sticking together. Kinda like us, up there stealing trees. We're pretty damn loyal too." Nathan's stench was all over this story. Charlie's shoulders stiffened. He stood and began pacing around the kitchen.

Henry leaned back in his chair and put his hands flat on the table. "Look, Annie abandoned her four-year-old daughter. What kind of mother does that? Folks wanted to protect that kid. I get it."

"Yeah? Well, maybe you don't know the whole story man. I mean it's not like I have this loving relationship with the lady, but Annie's a victim here too, I'd say."

"Yeah?"

Henry came from a pretty screwed up family from what Charlie could remember. There'd been a lot of drinking and some spectacular fights that became legend among the kids in town. Charlie could still recall the shock of witnessing Henry's mother drag his father out of the Bullhook by his hair while yelling, "you cock-sucking asshole somabitch." For nine-year-old Charlie, it was a first; he'd never forgotten that particular string of epithets.

Through it all Henry had kept his cool. He belonged to those people, but he wasn't really one of them. Charlie could never understand how his friend managed that.

Charlie stopped in front of the sink, looked out the window. "My father knocked her up, you know? And from what I heard, her husband, Warren, was not a guy to take that lightly."

Henry didn't move. The old clock above the stove ticked loudly.

"Nathan, the chickenshit, grabs her up and takes her away. Leaves me and my mom behind, by the way." Charlie's hands curled into fists and he began slowly pounding them—left then right—on the porcelain lip of the sink. "I'm not saying she had no choice, but man, her choices weren't good. An abortion without Warren finding out? Not likely. They leave. And then things get worse."

Henry stood now and walked over to stand next to this man with whom he'd shared a childhood. "What are you talkin' about?"

Charlie raised his eyebrows. He went over to the table and picked up the pack of cigarettes, took one, and lit it. "Look man, I need to be telling this to Grace. She's an adult, for fuck's sake. She deserves to know. I gotta go."

Henry reached out to put a cautioning hand on Charlie's arm. "I never credited it much, but there's people who say this town is cursed." He looked hard at his friend. "Good luck, Charlie."

The two men walked out of the house and Henry turned up the hill toward his own home, Charlie down toward the Hoot Owl.

But Grace wasn't at the café. Lyle said she was out of town.

Chapter 14

Grace dropped her backpack on the floor next to bed twenty-one. In her hand were a threadbare towel and a gray woolen blanket. She'd gotten these from the sullen guy who'd taken an uncomfortably close visual inventory of her physical attributes when he checked her into the hostel. After unfolding the blanket and wrapping it around her shoulders, she slumped down on the mattress.

It was after nine, but there was still some light in the sky and the rows of beds were empty. The place smelled of rank body odor and stale cigarette smoke. The walls of the long narrow room were covered with a thin coat of white paint that allowed the history of the old building to seep through. *Perfect*, Grace thought, *this hostel could be an orphanage right out of Dickens. I fit right in.*

A crushing fatigue suddenly took hold of Grace's body. She slid down on the bed and closed her eyes. When voices and footsteps roused her, Grace pulled the blanket over her head, and prayed for sleep.

In the morning, after finding her way to the bathroom and brushing her teeth, Grace walked down to the common room. There were a few people huddled over the remains of a meal. Was it breakfast or lunch? She picked up a cup from the tray by the coffee urn and poured herself the dregs. Then Grace forced herself to go over the previous day's events in detail. She needed to think, to sort out what Jane had told her and what it meant. But even after downing a couple of bitter cups, Grace's mind was still muddled. Her limbs felt weak, her stomach refused the thought of food.

She dragged herself back to her bed and buried her face in the pillow. Squeezing her eyes shut, she yearned again for sleep to bring the curtain down on her whirling distress. But it did not return. The stench of the room, the well in the middle of the mattress, the periodic slamming of a distant door, the blasts of static-laced music from the radio in the common room, the grumble of traffic, smoother and far more constant that the sounds of logging trucks passing her cabin— it all conspired to keep her aware of where she was and where she was not.

Grace sat up, slipped her feet into her boots, pulled out the sweatshirt she'd stuffed at the bottom of her pack, cinched it closed, and hefted the pack onto her shoulders.

"I'll be back tonight," she told the girl in the dingy flannel shirt, yards too big for her, who leaned against the check-in counter.

"Whatever." Not even a glance in Grace's direction. "We don't hold beds. Not a hotel."

"Right." Grace nodded as she stepped out onto the street. "Even I wouldn't mistake this place for a hotel."

The blue sky of the previous day had disappeared as if it had never been. The pavement was dark with rain that had fallen during the night. A backdrop of gray lurked behind everything, fogging her mind as well as her body.

Why didn't my mother come back for me? Maybe she tried. Maybe Jane lied to her too, maybe she thinks I'm dead.

She grasped at this shimmer of hope. *My mother is grieving; all this time she's believed I was dead.* There was fuel in this idea—a joyous reunion, Annie's arms around her, gratitude, relief, love—all this was possible still. All she had to do was find her. The fog lifted for a moment.

Don't be ridiculous. I was a healthy four-year-old. It would have been way too convenient for me to die just when she left town. No one would believe that.

Grace pulled the hood of her sweatshirt over her hair. *What kind of mother just walks away from her child? What kind of child was I? Why did she leave me?* Each time these questions circled through her brain, Grace felt more confused. If she were ever going to find an answer to any of it, she needed to start searching for Annie.

The phone hung inside a shelter of sorts, no sides or door, but a small plastic dome kept the rain from dripping down her back as she stepped up to lift the receiver. An empty chain dangled from the bottom of the phone box; the phonebook had likely disappeared long ago. Grace dropped a quarter in the coin slot and punched 411.

"Do you have number for Anne Tillman or, um, Anne Roberge?"

By the time she'd checked into the hostel for her second night, Grace had learned enough to take a bed at the end of the row by the back wall, where the constant shuffling of folks back and forth from the bathroom wouldn't disturb her. Aside from this kernel of street-wisdom, the day had yielded only frustrating dead ends. Telephone Information had no listing for Tillman or Roberge in Seattle. She'd had the same luck at the library, where she'd randomly pulled phonebooks from around the state. The world outside Prosperity seemed impossibly huge.

She dumped the contents of her pack on the bed and rummaged through the clothes and the few toiletries she'd brought for what she had expected would be a brief night at Jane's. She stuck her hand down to the bottom of the center pocket. There she found the little book she never went anywhere without. The edges of the cover were slightly swollen from the time she'd dripped hot chocolate on it as she wrote, several pages were wrinkled and smudged with greasy fingerprints. Grace thumbed through pages covered with small sketches of birds and trees growing out of l's and t's. There were a few dried flowers and bits of crumbling leaves stuck in the seams between the pages. Her diary. Just holding it settled her a bit.

Warren had given his daughter her first diary for her eighth birthday—a small blue book with white flowers on the cover. It had a leather flap that folded over the edge and locked with a key. The edges of the paper were gilded.

"Rose says girls like to write secret stuff, so it has a lock." He presented it to her with such an aura of seriousness that Grace came to believe only very serious thoughts belonged on those pages. From that first day she was diligent, recording in her diary before bed each night, taking care to lock it and stow the key in her dresser.

But one night the key didn't make it to the drawer. She searched for days, but the key was lost forever. Warren offered to use a knife on the leather flap and slit it open, but Grace wouldn't hear of it. She imagined the words inside that locked book had been sealed by some magical spell and it would be wrong to break it. She convinced herself that one day when she was ready to read those words the key would reappear.

The habit of writing in a diary had taken root by then, so Grace asked her father to get her another blank book—one without a lock. And Grace continued to record her thoughts, dreams, confusion of feelings about all the people in her life, and her sketches of plants and birds. Over the years, she filled several little books, though recently she'd become lax—writing only brief comments occasionally, so that one book covered years. The one she pulled from her backpack as she sat on the bed in the hostel dated back to high school.

> *September 10, 1987*
> *I can't believe it. I'm actually in high school!!! The same high school my parents went to. It makes me sad to think that I never got to ask Mom about her time at Cooper. I've asked Dad to tell me about those days, but he just brushes me off. Or he gets mad. Real mad.*
>
> *I don't want to think about that. Today is a day to be excited and happy. I wonder what it will be like to be in that huge place. I hope I don't get lost. Shauna and I have pretty much the same schedule, so we'll have each other.*

She thumbed through several pages to this:

> *March 15, 1988*
> *I can't believe Patrick wants to go out with me!! I've known him all my life. Is this weird? I wish my mom were here—I need to talk to her about this. My mom was pretty and funny and really popular in high school—you can just tell by looking at her*

yearbooks. I wish Dad would tell me more about her, but he never likes to talk about her.

There I go again. Every time there's something exciting happening in my life I think about my mother and get sad. Not today though—PATRICK!!!!

(Bright red hearts and yellow stars circle his name)

Not that I'm in love or anything. He is cute and funny and we know each other really well. That's good, isn't it?

Was that me? Grace slammed the book shut and closed her eyes. *It was all a lie. Who am I?* The question kept hammering inside her. *How can I be the same person I was before I knew my mother abandoned me?* She took a pen from her pocket, opened the book to its back page, turned it upside down, and began writing as if it were the opening page of a new journal.

August 17, 1991

Nothing will ever be the same again. Nothing. I can't even trust myself--I'm a gullible fool. What if I'd known the truth when I was four and still had my dad? Sure, it would have been awful, but having my mom die (?!) was pretty damn awful. Dad must have really hated her. All those years he would never talk about her. And Jane—her best friend ???!!! I try and try to remember every bad thing I can about my mom, but there's just nothing there. This morning I woke with a thought that I've been carrying around all day—maybe Jane is making this up. I don't know why she would do that, but it just doesn't feel real. I can't get my head around the idea that my mom is still alive. That she's been alive the whole time I've been growing up. I don't even know if I want to find her. She's never wanted to find me, apparently. If she'd been around, maybe Dad wouldn't have been so angry. Maybe. But maybe Jane was lying; maybe my mom did try to come back for me. I'm in a weird fairytale and Jane's the wicked stepmother.

"Sorry to bother you, but is this bed free?" The voice startled Grace and she looked up to see a young woman with thin strands of colorless hair dripping dirty water onto the bed next to hers. This new arrival grinned, showing gray teeth.

"Um . . . I think so." Grace stared as her new neighbor wiped her towel over her head.

"Great. I'm exhausted and it's pouring out there. I just need a warm, dry bed." She stuck out her hand, "I'm Marla."

"Hi, I'm Grace." The smile Grace offered in return felt forced and she looked back down at her journal.

"I really meant it—don't want to bother you. I know how important it can be to keep up your journal when you're on the road. Sometimes my journal is the only place where I can collect my thoughts. In fact, that's a great idea. I think I'll join you."

Grace lifted her eyes, alarmed, and noticed the dark bruises on the side of Marla's face.

"I mean, I'll write in my journal now too. I'm trying to make it a habit, but I still have to remind myself to do it." Marla sighed and sat firmly on the neighboring mattress. Grace tried to refocus on what she'd been writing, but the heaviness radiating from this new roommate distracted her.

Marla dumped her sack out on the floor and began rummaging through the pile of dirty clothes.

"God, I know some girls who write every day. One of my friends back home started writing in a journal when she was like five years old and still does it. Every day." She looked hard at Grace. "I tell ya, there are some days in my life I don't need a written record to remind me of. They're etched in the brain, along with the scars." Grace's eyes were drawn to the brownish-red band of thickened skin that circled Marla's wrist.

"But just imagine, you could go back and read all the other stuff you'd forgotten from your childhood. Some of it would probably be good, too. It's the good stuff you forget."

"Yeah." As this idea sank in, Grace sat up straight.

"Excuse me." Grace jumped up and began cramming her belongings back down in the pack. She tossed the blanket on the bed.

"I just realized I need to be somewhere else. Thanks!"

"Thanks for what? I'm telling you, it's raining like hell out there," Marla called after her.

Grace's backpack bounced on her shoulders as she raced out through the door of the hostel and up the hilly street, pushing through the rain, past the restaurant where she'd learned the truth. At the bus station, she found a pay phone and, just before boarding the bus, made a call. "Lyle? It's Grace. I need a big favor. Can you pick me up in Everett? I need to come home."

The trip north took Grace through a strange country. She didn't recognize landmarks; even the mountain peaks, whose names and contours she knew like she knew the streets of Prosperity, seemed to have rearranged themselves in the fading light. She'd traveled along these roads in blurring rain many times, but this evening nothing was the way she'd known it before.

She was surprised when the driver announced their arrival in Everett. As Grace disembarked, the sight of Lyle's pickup puffing exhaust through the wet air broke through her disorientation. She took a slow breath and tried to calm herself as she stepped up to the truck and threw her pack into the bed. She climbed into the passenger seat and looked at this man who had lived in Prosperity for only a few years. He had no part in keeping the truth from her.

"Thanks, Lyle, this is a huge help."

"Good to see you, Grace. Jane's been callin', wondering where you were."

"How'd you handle that?"

"I just told her the truth. I didn't know where you were. I didn't know when you'd be back home, but you'd promised me you wouldn't be away too long. What else could I say?"

"Yeah, well, the truth is a good way to go, I'd say. Thanks. I just needed to spend a little time in the city. Hope you managed OK without me."

He shrugged. "There wasn't much to do. Things were pickin' up there for a bit, but the last two days were pretty dead."

Grace shook her head. "And we have to get the taxes in this week. The utility bills. And we owe Bargreens. We can't go to the bank again, they'll just laugh." Then she stopped. She folded her arms across her chest.

"But, honestly, I'm not worrying about the damn café. I've got other things to deal with right now."

"OK. Worrying wasn't going to solve anything anyway." He put the truck in gear and began the trip out of the city. "Did something happen between you and Jane?"

She waved this off. "What's going on in town besides nobody eating pie?"

Lyle sighed. "Ran into Pat a couple of days ago and he asked where you've been. I told him you were visiting Jane in Seattle and he just gave me this smirk and said 'figures.' What's that supposed to mean, anyway?"

"Fuck Patrick."

"Grace! What the hell? I thought you and he were, like, a thing."

"Not for a long time, Lyle. That's old news."

He glanced over at her and shook his head. "Nobody's got any loyalty anymore."

"Yeah, well, loyalty's a pretty weird thing in Prosperity, I'm learning."

A silence settled between them as the pickup made its rattling way up the mountain. Grace let her head fall back on the seat and closed her eyes, slipping slowly into the blankness of sleep.

Lyle laid his hand lightly on her shoulder.

"You're home."

She sat up and rubbed her hands over her face. "Thanks for the ride. That really saved me." Grace stepped down out of the truck and reached into the bed for her backpack. It might be that nothing else was true, but this was home—her cabin, her jungle. And she was grateful to be here.

"Sure," Lyle said. "Get some sleep. I'll see you tomorrow."

Grace climbed the ladder and fell into bed too exhausted to remember the urgency that had driven her back home. The night was full of dreams. She wandered the forest, lost, disoriented; hidden birds called to her and small creatures scuttled beneath the undergrowth. Shadows and sounds drew her on till she was sitting on a patch of sunny grass in the middle of the Prosperity cemetery.

There were tears on Grace's face when she woke.

Brilliant sunlight blazed through her windows. Like an avalanche, all the confusion and shock of the last few days came rolling through her. Climbing out of bed, she dragged herself to the corner of the loft and pulled a battered cardboard box from the shelf above her clothes. The blue diary was buried beneath a collection of childhood toys, trophies, and favorite books she had packed when she left Jane's house.

Chapter 15

Gingerly, as if it might explode, Grace lifted the diary out of the box. She carried it down the ladder, stepped over to the kitchen counter and picked up a paring knife. She slid the blade between the gilded pages and the leather flap. The thin leather barely resisted her knife; the book fell open as if it had been waiting all these years for release. She took a deep breath and began reading the loopy, childish handwriting.

July 4, 1981
> *Dear Diary,*
>
> *Today is my eighth birthday and Daddy gave me the best present ever—you!! He told me you'd keep my secrets. That is good, because I have secrets and no one to tell. You have a gold lock and I have the key.*
>
> *Here's my first secret—I am sad. Everyone thinks I'm a happy girl because I smile and play and I'm good in school. But inside I'm really, really, really, sad ever since my mommy died.*
>
> *Love, Parrot*

July 5, 1981

    Dear Diary,

    It feels funny to read what I wrote yesterday. I'm not sad all the time.

    I love Daddy LOTS! I just wish he didn't get mad so much. He has a loud yelling voice that scares me. I miss my mommy at night. Here's my other secret—I can't really remember what she looked like.

    Tear drops wrinkle the paper here.

    That's all.

    Love,

    Parrot

July 7, 1981

    Dear Diary,

    I'm sorry I didn't write yesterday. I was busy! I went to bed it was late and I was tired. Yesterday was a fun day. Aunt Jane let me help her make pies at the café. Mr. Walt and Mrs. Rose and Mr. Jackson came in and they all saw me in the kitchen. It made them smile. They all were friends with my mommy. I think they miss her too. I wonder if they remember what she looked like. Mrs. Rose said I looked like I belonged in that kitchen. I guess I do.

    Grace looked at the clock. It was nearly noon. She picked up the phone.

    "Hey, Lyle, do you need me today?"

    "I'm managing. Forget it. Stay home and rest up. You gotta make a run up the mountain tomorrow morning. I'll pull the stuff together."

"Damn. I forgot those guys. OK. I'll come by early tomorrow and get everything. And thanks, Lyle. A lot."

He grunted. If his voice was colored with exasperation, Grace didn't notice. She made a pot of coffee and curled up on the sofa with the diary.

There were several short entries—a sketch of hearts or a line or two describing a bird's nest or just *I had a good day*. She turned the pages slowly, not exactly sure what she was looking for. Then this entry:

> *July 28, 1981*
> > *Dear Diary,*
> > *This is my first time writing in the morning. It feels strange, but I have to tell you about my dream last night before I forget it. I saw my mommy! In my dream she came and sat on the bed and talked to me. I was so happy! She told me that she missed me too and that I shouldn't be sad. She said she was watching over me. Like an angel, I guess. She was so beautiful—I can still see her face in my mind! That dream made me happy!*

> *July 31, 1981*
> > *Dear Diary,*
> > *I don't want to go to sleep ever again. I don't want to have the dream I had last night again. It was bad. You remember the happy dream when mommy sat on my bed and told me not to be sad? That's my favorite dream. Last night I had a different dream. My mommy was there again, sitting next to me on the bed. She put her hand on my head and she said she had to go away. She said she was really sad and*

*sorry she had to leave me, but Aunt Jane would keep
me safe. It was awful and I was crying and crying.
I think I had that dream before, a long time ago. I
don't want to have it again.*

That was the last entry. The key must have disappeared
that night.

Grace closed the book and hugged it to her chest. That
feeling of her mother's hand on her head. A cool breeze and
the smell of lilacs. It was so close. Grace held her breath and
squeezed her eyes shut. She tried to still her mind, tried to remember. Annie had vanished just before Grace's fourth birthday.
It would have been the end of June. The lilac bush outside
her childhood bedroom would have been well past its bloom.
Something important, something she once knew but had long
ago forgotten was right there, but it stayed just out of sight.

In the corner above where she sat, the yellow-green beak
of a toucan smiled down at her; on her right a black and orange snake wrapped itself around a thick vine and peered into
the room. This was the jungle world her mother had described
to her as they sat snuggled together on the couch. Annie had
whispered it into Grace's ears. "There is a place called the
jungle where there are monkeys and bright, beautiful birds.
The trees are all different, coconuts and papayas and mangos,
palms—and vines everywhere. I want to see that, don't you,
sweetie?"

Grace could feel the soft tickle of her mother's breath on
her ear. A sense of excitement sparked through the air, along
with a sense of panic. *I asked her if birds ever got lost! I remember
that. I was so afraid of getting lost.*

"The birds have their ways, their routines. You know
that pair of eagles that nest in the cedar next to the river?

They come back every year, don't they? They know where their home is. It's like they have roads in the sky that we can't see."

Grace climbed back up the ladder and dragged the box over to her bed. She turned it over and dumped out all the toys and junk she'd thought so essential to save. At the bottom was another black book—the journal she'd gotten after the key was lost.

> *August 15, 1981*
> *Dear Diary,*
> *I can't find the key to my blue diary, but that's OK. There are secrets in there that can stay locked up. But I want to keep writing. Yesterday Mrs. Rose took me shopping in Cooper and I bought you. I didn't get one with a lock 'cause I don't want to write secrets anymore. I'm just going to write happy things. You'll be my happy book!*

Grace flipped through the pages of this "happy book." The entries were all short and simple, "Today I made a pie!" "I found a robin's nest in the tree outside Daddy's window." "Mrs. Johnson put my picture of a parrot up on the wall. She said it was beautiful!" "Aunt Jane helped me with my arithmetic." Not a single reference to Mommy or to dreams, either good or bad. There were several long gaps between entries. The last several pages were blank.

Her current diary was still in her backpack. She grabbed it now. Sitting on her own bed, with her back against the wall of her own cabin, she turned the section she'd been afraid to read while she sat on that dingy cot in the hostel.

September 15, 1988

> *Daddy is dead. I know it's true, but it can't be. I keep expecting to hear his truck pull into the driveway. I am an orphan now. Why did this happen?*

On the next page, there were several aborted starts. *My daddy . . . Why couldn't it be someone else's dad? I hate the trees!!!! It's NOT FAIR!!!!*

Grace remembered writing those thoughts. She could taste the bitterness that lived inside her then, the helpless outrage.

Then this:

September 20, 1988

> *I had the dream again last night. That dream that Mommy came to me, she held me and let me cry and cry. She stroked my hair and told me she knew I was sad and that it was OK. It felt so real. I wonder if Daddy will come to me in my dreams.*

September 23, 1988

> *I dreamed Mommy was with me again, but I wish Daddy would come. I told her to tell him to come to me. She said she couldn't do that. She said Daddy was in a different place than she was. I got mad at her. It was such a strange dream, I could feel my fists pounding on her. I yelled "go away and let Daddy come back." I feel bad about that now, but if I have to choose between them, I want my dad.*

Grace put the book down and hugged her knees to her chest. Even now she felt that longing to see her father again, to hear his voice the way she heard her mother's.

That dream had been so real. The fury she felt when her mother said she couldn't bring her father back, the feeling of beating her fists against her mother's arms. She remembered thinking, *If I can only have one of you, I want him.* But Warren had not come to her in dreams. And after that night, neither did Annie.

Goose bumps covered Grace's arms and she shivered. Her body shook. She slumped over onto her side and wrapped herself in her sleeping bag. She closed her eyes and tried to shut it all out.

Chapter 16

The frustration and the waiting created the perfect opportunity for Charlie's fantasies to flourish.

What might happen once Grace knew who he was, once she learned the truth about her mom? Images of screaming homicidal rage with Charlie as its target, of suicidal wrist slashing and emergency teams called in, of the whole town hunting him down like a pack of betrayed hungry wolves. As he drove up and down the mountain, as he washed his truck compulsively scrubbing away at invisible dirt, as he rolled around in his bed trying to surrender to sleep, Charlie's brain worked through each potential disaster to its tragic end.

Friday night the job was winding down. It had been eight days and they'd hauled over a million tons of timber out of Jake Oliver's forest preserve, all they needed. Luck had hung around longer than they'd had a right to expect. No inspectors had sniffed them out. There had been no publicity. The last few nights they'd had to dodge lightning storms, kept their fingers crossed and watched the weather moving across the valley, but no storm had reached them. Another kind of luck.

When the last tree was bucked and hoisted off the mountain and loaded on the bed of Charlie's Peterbilt, the men fell into a stupor. They'd been moving like automatons, getting the job done, and now their batteries had all gone dead at the same instant. They looked up and found themselves aged. Tall and brawny men were stooped, sagging. Even the young ones carried their thick muscled arms like burdens, their heads bowed. No next job had materialized. No imaginable future. They avoided each other's eyes; they climbed into their pickups without bidding one another good night. The doors slammed against their withered hopes.

The next evening the men gathered at the mill for their paychecks. A thick mist had settled down over Prosperity, shrouding the waning moonlight. The crew agreed to wait to do the cleanup and bring the equipment down the next night when clearer skies were predicted.

Pat and his father stood outside the office, mumbling names and passing out checks. When they'd turned over the last one, Pat lifted his head and spoke loudly to the retreating crowd.

"All right now. We did it. Order's filled. Now who's ready to go another mile in and take some of those real monsters?"

The shuffling stopped and a few turned to look back over their shoulders.

"No way, man. We gotta get out of there," someone shouted.

"What are you thinking, son?" Burt Samson took hold of Pat's shoulders. "We've pushed our luck far enough. The government means business now. We get caught taking trees on a preserve, especially trees like these old-growth, we're going to jail." He waved his arm to encompass the men standing before them. "These guys have families."

"All the more reason we have to do this. I know a guy who can help us unload that timber at top price." Pat spoke loudly to the group. "This could be our last chance. We got the rigging up there. Anything more we cut is gravy. Who's with me?"

Most of the men turned back toward their trucks.

"Damn it, Samson. That's not what we signed up for," shouted one.

"Crazy fucker." Another.

A few stood silently and appeared to be considering Pat's challenge.

Burt walked over to his pickup and opened the door.

"Let's go home," he said to his son. Then he turned to the crew. "Be back tomorrow night and we'll get everything tidied up."

Pat stood a moment watching as the men turned to leave.

"Sleep on it guys. Think about it." Then he turned to his father. "You go on. I got some business."

Henry and Charlie stood at the back of the crowd. They saw Pat shrug off his father and stride across the yard toward town.

Charlie looked over at Henry. "What'd I tell you? Greedy son of a bitch."

Henry nodded. "Or more desperate than we are." He stuck his hands in his pockets. Henry was ready to head up north, try his luck in Canada. Charlie thought he might follow his friend, but he couldn't leave till he found Grace. The pressure to talk to her had boiled up the last couple of days. He could think of little else. If he could lay it all out for her and witness her reaction, whatever it was—stay there and accept her rage—he would be taking a step toward washing off the filth his father had dumped on him. Then he could leave

Prosperity and try to find some way to make a life that didn't leave any openings for Nathan to sneak back in.

As he surveyed the group leaving the yard, Charlie noticed a light on in the cabin. She must be back. Henry put a hand on his shoulder. "Check it out." Henry tilted his head toward the cabin.

Pat stood on the top step. The door opened and he disappeared inside.

Grace had awakened to the sound of truck doors slamming and motors starting up. It was dark outside her window and she felt, again, the sense of unreality that had stuck with her since her conversation with Jane.

Childhood mementos she'd pulled from the box were scattered around her bed; she sighed and began dumping them back in. The crackle of pickup tires over gravel caught her attention. She climbed down the ladder just as she heard the knock on her door.

"Patrick." Oh god, he'd probably known the truth all along too. She fought a desire to slam the door in his face.

"Hey, you're back." He smiled at her in that shy, tender way he used to.

"Yeah." How long had it been since she'd stood this close to him, close enough to smell his skin under the sweet scent of fresh-cut wood? That stubborn strand of hair begged to be tucked under his cap like always, the quizzical tilt of his front tooth shaping his smile into a seduction. Grace could feel her body soften. The exhaustion of the last few days, the whirling uncertainty, the terror of standing alone and disconnected from everything she'd known—it all cascaded through her again. The armor of rage she'd brought back from the city melted and left her defenseless against the yearning of her flesh for his. She gripped the doorknob, afraid of falling into his arms.

"It's good to see you." All she could manage.

"Listen, I need to tell you something. Could I come in?" He sounded hopeful, but also a little sad. "I hear you've done some amazing stuff in there. I'd like to see it." He was almost pleading.

"And you believed what people said? That's risky business in this town." A shock of bitterness boiled up again. But Grace stepped back and let him in. "Probably best to see for yourself instead of relying on what others tell you."

She stood watching him take in her artwork. Grace struggled to keep herself hardened. Up until a few days ago, she would have savored this moment; now she just wanted it over with.

This was a world where sun and shade danced together across the room, not a setting where anger and betrayal felt at home. Garlands of small electric bulbs strung between the logs shone spots of light on each of the colorful appliances. A tiny monkey peeked down from the top of the refrigerator; an orange-beaked toucan perched on the wall behind the stove. Glowing pink orchids and a green-and-orange snake wound around the ladder leading to the sleeping loft.

Pat stood dumbfounded in the center of the cabin. He slowly turned in a circle, his head tilted back. Then he let out a huge, "Yes!" His grin practically split his face. "It's too much, Parrot! Just wild!"

She knew if she stood there watching his delight, listening to his praise, she would be totally lost. "What did you want to tell me?"

He turned and his eyes sought hers. He put his hands on her shoulders.

"OK, look, I just heard this stuff from my dad and it seemed like you ought to know. It's pretty big. You might really want to be sitting down."

"What?" Mustering as much strength as she could, she stared at him fiercely. "Your dad just told you my mom is alive?" She watched his face. He knew, but she'd surprised him with this. He hadn't known she knew. "He told you that this whole lying, stinking town has been keeping her from me all my life?" She was grateful for the rage she heard in her own voice. She could ground herself with it, push him back. "When did he really tell you this? How many years ago, Pat? You're coming to me now because Charlie has come back, aren't you? Because you're afraid he'll tell me and you don't want to be left looking like a liar, like the rest of them." She bunched her hands into fists and started punching him in the chest, tears running down her cheeks.

He stood perfectly still and let her beat on him till it seemed she'd worn out some of her fury. Then he reached out and pulled her toward him. "He told me two days ago. I've been looking for you ever since."

At that, Grace dropped her arms. She leaned her head on his chest and sobbed.

Pat wrapped his arms around her. "I couldn't believe it when he told me. I don't know how they could do it. He said everyone thought it was the best thing for you."

Grace clung to him. "Why did he tell you now? "

"You were right about that. I didn't know who Charlie was, I swear. I hired him because Henry vouched for him. When I told my dad we had a new truck driver, he wanted to know if he was someone we could trust. I told him the name and he got real quiet. I let it go for a couple of days, but he was acting real weird around Charlie. I pushed on him till he told me. It totally blew my mind."

Grace pushed herself away so she could look at his face. "Wait a minute. Why are you hiring a truck driver? Does the mill have a new contract?" Before Pat could answer she shook her head. "Never mind. That's not important. I keep losing track. This whole thing is so crazy. What I really need is to find my mother. Do you think your dad knows where she is?"

"Are you sure? I mean . . ." Pat looked confused. "Sounds to me like it was a good thing for you she left. She musta been some rotten bitch. I mean, you were only a little kid, and your mother left you. That's fucked up."

Grace considered this. "I don't know. Maybe you're right. But I've loved her all my life. I mean, if she's alive, I just have to . . ."

Pat put his arm around her. "Maybe you need to give it some time." He took another slow turn, surveying the whole space. "Well, one thing I can tell you for sure: you're an artist, man. I always knew it. What's up in the loft?"

"Go on up." Grace followed him up the ladder. "Watch your head."

"Nice," he said as he crawled up into Grace's suspended bedroom. Next to her mattress was a sheepskin, its thick coffee-colored fleece still soft with lanolin. Years ago, Mrs. G had taken a trip to the other side of the mountains to visit her sister and she brought it back for Grace. Pat lay on his back on the soft fleece and watched Grace as she came up off the ladder.

She reached for the box of diaries. "I found my diaries from when I was a kid."

"Yeah? Do you really want to relive all that?"

"You're probably right." Grace's head was swirling now. If her mother left her and didn't come back, maybe she was a monster. Maybe it would be a mistake to track her down. It was so hard to imagine. As a child, Grace believed her mother was an angel looking out for her. But that was all a fantasy. Truth was she didn't know anything about her mother. Not really.

Thinking about Annie was exhausting and Grace longed to forget about all that for a while.

She pushed the box aside and sat next to Pat on the fleece.

Could she ask him what was going on at the mill? She feared where that might lead. She didn't want to fight with him again. Holding onto all that anger was like hiking up a mountain with a ten-ton pack. She ached to put it down. Grace shoved away the questions that had been plaguing her and leaned her head against his shoulder. He put his arm around her and laid her back on the fleece.

Leaning over her he whispered, "I've missed you."

She started to tell him how she didn't know who she could trust anymore, but he put his finger to her lips.

"Shhhh." He brushed the hair from the side of her face. His lips slowly traced a line down the side of her neck and she wrapped her arms around him, relishing the contact.

Pat and Grace had first had sex in the cab of his truck when they were juniors in high school. It was awkward and fumbling and mostly embarrassing. But Pat had laid claim to Grace with his body and to Grace that felt like love: the kind of love that anchored her and reminded her where she belonged. When the shifting tide pulled hard against that anchor, the tether had stretched and thinned. Pat had turned to spite and bitterness, Grace to denial. But now, completely unmoored, Grace recognized the safe port of their mutual history and longed to return.

She let her lips find Pat's. She closed her eyes. Melding her body to his, breathing in his smell, tasting the cedar-salt of his skin, Grace yearned to forget everything she'd learned in the last days and return to the shelter of what she'd always believed. Pat invited her to come back home and Grace let her body decide.

SECTION 4: LOST AND FOUND

Chapter 17

Pat's arm lay across her stomach. Grace opened her eyes and took a deep breath. What had she done? She forced herself to rewind the last day and night. The urgency and the surrender; the fury, the betrayal, and the comfort of Pat's arms around her. She looked at the clock.

She lifted Pat's arm to free herself. "Patrick, you need to go." She shook him.

"Huh?" He picked up Grace's alarm clock from the floor by the bed. "It's only five a.m. I don't have to work today." Then he rolled over and put his hand on her back. "We can spend the day right here."

"No. No we can't. I have to get to the café. Lyle's been covering for me and I need to give him a break. You need to go. Now." She was up, grabbing her clothes, climbing down the ladder. "I'm going to take a shower and you'll be gone when I get out," she called to him as she walked to the bathroom.

"What's the big rush? You know no one is going to be there this early."

"You never know. We can't afford to miss a single customer." She pulled the bathroom door closed behind her.

When she stepped out of the bathroom with a towel around her hair, he was dressed and standing by the fireplace.

"I think I'll have breakfast at the Hoot Owl this morning. How's that?"

She retreated into the bathroom and busied herself rubbing the towel over her head. He poked his head in the doorway to check out the underwater paradise she'd created around the blue toilet. The whole space was painted in multiple shades of blue and green. Bubbles rose along the edges of flowing seaweed. Tropical fish swam across the floor and walls. Grace tried to avoid his eyes as he looked at her in the mirror.

"I don't know how we're stocked. I gotta make pies and stuff. On second thought, you should just stay here. I'll call you when I have a break."

"Naw. I'm up now. I'll walk you over." He picked up his jacket from the couch.

"No. Listen, Pat. I'm not ready for everyone seeing us together again." She was beginning to panic. She had to get up the mountain and deal with Chelsea. If Pat found out—she just couldn't think about that now. "This is all so . . ." She looked down at her hands. They had curled into fists without her realizing it. "I mean, you need to give me time."

"Whoa. What was that all about last night?" He put his hand under her chin and turned her face to look at him. "Am I missing something here? You sure seemed ready to get back together last night."

Grace twisted away from him. "Yeah. Well, now I'm not so sure. Everything is just so strange right now. Can't we back off a little while I figure things out?"

He started at her, his lips open, his eyes full of hurt. "OK. That's fine. I understand." He turned his back on her. "When you come from a family that lies to you, I guess you have trouble being straight about things," he said as he walked to the door and put his hand on the knob. "If you ever make up your mind, think twice before calling me, Grace. I don't need to go through this again."

Damn.

Could that be right? Did dishonesty run in her family? Pat might be one of the few people in Prosperity Grace could trust and she'd just pushed him away so she could hide her own secret from him. Had she inherited her mother's lying, cheating ways, or had the whole world gone crazy, including her?

Whatever her mother was or wasn't, Grace was still responsible for at least part of the craziness. Feeding the protestors had been her decision. Maybe she'd made it out of desperation, but she had brought that problem on herself. And now at least she could try to fix that one thing. She looked at the clock on her stove. It was getting light now and she needed to get up the mountain and back before anyone noticed. Luckily the rain they'd had in Seattle a couple of nights before hadn't reached the Cascades. The trails were dry.

She went into the café through the back door. Lyle had stuffed the pack and left it for her with a note: *Make sure they pay you!!!* On the counter blueberry muffins were cooling on a rack. She grabbed one and pulled the pack onto her shoulders.

Grace was halfway up the mountain when her mind began to clear. She couldn't go on acting like nothing had changed, like she was going to keep struggling to pay the café's bills, like she was going to stay in Prosperity and serve food to all those liars. And there was no way she could keep this huge secret from everyone, as if this wrong would cancel out the wrong they'd committed.

She stopped dead on the trail and looked around. She'd always felt so comforted by the forest, but why? The trees didn't give a damn. Whether she was just as much a liar as everyone else didn't make a bit of difference to them. They'd just stand here growing until some man with a chain saw decided their time was up and then they might prove to be just as full of treachery as any human being. That's one lesson her father's death ought to have taught her—you can't even trust the forest.

She adjusted the straps on her back, took a deep breath and headed up the trail the rest of the way to the camp. This time she made plenty of noise when she arrived.

"Hey, Chelsea!" She called when she saw the first glimmer of light on the plastic tarps. "Food delivery!"

"Shut up, it's too early," someone grumbled from within one of the tents.

Chelsea stuck her head out of another. "Hey, Grace," she whispered. "Just leave everything there by the fire pit, OK? Here's a list for next time." She held out a piece of paper.

"I need to talk to you, actually," Grace stood in the center of the encampment and turned in a slow circle, "I need everyone to hear this." She waited a moment, listening to the sounds of people unzipping sleeping bags, grumbling as they shook one another awake.

"This is my last delivery, guys." She set her pack down and started laying out all the food Lyle had packed. "Nothing personal, but I'm not doing this anymore. And," she saw a few tent flaps lift, a few scraggly heads stick out. "I need to get paid. Everything you owe me. Now."

Silence. After several seconds, Chelsea stepped out of her tent. "Bummer for us. Does this mean your business has picked up?"

"Not really. But it's not about that. I just need to stop doing this."

"Your conscience finally get to you? Feeling like a traitor to your roots, logger girl? I knew you didn't really give a shit about the environment." Jason now stood across the fire pit from Grace.

"Yeah, well maybe and maybe not, as my friend Kev would say." Grace did not have the energy to argue with this jerk. "Right now, what I care about is my money, so I guess I'm just like everyone else in Prosperity—according to you. Here's the bill." Grace handed it to Chelsea.

Chelsea rummaged through a string bag that hung over her shoulder. She pulled out a roll of bills that shocked Grace. "Here. This money is supposed to last us till these trees are safe. It's probably just as well we aren't tempted to buy any more of your delicious food." She handed Grace more than she owed. "Keep the change. And good luck, Grace." Chelsea smiled and opened her arms to give Grace a hug. "Blessings on your journey."

Grace let herself be embraced and then picked up her empty pack and headed back to town. *Whew.* That was over and she'd gotten out of the enemy camp unscathed. Except she had no idea if the people she'd just cut out of her life were, in fact, her enemies or not.

"D'you get the money?" Lyle said as she came into the kitchen from the back.

Grace gave him a mock salute. "Yes, sir."

Lyle laughed as he began emptying the dishwasher. "I'm just hoping to save my job here. It's about survival."

She threw the bills on the counter. "More than they owe us, I'm betting. I didn't stop to count it." Dumping the pack on the floor, she rubbed her eyes with her fingertips. "Listen, I hate to do this to you, Lyle, but I just can't handle the café right now. I got some stuff I need to do, and I'll have to leave town for a while."

"I'm listening." He turned toward her, leaned back against the counter, and folded his arms across his belly.

"It's a long story and I don't want to go through it all now. But I need to track down someone. And, honestly, I don't know what's going to happen when I find her." Grace sat on the one stool in the kitchen and wrapped her feet around the cross pieces to keep her knees from bouncing. She was having trouble sitting still.

"And the café?"

"It's up to you, I guess. If you want to stay and run it on your own, go for it. You can tell Jane I've turned it over to you. I can leave you a few signed checks to cover things till I get back." For someone who just learned that all the people she'd trusted with her life up to this point had been lying to her since she was four years old, Grace couldn't ignore the irony of giving him free access to her money. But Lyle had nothing to do with the big lie, as she'd begun to think of it. Plus, he was well aware that the café account was practically empty.

"What's Jane have to say about this?" Deep furrows formed on his brow.

"Yeah, well. I'm not actually talking to her at this point. You can tell her if you want to. She's not going to be surprised. She'll probably be grateful to you."

Lyle pushed himself away from the counter. "How soon you leaving?"

"Not sure, but soon. I told Chelsea the catering service is over." She jumped down from the stool. "You think about it. I'll check in with you later. If you don't want to take it on, we'll just close the place and let Jane deal with the bills." It would mean bankruptcy for sure. Putting Jane through that humiliation might just be worth it, even if she got dragged down with her.

"Why, Dad?" Grace put her hand on the cold marble that marked Warren's grave. "How could you let me believe she was dead?"

She lowered herself onto the grass and let the memories wash over her: her daddy kneeling down to see the world as near as he could through child eyes and then offering her a peek through his binoculars; his finger to his lips as they stood in the duff above a stream and watched a doe nudge her fawn to drink; standing together staring up into the ancient tree as he introduced her to their owl. Her eyes were dry. The sharp stab of betrayal cut off the comfort those memories used to bring.

Then another memory, this one foggy and dark, made her pull her hand away as if the gravestone had bitten her. Her father's huge hand whipping toward her face with the suddenness of a rattlesnake striking, the stinging crack that seemed to ring in the air for hours, the numbness that settled over her as she watched him turn and walk out of the house. Years of practice had embedded a habit of pushing that memory away, unexamined, so that when it rose now, it felt as if it did not belong in Grace's head.

Jane's confession had knocked the world out of kilter and then Pat had sent it into a new orbit. Grace couldn't get it to slow down enough to tell what was real anymore. Was her mother the angel she'd always believed, or was she some horrible woman who walked away from her own child? Was her father the loving, kind man she wanted to remember? Or was he a violent abuser? Did she still love Pat or was what she felt last night merely a reaction to all the turmoil and shock? Right now, she barely recognized herself.

She couldn't shake the sense that the only way to get her feet under her again was to find her mother. Yes, that might mean tracking down a monster, like Pat said. But Annie was alive and owed Grace an explanation. Besides, now that she knew the truth, Grace couldn't go on pretending her mother didn't exist. That would be just another lie, wouldn't it?

But how to find her?

She could go to Walt or Rose and demand what information they had. They'd be full of feeble apologies and self-protective explanations. The thought disgusted her. Before she resorted to them, she needed to search the one place Annie might have left a clue.

Chapter 18

Leaving the cemetery, Grace walked up the hill toward town, stopping to stare at the house everyone called "the Tillman place." This was where Jane and Warren grew up. This was where Warren and Annie lived with their baby. This was where Grace stayed with her father after Annie left. And this was where Jane had returned to help her brother care for his daughter and to repair the damage his wife's abandonment had caused. Until she moved to Jake's cabin, this was the only home Grace had known.

The flowerbeds that ran on either side of the concrete path up to the front porch had been recently weeded; dark pansies bloomed in the churned earth. But no one in the Tillman clan had ever had the patience to make a garden. The flowers were Sherrie's work.

As Grace climbed the front steps of the house, a flood of memories fought against her determination. Sherrie had been part of her life as long as she could remember, so Sherrie was undoubtedly part of the lie. Grace must remember that. She steeled herself and raised her fist to knock.

The door swung open before her knuckles reached it. Even now, fully grown, Grace had to look up at her. Nearly six feet tall, Sherrie leaned against the door, her body in shadow.

Strands of her pale hair stuck out, backlit by the gray day pressing in through the kitchen window.

"Oh, sweetie." She opened her arms to Grace. "Jane called. She told me."

Grace stood still, her eyes focused just beyond Sherrie's shoulder. This offer of comfort and condolence stunk of guilt, a sinister stench. "I need to look around."

Rebuffed, Sherrie stepped back and lowered her head. "Of course."

Grace walked into the familiar room. The brown shag rug from her childhood was gone and a brightly colored braided one sat in the center of the room. Photos of Jeremy—here flanked by his parents, there standing alone on top of a huge stump, feet spread, arms akimbo—sat on the mantel where Jane had kept Warren's picture. But the overstuffed chairs by the fireplace, the tired couch with its arms darkened by years of Tillman heads and feet, were part of the landscape of Grace's childhood.

Sherrie watched Grace take in the room. "I'm so sorry, sweetie. We really believed it was the best thing."

Grace held up a hand to stop her. Shook her head. "Do you know where she is?"

Sherrie's eyes widened. "She? Your mom? God, no. Not for years."

Grace nodded. "Yeah."

She walked through the front room and stood a moment by the hallway entrance. "Jane must have left some stuff, papers? Pictures? Where?"

"Parrot, sit down a minute. Let me get you some coffee. You need to understand."

"Please." Grace folded her arms over her chest. "What I need is to do is figure out where my mother is. I'm not in the mood to listen to excuses. If Jane left anything, I want to see it."

Sherrie squeezed her lips together and shrugged. "I haven't found anything."

"OK. I'm going into my bedroom. I'll need a stepladder."

Sherrie nodded slowly. "Huh. I think there is a ladder in the closet in that room. I wondered what is was there for. Just left it."

"There's an access to the attic space." Grace turned and hurried down the hall.

Sherrie walked into the kitchen and rummaged in the drawers.

"Here's a flashlight," she called, following Grace down the hall.

Without the bed and dresser that now stood in Grace's cabin, the room was nearly bare. She opened the closet door. In the ceiling, next to the bare bulb, was a recessed panel, access to the storage space above.

"You might need this." Sherrie handed her the flashlight. "Want some help?"

"I'll manage."

"Oh, honey, I'm so sorry about the whole thing. I just . . ."

"Don't bother, Sherrie. I don't want to hear it." There were a few people in this town who didn't deserve her fury, but Sherrie wasn't one of them.

Turning her back to Sherrie, she pushed aside the few things she'd left hanging, unable to choose their ultimate fate—Pat's letterman's jacket, a tattered chenille robe that had once belonged to Annie, and two dresses far too small for her adult body. There had been a time in her middle school years when Grace had worn nothing but dresses. As she crammed the hangers aside, she grabbed a handful of one of the flowered prints and crushed it in her fist. How many ways had she tried to imitate her absent mother?

The stepladder leaned against the back wall of the closet as it always had. When her father explained its presence, he'd been matter-of-fact about it. "That's how I can get up to the roof if we have a leak or I need to fix something. It's just a small space, all dusty." He'd pushed the panel aside and held her up, so she could peek into the darkness. She'd put her hands on the rim of the square opening and they'd come away covered with black scum. "Yeah, it's pretty dirty up there."

Grace had squirmed in his arms, "I want down." She'd never liked the dark.

Grace pulled the ladder's legs apart and stood it below the access panel. Then she climbed the few steps, reached up and pushed the panel aside. She stood on the top step of the ladder and stuck her head into the opening. A shiver of panic passed through her as she peered into the darkness, then she pulled the flashlight from her back pocket and switched it on.

"Frankly, I think this town is cursed." Sherrie's voice from the doorway startled Grace. Her foot slipped.

"Damn it." She grabbed the edge of the opening to steady herself, the flashlight still firm in her other hand.

"Oh, god, I'm sorry, sweetie." Sherrie had grabbed Grace by the legs. "You OK?"

Grace looked down. "Yeah. You can let go." She lifted her hand from where it rested, her palm coated with black dust.

"See? That black stuff? It's probably all over up there. Ashes from all the fires over the years. The forest burns and takes its revenge." Sherrie's voice softened. "Just plain cursed."

Not long after Annie disappeared, smoke and ash coated Prosperity in a ghostly dust and a hot wind blew even at night. Firefighters came and pushed everyone onto buses. Sitting on her father's lap, Grace had pressed her face against the bus window and heard the noise of hungry fire.

Four-year-old Grace had identified that hot roar as the sound of her grief.

Grace shone the light across the attic, revealing the skeleton of the house—raw planks with battens of Rockwool shoved between them. No actual floor, just the ceiling joists of her room below, and a cardboard box balanced on those joists, illuminated by the narrow beam of light. The box sat within arm's reach of the opening, as if hoisted quickly out of sight with no time to push it farther in. She set the flashlight down and stretched up onto her tiptoes so she could gather it into her arms. She looked behind her and put one foot out, searching for the next step down. "Sherrie? Are you still there?"

"Right here, sweetie." Sherrie stepped up to the closet door, her hands in her pockets. Grace passed the box down. "Put this on the floor for me."

"Yuck. This stuff is going to get all over your clothes." Sherrie placed the box under the bedroom window. "I'll get some paper towels."

Grace climbed down and stood over the box. "Don't bother." She wiped her hands on her pant legs. "If there's anything in here I need, I'll take it home. Just give me a minute."

Sherrie stepped back out of the room.

A wave of vertigo rocked Grace as she stood looking down at the box. She put a hand out to steady herself against the wall and reached over to raise the window. The latch had always been tight. As a child she'd needed to get her father's help to release it so she could let fresh air into her room. In recent years she'd kept a hammer on the windowsill for assistance, but there were no tools in the room now. Grace clamped her lips together and pushed the heel of her hand against the latch as hard as she could. It gave and her own force knocked her backward. She stumbled over the box and landed hard on her rear, the heel of her right foot denting the top of the box. As she pulled her foot off, she spun the box toward her and, on the side that she had not seen, the letters *A N N I E* were scrawled in faded pencil.

She scrambled to her knees and yanked apart the overlapping flaps that sealed the box. A blast of dust and mold hit her in the face. The vertigo returned. Grace scrambled back to the window and pushed it open wider. She stuck her head out and closed her eyes, inhaling. The box was real. It had her mother's name on it.

Grace pulled her head back into the room and looked down into the box. A jumble of envelopes, different sizes and colors. She inspected her hands and once again wiped them, this time slowly and carefully, on her pant legs.

She reached in and picked out the top envelope. It had been ripped open; a single piece of paper inside. Her hands began to shake as she looked at the name on the front of the envelope: Parrot Tillman, 137 Second St., Prosperity, WA.

There was no return address. The postmark said July 14, 1977, Seattle WA. Grace pulled out the folded sheet of white paper. She unfolded it and read the loopy script:

> *Dear Parrot,*
> *I love you so much and I miss you. Today I saw a beautiful yellow butterfly and I wished I could show it to you. I am so sorry.*
> *Be a good girl.*
> *Love, Mommy*

Grace's hands were shaking violently now and the paper rattled. Her head filled with a rushing sound like fire moving through trees.

Grace began pulling everything from the box. There were twenty, twenty-five, letters. She shuffled through them frantically. Most were addressed to her: Parrot Tillman; Grace Tillman c/o Warren Tillman; Parrot Tillman c/o Jane Tillman. As if the right name would make the difference. The postmarks told their own story. There were ten letters that had been mailed every other day for the first three weeks after Annie left, all from Portland. Then they began to space out, every three days, then once a week. The last date she found was seven months after Annie disappeared. What happened? Why had she stopped writing?

Beneath the envelopes, she found several framed photographs, some with the glass cracked. Here was a young man in a Cooper High letterman's jacket, grinning as he leaned against the side of a pickup, his arm around a skinny blond girl. Grace recognized her father. The girl was so tiny he could have carried her in one hand. She was looking up at him with such vulnerability. She adored—no—she worshiped him. Grace recognized that look. The girl was her mother.

In another snapshot a much more somber Warren sat with a beer in his hand; behind him two women, arms around each other, made faces at the camera. Jane and Annie.

Throughout her childhood, Grace had complained that there were no pictures of her mother in the house. It had been Sherrie who'd shown her the few she'd seen.

"Daddy, Mommy was pretty. Sherrie has a school book with her picture."

"What are you talking about, Parrot? What school book?"

"The one with everyone's picture. She showed me your picture too. When you were in high school."

Warren slammed his fist on the table and stomped out of the house. Grace hadn't gotten it. Not then.

She tipped the box over and a few more photos fell onto to the floor. From the bottom of the box a large book slid partway out—a Cooper High School Yearbook, *The Clarion 1968* in gilded letters on its cover. Grace pulled the book out, threw the empty box into the corner of the room and sat back on her heels. She lifted her head and raised the back of her hand to her cheek. She closed her eyes, but she could not hold back the tears.

She reached out and picked up an envelope that was addressed to her father; it was postmarked, June 1979, just before Grace's sixth birthday. Like the first, it had been ripped open; it contained two sheets of paper.

She unfolded the first sheet. The handwriting was her mother's with its characteristic adolescent flair, but this message was not intended for her.

> *Warren,*
>
> *Your sister promised she'd bring my Parrot to me and I trusted her. I'm a fool and I don't even have a word for what you are.*
>
> *Where am I supposed to get the money for a lawyer?*
>
> *If you ever hurt my daughter I will know and I will kill you. Believe me.*
>
> *If you have any decency left, at least let Parrot read my letters.*
>
> *A*

A cold chill ran through Grace's body. What was this? *If you hurt my daughter I will know and I will kill you.* Were those the words of a monster or of a desperate mother? Or both? *Believe me.*

Numbly, she unfolded the second piece of paper and read it.

> *My sweet Parrot,*
> *I think about you all the time. I wish you were*
> *here with me.*
> *I'm going to find those beautiful birds, baby.*
> *Love,*
> *Mommy*

Was her father afraid of her mother? Or was her mother afraid of her father? Was this an idle threat, or the words of a crazed woman? Could she have meant it?

Outside the trees were still. Grace stared into the stillness trying to slow her breathing. The memory that had seemed so foreign to her just an hour ago as she stood at her father's grave now emerged in full detail like a photograph developing in a chemical bath.

The summer before Grace started high school she'd been full of questions. She bugged her father.

"What was it like, Dad, when you first went to Cooper? It's so big . . . did you get lost? How did you find your locker?" And on and on. At first Warren just shrugged his shoulders and said, "You'll be fine."

But Grace wanted more. "Tell me about how you met Momma. Were you in a class together? Did she help you with homework?" Those last questions changed everything. It was like she'd jabbed her father with a hot poker.

"SHUT UP!" Warren jumped to his feet and screamed in Grace's face. He brought his hand back, his right hand. Big and red. The hand came toward her with such force that she was knocked from her chair. She froze on the floor, numb. Her father turned away and walked out the front door and didn't return for two days.

Neither of them ever said a word about what had happened. When Jane asked about the bruise on her face, Grace told her she'd run into a door.

The letter fell from Grace's hand. Her stomach lurched. She made an instinctive calculation, raced across the hall to the bathroom and slammed the door behind her just as her abdomen convulsed and she retched. Her body quivered as she spat bile from her mouth; then she slumped to the floor and leaned against the thin wall, her forehead on her raised knees. *If you hurt my daughter I will know and I will kill you.*

"Are you OK, hon?" Sherrie's voice startled Grace.

She reached over and pushed the button on the doorknob, locking it. Then she stood, washed her hands and splashed cold water on her eyes.

"Fine," she said as she opened the bathroom door and walked back across the hall. She needed to take all this to the cabin where she could be alone and think. Retrieving the box from the corner of the room, she laid the yearbook carefully at the bottom, next the framed photos, which she stacked gingerly, followed by the letters and the empty envelopes, the stray photographs.

Swallowing the bile that continued to rise in her throat, Grace looked around the room for anything she might have missed.

A photo stared up at Grace from the floor: Annie standing in the kitchen of the café, her hands covered in flour, her body wrapped in a green apron. Grace stooped to pick up the picture and she felt a chill go through her body. It was like looking at a picture of herself with blond hair. For years people had been telling her how much she looked like her mother. At least that was the truth. She placed the stray photo on the top of the box and overlapped the cardboard flap, picked it up, and walked out of the room.

Sherrie stood by the stove. "You OK, kiddo?"

"Not exactly." Grace couldn't bring herself to tell one more lie. "I've got what I came for."

She opened the front door and without saying anything more, she left.

Chapter 19

Grace carried the box down Main Street past the post office, the café, the tavern. She kept her eyes straight ahead, armored more fiercely than she'd ever been in the city. At the curve in the road she stopped. Someone sat on the steps of her cabin, his head turned away from her. His boots weren't logger gear, his jacket not one she knew; something about the hunch of his shoulders was familiar though. Curiosity was no match for her need to be alone with the evidence she held. Resentment gathered around her as she walked to her door. She opened her mouth to scream an obscenity at this loiterer when he turned to face her.

"Charlie."

"I need to talk to you." They both said simultaneously. Charlie opened his mouth to begin his confession, but Grace put her hand up to stop him.

"Come in."

Grace knew that once Charlie caught a glimpse of the interior he'd do what everyone did when they first saw the place. And he did. He stepped through the doorway, his jaw dropped, he tilted his head back and he spun around. Predictable.

"Wow. This is incredible . . . Did you . . .?"

She cut him off. "Yes, yes. I painted it. Sit down over there." Grace set the box on the floor and plopped down onto the couch.

Charlie had trouble pulling his eyes away from the ceiling, as if he expected something to fly out of it.

"Charlie, come and sit," Grace repeated. She looked at him with an evaluative eye, remembering what Jane had said about them not being blood relations. "Now that I know the truth, or at least part of it, I realize you may be the one person in town who can fill me in on what I don't know." She held out her right hand. "Glad to meet you, Charlie Roberge, I'm Grace Tillman, otherwise known as Parrot."

"Yeah. I finally figured that out."

"Well, I had no idea you existed until a few days ago. But if you hadn't showed up, I probably would never have found out that my mother is alive." She gave him a soft smile. "So, thanks, I guess."

Charlie's eyebrows rose and he squinted. "Wait. You do know Annie's alive? I thought . . . I mean, up until a week ago I had no idea you *didn't* know she was alive. I mean . . ."

"Don't strain yourself, Charlie. It's flat crazy." Grace shook her head and chuckled in spite of herself. It *was* flat crazy. "It took a trip to Seattle and practically pinning my aunt to the wall to get the truth out of her, but I did it. That was all just three days ago." She could hardly believe this, but it was true; only three days before she'd been an orphan. Now she had a living mother. "Up until then I really did believe my mother was dead."

"Whew. That's a hell of a thing." Charlie looked around the cabin as he pulled his Marlboros out of his pocket and held it out to her. "You OK with this?"

"Not really. It's not good for the paint." She gestured at the walls. Her art was real—maybe it came from her imagination, but she could trust every brush stroke—and she wasn't going to let it get covered with smoke.

"No, no, of course not." He stuck the pack back in his pocket. "Just as well." He nodded. "Henry kind of filled me in. I'm just beginning to understand. But there's more to the story than I think you realize. I've been trying to find you to tell you what I know."

She nodded and held her hands out as if to say, here I am.

"Right." Charlie took another look around and swallowed hard. "My father is a son of a bitch, you should know that from the get-go."

Grace grinned. "Oh, I have no doubt about that. My father could barely say his name without spitting." She shook her head, "but then, my father wasn't . . . Hell. I don't know what my father was."

"Well, I don't know much about your dad or why your mom would get involved with my father in the first place, but he knocked her up. You knew that, right?"

Grace nodded again.

"OK. Well, she lost that kid," Charlie paused and looked down at his hands. "Nathan never talked about it much, but when I was sixteen I went to spend the summer with him. Annie was still there, physically anyway."

"What's that supposed to mean?" Grace had wondered about this child. Thoughts of having a sibling, even a half one, somewhere out in the world had swirled beneath the surface of the shock and the chaos of emotions she'd lived with for the last several days.

Charlie interlocked his fingers, the tendons on the backs of his hands and his forearms looked like the roots along the trails. The thought flashed across Grace's mind: *this man is praying.*

"She was like a zombie, Grace. She hardly spoke. She moved around the house like a ghost. It was so weird."

Those words seemed to break something open in him. He jumped up and began walking around the room and words poured out of him. "I couldn't handle being in that house. I'd wanted to be with my dad for so long, but once I was there and saw all that . . . I just took off, and Dad came after me. He told me later that he was afraid to leave her alone, like she might kill herself or something. She'd been like that since she lost the baby." He stopped, took a deep breath and looked over at Grace, who stared back, speechless.

"Then she disappeared." Charlie's face flushed, and he slumped down into the rocking chair across from Grace. "I never got a straight story from my father. He said she was sick and went into a hospital. But I never saw her again." He put his head in his hands. "After a while I just stopped bringing up her name."

"Oh, my god." Grace said. Whiplash again. She was getting familiar with the sensation. One minute Charlie knew where her mother was, the next she had disappeared. Once again numbness encased her. "Do you think she's still alive?"

Charlie shook his head. "I don't know." He gave her a weak smile and shrugged his shoulders. "I know this sounds awful, but I was a pretty self-centered kid then and I just didn't care. My dad didn't have any time for me and I blamed Annie for that. I didn't really care what had happened to her."

"But your father's still alive, isn't he?"

"I'm afraid so."

"So, he'd know where she is, if she's alive, right?"

Charlie shrugged again. "I haven't seen him, or her, in over ten years. He calls me once in a while to steer me into some scam or another. Like this one. I try to avoid him, but when I got desperate . . ." He rubbed his hands over his face. "When I got desperate, I'm his son, and I took the bait he offered."

"Could you pick up the phone right now and call him and ask him where my mother is?"

"Yeah. If you want me to, I could."

Grace looked around at her walls. This had all been in memory of the mother she'd believed dead. Her whole life had pivoted around that belief. As awful as that had been, maybe the reality was actually worse than death. She tried to imagine it. Annie had abandoned her, left her with a man she thought could harm her, and ran off. Did losing Nathan's baby make her crazy or had she already been crazy? Again, she thought of what Pat had said. What kind of woman left her child?

"Yes. I want you to. Now." Grace stood and walked over to the telephone, picked up the receiver and held it out to him. When he took it, she thrust her hands deep inside the pockets of her jeans and walked stiffly to the window that faced the mill. The cage of her ribs was shrinking, squeezing her heart. She closed her eyes and pressed her forehead against the window.

"Dad?" Charlie spoke into the receiver.

Grace gasped, her eyes popped open. No. She wasn't ready. Not on the phone.

Charlie had his back to her. She wanted to run to him, to yank the phone from his hand, slam it down. But time had stopped and her feet refused to move.

"I need some information fast. Call me at Walt's." He put the receiver down and turned back to Grace. "All my life— same deal. He's never there when I need him."

She put her hand on her chest and exhaled. "I've never fainted in my life and that's as close as I want to get." She stumbled to the kitchen sink, turned on the cold water and splashed it over her face. As she brought her head up, she looked out the window.

The mill. What was going on there? Pat and Charlie were both trying to tell her something wasn't right. But damn. One more thing. She shook the water from her hands and looked over at Charlie.

"I . . . look, I don't want to know, OK? I just can't take anything else right now."

"You don't want me to talk to my dad?" Charlie looked honestly puzzled.

"No, no. I mean whatever's happening, whatever you guys are up to at the mill." She tipped her head back and pointed out the window with her chin. "Just keep me in the dark a little longer." The she grinned. "That shouldn't be too hard."

She stepped over to the sofa. "I've got something I want to show you."

Charlie watched her open the cardboard box she'd laid down when they first came into the cabin. The photo of Annie in her green apron stared up at them. He picked it up.

"Wow. I'd forgotten how pretty she was."

"Is."

"Right. Is," said Charlie looking from the photograph to Grace.

"She was behind all this." Grace said, waving her hand to encompass the world she'd overlaid on the raw logs of the cabin. "She had a thing about the jungle."

Grace handed him the letters. Slowly he unfolded and read each one in silence while she sat staring at the photos. The fierce energy that had driven her all day was beginning to fade. She looked at his face as he read, and felt a bone-aching desire to turn all her pain, all her sadness and confusion over to this man. This kind man who was, after all, a sort of brother to her, wasn't he?

"Do you think she was crazy enough to kill someone, like she threatens in that letter?"

"Not the lady I saw. She was more like someone who'd been beaten down. Not angry, more kinda dead herself." Charlie gently folded the last of the single-page letters and slid it back into its torn envelope. Then he turned to Grace and put his hand on her shoulder.

"I'm going back to Walt's. If Nathan doesn't call soon, I'll call him again. It's getting late. Try to get some sleep. Call me in the morning."

Grace nodded slowly. She stood and walked him to the door. "Thanks."

After Charlie left, Grace stacked the letters and tucked them back in the box. She folded over the flaps of the lid and put it on the floor where it she didn't have to see it. Then she made herself a sandwich. She would pretend life was normal. She would eat and then she would sleep. *I hope*, she thought, *I really hope I can trust this man.*

Grace woke on the couch, still dressed in the clothes she'd worn since leaving the house so long ago to hike up to the protesters' camp. The sun was bright. How long had she slept? She stretched and slowly reviewed the events of the previous evening. A loud banging on her door made her jump. Was it Charlie? Had he talked to Nathan already?

She was up and at the door before she had time to consider what news he might be bringing. But it wasn't Charlie; it was Mary Bigley who filled the open doorway, her gray curls sticking out in wild tangles, her shirt buttoned un-evenly.

"Mary! What's wrong?" Grace had never seen Kev's mother so pale. "Come in, sit down. Are you OK?"

Mary was a large woman, encompassed in pillowy fat. It took a lot out of her to move fast and she'd obviously been running. Her face was flushed, her breathing labored. She grabbed hold of Grace's hands. "When did you last see Kev?"

"I . . . um . . . I don't know." Grace pulled her hands out of Mary's sweaty grip. Mary had gotten hysterical about her son before. "What's wrong?"

"He wasn't in his bed when I got up. I thought he'd gone to the café, so I didn't worry about it. But it's afternoon now and no one's seen him."

Grace's exhausted brain could not process this. "What do you mean?"

"He said you invited him to the cabin yesterday, but when he knocked on your door, you weren't there."

"Oh my god." Grace slapped her forehead. Kev. "I did invite him. I totally forgot."

"He was pretty upset, but I told him he must have gotten the day wrong. Then he went on and on about how you were hiking in the woods, but you hadn't come back down, and maybe you were lost or something. Were you?" Mary braced herself against the doorframe and stared hard into Grace's eyes as if she might be able to read something there that Grace wouldn't say.

Mary's own eyes were red-rimmed, dots of sweat stippled her forehead, and her breath smelled of stale coffee and some-thing sharp and metallic. "What are you saying?" Grace said. "Kev's missing?"

Mary nodded, bending forward and bracing her hands on her knees.

"Come inside. Sit down." Grace put her hand under Mary's arm and guided her to the couch.

Mary made a frantic survey of the cabin; nothing but Kev's absence seemed to register. She swallowed hard and her words rushed out. "Things have been so crazy with this night job Kevin's been doing for the mill. I don't like it and it makes Kev nervous. He knows something's not right. And he's all worried about you. You weren't at the café the last few days and he wouldn't stop talking about it. 'Parrot didn't give me my pie.' Over and over." Her fingers tugged desperately at the hem of her flannel shirt as if to keep herself anchored on the ground. "Last night after Kevin left, Kev ate his dinner and went to his room. I looked in before I went to bed and he was asleep, at least I thought so. But this morning he was gone. His orange sweatshirt wasn't on the coat rack where he always puts it. I thought he went to the café, but he'd be back by now. No one's seen him. I'm going a little crazy."

Grace began racking her brain. Had she seen him since she'd come back from Seattle? When was that? "What day is it?"

"Sunday."

"I asked him to come to the cabin on Saturday, but I forgot about that. I wasn't here most of the day. Damn it." She balled her hands into fists and knocked them against her skull. "Oh, god, Mary. I don't think . . . I didn't see him. Not yesterday and I haven't been anywhere yet today." Grace felt the panic now. "I've been so distracted! What can I do?"

Mary took a deep breath. "His dad is rounding up some guys to search the woods. They're over at the mill now. You didn't go hiking this morning? So he couldn't have followed you?"

"Not today. But yesterday I went up the mountain early. But I went around the mill, not by your place. Kev did see me when I went your way a few times. He told me." Everything that had filled her mind for the last seventy-two hours now seemed trivial.

Mary was pacing, her hands running through her hair. "He told me you weren't where you were supposed to be. I told him you were fine. Oh, god!" She stopped dead. "Where did you go? Were you up where the guys are cutting Jake's trees?"

Grace's jaw dropped. "What?"

"You must know about it. It's been going on a while."

The shock that flushed across Grace's face made it clear she had no idea what she was talking about.

"Rose told them to take what they needed to fill that last order. They've been logging in Jake's preserve."

"Oh, my god." Grace's head was spinning. Nothing was in focus.

"Weren't you up there, too? Taking the guys food? Kev probably followed you."

"No, Mary. I wasn't taking food to the guys stealing trees from the preserve. I was taking food to the kids trying to save the old growth in the national forest." Would the jumble of lies and betrayals ever stop mounting?

"Those protestors? Oh, my god. Why?" It was Mary's turn to be shocked.

"Hell, Mary! I was trying to survive!" She grabbed her jacket. "But it doesn't matter now. If Kev did follow me, I know where he might be. You can tell those guys at the mill I'm heading up to the protestors' camp." Grace opened the door.

"Wait!" Mary pulled something from her pocket and held it out. "I found this on the floor of his room. He must have worn those stupid jeans with the hole in the pocket. He never goes anywhere without it."

Grace reached out and took the metal whistle in both her hands. "We'll find him. I promise."

Chapter 20

"Nathan." Walt held his hand over the receiver and whispered to Charlie, "You want me to say you ain't here?"

Charlie grabbed the phone. "Dad? Tell me where Annie is."

Walt leaned against the back of his kitchen chair and shook his head.

"No, I'm not asking, I'm demanding. Now." Walt's eyebrows rose and he stared at his nephew.

"Where's that?" Charlie opened the drawer next to the phone and picked out a pencil. He began writing on the wall. "And you just left her there? Jesus, Dad." Charlie shook his head. "OK. OK. But she's still there, right? You got a doctor's name?" He wrote something more on the wall. "Got it. Yep." He hung up the phone.

"You'll want to check out the pickup and make sure she's ready for a trip to SeaTac." Charlie called over his shoulder to his uncle as he strode out the door and down the porch steps.

Back at the cabin, he got no answer to his knock; he tried the knob and found the door unlocked. "Grace?" Charlie stepped in and called her name into the empty space. Puzzled, he stepped back outside and saw a pickup pull into the mill yard. Paul, the other log truck driver who was working on the operation, got out and ran into the office. Then he noticed five other pickups parked at chaotic angles around the mill office.

Charlie walked over and climbed the office steps.

"Hey, Charlie." Henry looked up from the trail map spread across the desk.

"Good. We could use another pair of eyes."

"For what?"

"We got a lost kid."

Charlie looked around the small office. Pat leaned against the back wall, bleary-eyed, with his arms folded over his chest. Paul, Mel Parker, Burt Samson. Even the guy with no thumbs who hung around the millyard, Clett. Familiar faces—all these men were thieves too.

"I don't think he could have made it over the ridge. He's a pretty slow walker," said a fellow Charlie recognized as one of the choke setters. He'd never gotten the man's name.

"Right. Let's go. We can fan out, cover all the trails," Henry said.

"Anybody know where Parrot's been hiking?" the choke setter asked. "Mary says Kev's been talking about Parrot going hiking in the mornings. Mary thinks he tried to follow her."

Before Charlie could get a word out, Pat spoke up. "She could of taken any of the trails out of town. I can run over to the cabin and check with her."

Charlie cleared his throat. "She's not there. I was just there looking for her. But a couple of days ago I ran into her on the trail above the junction where four trails converge. She was headed downhill. I think she stayed to the north, on the trail that ends right out here." He pointed across the mill toward the trailhead.

Pat raised an eyebrow and pushed himself off the wall. "You know Parrot?"

Charlie grinned. "She was taking a piss when I walked by. Made for a quick introduction."

The choke setter Charlie didn't know turned to him. "Thanks for helping. It's my son that's missing. He's disabled, but he's not stupid, and he'd do anything for Parrot." He held out his hand. "I'm Kevin Bigley."

Charlie reached out and shook Kevin's hand and nodded. "Charlie Roberge."

Before Kevin's look of stunned recognition formed itself into words, Henry straightened up from his concentration over the map and said, "OK, let's move it." He pointed to each of the men and directed them to the three main trailheads that all led out of town and up. "You," he said to Charlie, "take me to where you saw Grace."

These men had all been through this before. Scouring the woods for a missing buddy or a stranger—it was never a good thing, but there had been a few searches that had ended with a rescue.

"If you find anything, stay where you are and use your whistle."

"Why don't they call in the search and rescue team?" Charlie asked as he and Henry hurried to the trailhead at the far side of the mill yard.

"Kevin's not willing to risk someone finding out about the operation in the preserve."

"Shit. That's crazy."

"It's the man's son. I figure he gets to decide."

"Jesus." The thought of any father making such a choice set Charlie's brain spinning disastrous possibilities. A disabled kid lost in the woods and bears feasting on the wild huckleberries that grew upslope. The kid could have stumbled on an animal, startled it into charging. Or just a slip near the edge of the trail; he could have broken a leg, hit his head. It was August, but the nights never really warmed in the mountains. Hypothermia. If he got hungry he could mistake a poisonous mushroom for something edible. But the primary storyline, the one that felt most likely and most tragic, was that he had wandered off the trail and would simply never be found.

As they reached the trailhead, Henry looked over his shoulder to watch the other men move out of sight. "There's Mary. Looks like she's barely hanging on."

Charlie watched Kevin hold Mary in his arms a moment, nodding as she spoke, and pointed up the mountain.

"Goddamned curse." Henry muttered under his breath.

Without a pack Grace was able to bolt up the steep two miles to the camp. She was gasping for air when she got to the clearing and could barely get out a single "Guys!"

Jason was perched on a stump at the far side of the camp strumming his guitar.

"Where is everybody?

He looked up. "They all decided to hike over the ridge." He played a few descending chords. "My turn to guard the trees. Why?"

"I need your help."

Jason's hands dropped from the strings and looked at her. "Yeah?"

"There's a kid lost on the mountain somewhere. He might have tried to follow me up here. He's not a good walker, probably got off the trail somewhere down below."

"Don't think he's been around here. If anybody had seen someone wandering around here they would have said."

"Well, there's a lot of mountain to cover. His father and some of the others will probably head up from the trailheads in Prosperity, so if we can start from up here and work our way down . . ."

"We?"

"I was hoping everybody would be here, but it's just you, so let's get going."

Jason held up his hands. "Look, I'm sorry about this, but I gotta stay here with the trees."

"Jesus! This is a disabled kid lost in the woods, he could be hurt. Forget the damn trees!" She leaped over the distance between them and grabbed his guitar and threw it onto the tarp. "What's wrong with you?"

"What the fuck? How am I supposed to know this isn't some trick to get me to abandon my post, so those chain saws can get in here?"

Grace shook her head. This was a waste of precious time. "Kev!" she yelled as she scanned the woods around her—there were too many shadows, too much undergrowth. She stepped close to Jason and gripped him by the shoulders and screamed in his face.

"Dammit, Jason, listen to yourself! If Kev dies because we don't find him in time, I will personally cut these trees down and make you watch!"

She pushed him backward. He fell off the stump and landed with his feet in the air. Grace began retracing her steps out of the campsite, shouting, "Kev!"

She concentrated on the dirt as she moved downhill where a complicated story of foot and paw prints played out. Kev's contorted gait would have created a distinctive track in the dirt. He dragged the toe of his right foot with each step.

When her son was younger Mary had torn her hair out as he wore through the top of each right shoe before coming close to outgrowing them. She'd hit on the solution of having a shoemaker down in Everett cover the toes of his shoes with a thick piece of rubber. Kev loved the look. "I got boots like Dad's," he crowed.

Grace crouched down and looked closely at the marks in the dirt. Could he have made it up this far? He would have tried to come this way if he thought she had. Once the trail began to climb, the roots of overhanging firs and hemlock crossed it like thick veins on the back of a hard-working hand, uplifting the surface. Able-bodied hikers frequently hobbled down to town with twisted ankles and bunged knees. For Kev, this would have been a nightmare.

While Grace was fighting with Jason, a cloud had crept in among the trees. The shadows had vanished; all around her was gray and mist.

"Kev!" she cried again. But the forest had withdrawn its cooperative silence and no longer allowed her voice to carry farther than she could see. Instead, a cacophony of drips and splashes filled the air as water fell through the many shapes of fronds and needles to the resonant ground. The dirt began to soften and turn muddy.

All she had now was her instinct. And her memory. Could she trust any of that? She stood still, took a deep breath, and in her mind began tracing the route she'd hiked so many times. To her right off the trail about ten yards, a boundary marker indicated the end of national forest land and the start of Jake's preserve. Peering through the veil of fog into the untended darkness of the preserve, Grace could barely make out the pale form of that marker. Just beyond it, she knew, lay the trunk of a huge tree that had long before fallen across the steep valley running parallel to the trail. She took a few steps toward where she thought that valley began; her boots sank slightly into the soggy layers of soil. She shielded her face with her hands. Stinging nettles hid in the mist, appearing only when they were close enough to brush against her skin. She'd never challenged her father or any of the men in town, but she'd felt a secret gratitude that Jake Oliver had set this area off limits. It had been her haven. Today, though, she saw only the traps and dangers it harbored, and she wished the loggers had gotten in here and made space for the light.

Far on the other side of these woods was where the spotted owl had made her nest. A sharp bitterness filled Grace's mouth and she spat to rid herself of the taste and the memory of that slap. Had her father been angry and dangerous, or strong and kind? And what kind of person was her mother, really? She blinked away tears and shook her head to rid it of the sensation that she was just as lost as the boy she searched for.

"Kev!" she called.

Charlie scanned the woods as he and Henry headed up the trail from the back of the mill. Henry kept a close eye on the ground..

"I don't think he came this way." Henry spoke softly. "It's pretty far from his house. But this trail meets the others after that next turn."

"Right." Charlie said, and took this as direction to hustle up ahead to the junction.

He quickly reached the point where four trails converged into a single track switchbacking up toward the ridge. When he'd hiked up a week ago he'd met Grace above the junction. She could have gotten there via any of the trails that led out of Prosperity.

Charlie tried to reconstruct the rest of that hike. Where had he turned to get to the ridge? How had he come down?

"Hey, Henry," Charlie called down. The trees were thick along the sides of the trail and the switchbacks hid Henry from sight. "How big is this kid?"

"Kinda small and scrawny. He's probably ten or so, but seems younger."

"I got an idea. I'll whistle if I find anything."

Charlie sprinted up the mountain along the single trail. He was breathing hard; images of an injured boy sent adrenalin pumping through his body. He needed to reach the ridge so he could backtrack slowly, looking downhill.

Chapter 21

As Grace made her way through the undergrowth, the forest closed in on her and fingers of panic ran up and down her spine. She reached the downed tree and braced herself against its moss-coated bark. She tipped her head back and let the mist wet her face; she had to clear her head and think. She pushed herself off from the trunk and took a few steps down where the contour of the land began to slope into the valley. The fog was thicker here and there were no familiar landmarks.

If you hurt her, I will kill you. Believe me. Grace edited her mother's warning and directed it toward the wildness around her. *If you hurt him, I will . . .*

"Kev! Kev! Where are you?"

What was she doing? This made no sense. Kev couldn't maneuver on this soft ground. Unless he'd fallen and slid down, he would have stayed on the trail or much closer to it.

A picture began to form in her mind. He would have gotten to that first bend, where the trail that ran from the end of his street into the preserve went from a gradual slope to a steep climb. At that point what would he have done? Followed an animal track off the trail? Gotten down on all fours and dragged himself up the mountain?

Grace strained against the panic. Think like Kev would. He's practical. He thinks I'm lost. He's looking for me. She cupped her hands around her mouth and shouted into the woods.

"Kev! Kev! It's Parrot!"

Charlie rounded a switchback and looked up where the trail continued on to the ridge top. Strange. Above him fog lay heavily across the forest. The old guys would have called it a brume—a dense cloud that hushed the birds and hid the foliage. He'd rarely seen it so thick in the summer. If the kid were caught in that he'd be wet and cold and surely disoriented.

His hunch might be pretty far-fetched, but he had to act on it fast. If that cloud moved farther down the mountain, they'd all have trouble staying oriented. Charlie spun around and began heading down, scanning the trail as he went, looking for the tracks of a kid's shoes.

Every ten feet or so he stopped and bent low, looking up into the forest from a nine-year-old's perspective. It was probably ridiculous to suppose the hole was still there.

As he approached the trail junction from this vantage, everything looked different from the way it had on the way up. The trail he was descending met three trails that fanned downhill like the fingers of a hand. The webbing between the fingers was filled with dense undergrowth. The fog had crept down the mountain behind him. As it descended, the cold mist condensed into droplets and while Charlie stood at the junction, it started to rain. The sound of water hitting the earth, soaking the duff that covered the forest floor, alerted him, and the darkening the colors clarified his vision.

Instinct drew him to the area between the eastern-most trail and the center one. He stepped over the log that marked the boundary between woods and trail and began picking his way downhill. Every few feet Charlie crouched down and surveyed the territory, looking for a pine with a low branch that curved back on itself. What were the chances it would still look the same? An erratic branch like that was vulnerable; in twenty years it almost certainly had broken off, or more likely, the whole tree had fallen. But there was something about the slope of the earth here and the sense he recalled of being far from town, in the wild.

Charlie walked farther into the woods, calling, "Kev! Kev! If you can hear me make some noise."

He reached a small clearing where a cushion of thick fir needles had offered a bed for deer, the imprints of their bodies still visible. "Kev!" He stopped and waited.

A faint sound. Maybe the movement of a small animal. It sounded like panting, or a breath expelled forcefully through pursed lips. It seemed to be coming from the other side of a small clearing ahead.

"Kev!"

Again, the blowing sound.

Charlie moved slowly into the open space, stepping gingerly, his eyes fixed on a gap between the giant firs on the far side. As he got to the edge of the thick woods, he squatted and looked up from the angle of his nine-year-old self. There it was. Straight ahead. The ancient pine and the S-bent branch. When he stood up he could see the edge of the eastern trail where it curved in toward the other forks. The hole must be much closer to the trail than he'd thought, but he still couldn't see it. Charlie inched forward, looking at the ground, calling "Kev! Kev! Don't be scared. I'm here to help you. You're going to be OK."

The large bushes between the trees had been sprouts when he'd last been here. From the eastern trail anyone could have reached the spot easily, but from where Charlie stood the only way was to get down on all fours and crawl through the undergrowth. Charlie threw himself onto the ground and began clawing his way forward. The rain pelted his back. He hadn't been surer of anything in a long time. As he emerged from under the tangle of hazel and ferns, he nearly fell into the pit himself.

"Kev?" Charlie kept his voice soft. If he hadn't been looking for a boy, he might have walked past this lump coated with mud and duff except for the spots of Day-Glo orange that shown through the filth. "How you doin', buddy?"

A scrambling movement, like a terrified animal, tightening into a smaller ball.

"It's OK, Kev. I'm a friend of your dad and Parrot. We're all looking for you."

The bundle of boy pulled deeper into the mud and whimpered slightly.

Charlie sat on the ground and let his feet dangle over the edge of the hole. "I'm Charlie. I once spent the night in this hole. In fact, I dug the thing." His arms had ached for days. How long had it taken?

"Aaaah!" Kev's head shot up and he screamed.

"It's OK, Kev." Charlie tried to keep his voice calm. This child was terrified and there was blood on his face. "I'm going to blow this whistle," he held his palm open with the whistle in it. "Your dad and Parrot are nearby, and they'll come when they hear this. OK?"

A faint movement of the boy's head gave Charlie permission. He blew. Again.

"I found him! Over here, by the easternmost trail." He shouted.

Grace took a few more steps downhill before her toe hit hard against a rock. Momentum carried her forward, downslope, and she lost her footing. She thrust her hands out in front of her, but found nothing, no branches or even the thin stickered threads of nettles, to grab onto. Her right knee smacked the ground and she sprawled flat on her stomach, but she kept sliding, head first downhill. She pressed her toes down into the mud, adding friction to slow her descent; her right ankle slammed against a rock and sent her skidding to the left. Again, she threw her hands in front of her, groping for a root, anything solid, unmoving. It wasn't far, but it was dark and it was wet and it was hard.

By the time she finally stopped moving, her body had managed to twist itself around, so she was sitting upright, facing downhill; her legs were somewhere out in front of her, but she couldn't see them. Her view was blocked by an enormous log that lay crosswise to the slope. It took her a long, panicked moment to realize that this log was what had stopped her slide, preventing her from falling over a cliff, off the edge of which her legs now dangled. The log, her savior, sat just a foot above her lap and close enough to her face for her to make a microscopic lean forward and kiss it.

Resting her cheek against the mossy surface of the log, Grace began to take stock. To her right she could just make out the massive tangle of the fallen tree's roots clawing the air maybe ten feet away. Slowly, carefully, she turned her head to the left. The top of the downed tree was hidden in the fog, but she sensed open space beneath it not far from where she sat. In order to maneuver herself to safer ground, she must move back and to the right. The soil on which she sat was layered with slippery fir needles and cones. Placing her palms flat on the duff, pushing up and back, she gingerly scooted her butt away from the edge. As she inched backward, the forest debris on the surface began to move in the opposite direction and she could hear cones and dirt falling into the valley below, crumbling bits of the cliff as it fell. Grace tried to slow her breathing, to make each movement count. If she moved too slowly, too tentatively, the slope where she sat could collapse beneath her. A decisive, strong push in the opposite direction was her only hope. The log prevented her from bending her knees and pushing back with her feet, so she bore down on her hands, took a deep breath and wrenched her body backward as hard as she could.

Once her feet touched soil, she began to roll onto her right side and that's when the pain hit. Her right leg furiously protested the slightest movement. "Shit!" She let her head rest in the mud and held her leg as still as she could, waiting for the pain to dull.

As she lay there, the damp cold soaked through her jeans and combined with the jagged ache in her leg; she began to shiver. She had to move; she had to get to farther away from the edge or she'd start sliding down again. She bit her lower lip hard between her teeth. Just above her a branch, about the size of her arm, protruded from the log. The force of the tree's fall appeared to have shoved the other end of the branch into the earth. If it hadn't been shattered by the collision, it might be anchored deeply enough to offer a solid grip. She stretched her arms out over her head and lifted her upper body as high as her injured leg would allow. She grabbed hold of the ragged branch and, whispering a plea for the right kind of luck, just this once, Grace pulled with all her strength.

The hole had gathered layers of detritus over the years and its bottom was soft. Kevin Sr. dropped down into the pit and immediately sank to his knees.

"Oh, son, you gave us a scare." He reached out to take his son in his arms, but Kev didn't move toward him. "Are you hurt, boy? Let me see."

The child turned toward his father and held out his arms. He was shivering and a large, mud-caked wound seeped dark blood over his right eye.

"OK, son. Let's get you out of here."

Seeing now what they were dealing with, Charlie pulled Pat aside. "Get down to town and bring that Doc up here. Tell him the kid's hurt his head and maybe his eye. It doesn't look good. And stay away from the mom, if you can. No need to scare her more." Pat was younger and faster; both men understood that.

Paul and Burt worked together to hoist father and son out of the hole. Still Kev hadn't spoken. Kevin Sr. took a few muddy steps to a nearby stump and sat, cradling his boy in his arms.

"Pat's gone to get Doc Janson." Charlie said, handing Kevin a clean handkerchief. "Henry's got some water."

But Kev fought against his father's efforts to clean the wound; it seemed a better idea to just give the boy some time to calm down. Kevin simply held him and spoke in soft whispers.

The men stepped back, giving father and son some private time. Henry motioned for the crew to circle round out of earshot of the boy.

"Thank you, guys. I'll stay till Pat and Doc get here, but you all can go on home. I'm sure we can get them down. And if you see Mary, tell her we found him and he's OK. No need to alarm her."

The men nodded and, as they began dispersing down the trail back to town, Charlie asked, "Any of you see Grace?"

The group stopped and looked back at him. "Oh, right, that's what got Kev all out here in the first place. Where the hell is that girl?" asked Terry Childers.

"She hasn't been at the café the last couple of days. Lyle said she went to Seattle or something," Clett offered.

"Well, I saw her yesterday," Charlie said. "She's back from Seattle, but I went by her cabin this morning and she's not there."

"When we couldn't find Kev this morning, Mary said she'd check with Grace," Kevin called out to the group.

"Oh, shit. With all this commotion, I forgot. Mary told Grace about Kev and she went up the other way to look." Burt raised his chin to indicate the path farther up the mountain. "Mary said Grace was going up to the protesters' camp, somethin' about thinking Kev had followed her up there."

Just then Pat came sprinting up the trail with Doc Janson at his heels. He pointed to where Kevin sat with Kev, still silent, on his lap. "He's over there, Doc."

Burt grabbed his son's arm. "Turns out your girlfriend's been taking food to those assholes camped in the old growth." He shook his head and spat. "D'you know about that?"

"Are you crazy? No, I didn't know a thing about it and why would she do that, anyway?" Pat was indignant. The other men stared at him.

Charlie interrupted this brewing conflict. "The problem right now is that she's gone looking for Kev and no one knows where she is."

"Well, if she went up there, she can damn well find her own way home," Pat muttered.

Kevin and Doc picked the boy up and began walking back to the trail. As he passed the group, Kevin said, "You know, we haven't treated that girl right. She might have reason for what she did."

Chapter 22

Grace shook like a traumatized animal. She'd managed to pull herself back from the edge; the echoes of stones and broken branches bouncing off the cliff as they fell had faded. The danger of her own body dropping into the valley below was no longer immediate. She squeezed her eyes shut and bit hard on her lip, leaned back against her arms and took a deep breath. When she opened her eyes again, the fog had thinned enough for her to make out the area around her a bit more clearly. She looked up the steep mountainside down which she had slid.

Shit! What have I done? How am I going to get up that slope with this leg?

What was I thinking? Kev would never have made it up the trail this far. I am an idiot.

The thought of Kev brought the search back to her mind and she reached in her pocket. *God bless you, Kev!* She put the whistle to her mouth and blew as hard as she could.

Charlie started to follow the rest of the guys back down the mountain when he remembered how the day had begun. "Hey, Pat. Can you show me where that protesters' camp is?"

"Why?" Pat looked skeptically at Charlie. "She's not worth it, man. I ought to know." He spoke a little too loudly.

"It's not like that." Charlie was in no mood to humor this jerk. "I just need to find her."

Pat narrowed his eyes, stuck his fists into his pants pockets and looked over his shoulder at the men who were descending the trail. He waited till his father's back had disappeared around a curve, then he nodded. "Follow me."

The two men walked swiftly, but took care where they placed their feet. The rain had stopped, but the trail was slick and muddy—the kind of muck they both knew well. It looked benign enough, but things went wrong in this kind of wet. Especially when you moved too fast.

"What's your deal, anyway?" Pat kept his head down, eyes on the trail as he asked.

"Long story." Charlie knew there was something between Pat and Grace; he could feel the jealous energy radiating off the guy. "I'm probably the closest thing she's got to a brother, if that helps."

Pat stopped. "What's that's supposed to mean?"

Charlie gave him a brief version of what had gone on between Nathan and Annie. "You guys are a couple, right?"

"Were. Man, I thought I knew her, but that's all over. Done. This whole thing with feeding the hippies? You knew about that?"

"Hell, no. That's news to me. I've only had one conversation with the lady. And it wasn't about saving trees."

They were at the steepest point in the trail now and they'd stopped talking. Charlie was feeling winded and cursing himself for his cigarette habit. It was damned embarrassing, panting in front of this kid.

Then the sound of a whistle, sharp and clear, coming from somewhere to their left and down.

"What was that?" Charlie looked toward the sound. "Who's there?" He shouted.

"It's Grace! Down here!"

"Grace?" Pat shouted. The frantic tone in his voice gave him away. This guy was not close to being over her. "I fell off the trail. I think I broke my leg."

The two men raced toward the sound of her voice.

"Careful!" she shouted. "There's a nasty drop off right by the edge of the trail there!"

Pat and Charlie stood at the lip of the valley looking down to where Grace sat. The fog had lifted, and they could see all the way to the valley floor. Her predicament was clear.

"Jesus." Pat was trying to sound matter-of-fact, but the tender concern was apparent. "I'll send Charlie here back for some rope. We'll haul you up." He looked over at Charlie who gave him a thumb's up and headed back down the trail.

"I'm pretty cold." Grace said through jittering teeth.

Pat took his jacket off and rolled it into a bundle. Just before he threw it, he stopped.

"I can't get it down there, Grace. It'll get hung up on the bushes or it'll go over the edge. Hold on." He bent low and scanned the slop, looking for the tracks of her fall. Then he pulled up a thin blackberry vine growing along the trail and, standing in the middle of it, dragged it back and forth under his instep to strip it of its thorns. He tied the vine tightly around the ball of his jacket. Then he jammed a rock into the center of the whole bundle to give it some weight. "OK, I'm going to roll this down to you. Look out for the stickers on the vine."

"Genius," Grace shouted as the jacket bumped and slid down the side of the mountain, right into her hands. "Thanks." Gingerly she tore off the vine and slid her arms into Patrick's sleeves.

"Jesus, Parrot. How did you manage this stunt?"

She didn't reply. Now that she'd been found, now that she was warmer, now that she was covered in Pat's scent, she relaxed just enough for the pain in her leg to overwhelm her.

Charlie was puffing hard when he got down the mountain to the mill. The crew was still crowded around the yard, soaking in the relief at Kev's rescue. Grace's name stood out from the jumble of chatter. "She was bringing them food? How could she?"

"Grace is down a cliff." Charlie panted. "Need some rope."

All the men turned to him and nearly in unison demanded "Is she OK?"

"She's hurt her leg." They crowded round him and asked for details.

"She's off the trail on the north, where it gets steep, near the hippy camp. Pat's up there with her."

Clett raced to the shop and pulled a coil of rope off a hook and hoisted it onto his shoulder. Back where the men had gathered, he started to hand the rope over to Charlie, but it was obvious Charlie wasn't going to make fast time up the trail carrying any extra weight. Without a word, Clett took off with five of the other men trailing him. Charlie started to follow, but Henry came over and put his hand on Charlie's back.

"Let them go, man. They've got something to make up to Parrot. Give 'em the chance to do that."

"All of them?"

"Hell, yes. Everyone in this town was part of it."

As they waited, Pat kept talking to Grace even though she said little. "We found Kev. He was in this hole—something Charlie says he dug when he was a kid. Weird that it's still there."

"He must have been terrified. I feel so guilty." She winced.

Pat was sitting on the ground now, studying her from above.

"Yeah, seems like you have a few things to feel guilty about."

She tilted her head to look up at him. "Is this the best time to go into that?"

"It's true then? You betrayed the whole town feeding those damn hippies? I never would have believed it."

"Oh god, Pat. I was desperate." She gave in and laid her head back down in the muddy duff. "If it helps any, I felt like a traitor the whole time."

"You're damn right! You were working for Jane, weren't you? Doing just what she would have done!"

"Goddammit!!" The fury at herself, at Pat, and at the predicament she'd gotten herself into boiled over, and Grace screamed, long and loud. "I can't believe you're doing this now!" In her rage, she tried to stand. "AHHHHHH!"

"Oh, shit, Parrot! OK, OK. Forget it. Those guys'll be here with the rope soon."

There was no denying the pain. She was stuck—dependent on Pat, but furious at him; angry at the whole town, but guilty and embarrassed by her own betrayal of them; wanting desperately to find Annie, but terrified of learning who her mother had become. And on top of all that, it now looked like she'd hurt herself badly enough that she wouldn't be going anywhere very soon. Grace sank back into the muddy duff and let the tears come. She kept her head down, not wanting Pat to see her cry.

The sound of his frustrated steps, as he paced along the cliff edge, added another layer to Grace's distress. If she could get him to calm down, it might calm her a bit too.

"Yeah, you're right, it was Jane's idea." But as soon as she started to talk, her fury surfaced again. "Back then I didn't know what a horrible liar she was. And speaking of not knowing the truth about people I trusted, I heard about you cutting trees in the preserve." Her initial shock over Mary's revelation had been simmering all day. Yes, not more than a couple of hours ago she'd wished for a chain saw to clear out these same woods, but that had been in a panic over Kev. This man she'd once loved, who maybe she still did love, had actually done it.

Pat stopped pacing and stood, arms akimbo, shouting down at her. "I was doing just what your father, or any decent logger, would have done. Rose knew how much we needed to fill that contract. She was OK with it. Who are you to get on your high horse? At least we're keeping this town alive. You've been aiding the enemy."

"Dammit. It's always about taking sides with you, isn't it? You're never going to get over it." She tried to get her good leg under her. Maybe she could stand. But as soon as she sat up and bent her knee, she groaned. A cascade of fir cones, rocks, and mud slid over the edge, bouncing off the boulders below.

"Jesus! Be still. Don't act like an idiot."

She wanted to grab him by the shoulders, to slap his face, to shove him off this cliff, but she could do none of that. She couldn't even look him in the eye. She put her hands over her ears she refused to listen to anything more from him.

By the time the men arrived, the silence between the two lovers was thicker than any rope.

The men lowered Pat down to where he could stand next to Grace. Silently, he removed the rope from his waist and looped it around hers. Afraid of what might come out of her mouth, she clenched her teeth to keep from saying anything.

She grabbed onto the rope and started to lean back till her leg screamed at her.

When he saw her flinch, Pat stepped over and took hold of the rope. "You're going to have to let that leg hang, Parrot. Push yourself away from the trees with your other leg."

The pain was wearing her down. She nodded, pulled the rope away from him, and clenched her hands around it. "Ok, I'm ready," she yelled to the men standing above. As soon as the rope tightened and her feet lifted off the ground, she instinctively clenched her lips tight and tried to hold her body as straight and still as possible. There was no way to avoid being bumped against the branches and boulders that covered the slope; all she could do was try to protect her damaged leg as Pat had said. Not easy. Pushing off from a large cedar bough a bit too forcefully caused her body to spin around on the rope, slamming her injured leg hard against the higher branch. She couldn't keep the groan to herself.

"Sorry, Parrot! We've almost got you. Hang on." She didn't need to look above her to know that Clett was holding the other end of the rope with his thumbless hands, and that Burt was there, and Paul. Men she'd trusted all her life; men she still trusted.

Pat made his own way up, tugging on branches and leaning into protruding rocks. Once they were both at the top, the group took stock. Grace's leg was starting to swell, and she couldn't bear her own weight. They wanted to carry her, but she insisted on throwing one arm around Clett and leaning the other on Pat in spite of the angry sparks that flew between them.

After the second switchback, she asked for a break. "Just give me a second." And she slumped down on a fallen log, sticking her injured leg out in front of her.

"When you were a little girl," Clett said, "I carried you on my back, you and Shauna. Want to try that again?" He grinned and stooped down for her to grab hold of his shoulders.

She laughed and shook her head. "I'll be OK in a minute."

"We trusted each other back then. We stuck together," Clett went on. "Then your dad died, your aunt started all her environmental bullshit, and now I don't know what we are. It just seems like a lot of apologizing is in order, all the way around. I'm sorry, Parrot."

Grace looked hard at this man, whose scars bore witness to the brutality of life dependent on the forest.

"Yeah, I'm sorry too, Clett."

Once they were up and moving again, Pat whispered in her ear. "We can still make it work between us. Don't follow Jane, Parrot. Don't turn your back on all of us now. Don't run away."

His breath was tender on her neck and she heard the plea for forgiveness in his words, but Grace's anger was holding her together and she knew if she let it go she'd break down.

"If searching out my own mother is running away, then that's what I'm doing. But I'm not following anybody. And I'm certainly not sticking around here with a thief who's stealing trees from the preserve."

Doc Janson wasn't able to do much for Kev. He cleaned the wound and helped get him down to town, but it was clear the boy needed to be taken to the hospital. Sherrie Thomas piled the Bigleys into the back of her van and drove them down the mountain to Everett.

By the time Grace got to her cabin, her leg was swollen and she was exhausted. Clett got her settled on her sofa and Pat went for Doc Janson. She started to protest; now that she was home, lying down, maybe it wasn't so bad. But the shivering had started again. Clett wrapped a blanket around her.

"Looks to me, you've got a broken leg, Parrot, and you're in shock. It's one thing the doc can do something about. You need to let him do it."

In the end she was grateful for the doc's attention. She just wished Pat hadn't been the one to fetch him. One more thing she owed him for.

It was well past dark when Sherrie's van appeared on Main Street. Folks poured out of the Hoot Owl and surrounded the car. Sherrie turned off the engine and got out.

"They're keeping him for a few days at least. Kevin and Mary are sleeping on chairs in his room. The docs think he may have damaged his eye and they're worried he isn't talking." Someone offered her a beer, but she shook her head.

"We've got to get them some clothes and their truck tomorrow. Can one of you drive it down and I'll pick you up at Everett General?"

"I'll do it," Pat volunteered. "And Charlie can follow me down. You don't need to, Sherrie. Right, Charlie?"

"Sure. I'll take Walt's truck."

Over the next few days, the absence of the Hoot Owl's most loyal customer created a vacuum that sucked in most of the town. By the time Lyle got the coffee going in the morning, at least half the tables were occupied by anxious people awaiting news of Kev. Even Grace, who the doc had taken into Cooper to get her leg x-rayed and set, managed to hobble on her crutches over to the café on the third morning. Her concern for Kev outweighed her conflicted feelings toward everyone else in town. She perched on the kitchen stool where she could serve the folks at the counter and handle the register. This was hardly like old times, though. Grace's smile was strained and there was no teasing banter. After that first morning filled with awkward apologies, Grace put a sign on the back of the register:

"If you know where Annie Tillman is, tell me. Otherwise shut up about it. You all know how to do that." This elicited a lot of raised eyebrows and mumbling, but folks kept their explanations and regrets to themselves.

Pat had been coming in most days and sitting at a table toward the back of the café nursing a cup of coffee he fetched for himself. He avoided making eye contact with Grace.

On Thursday morning when Kevin Sr. called the number at the Hoot Owl, Pat waited tensely with everyone else to hear Grace relay the conversation. The doctors were releasing Kev. His eye was healing, and he could see again, but he still wasn't talking. They thought it was shock and that he'd be better off at home. The docs warned them to keep things quiet, avoid a lot of fuss.

Mary thought Kev would like to see Parrot.

There was a collective sigh of relief. Mrs. G offered to take some flowers over to the Bigleys'. Sherrie said she'd put

up a welcome home sign. Pat offered to make a run down to
Cooper to pick up some groceries for them. Did anyone know
Kev's favorite foods? Grace grabbed a pen and paper and wrote
a list. "I'll be sure we've got chocolate cream pie, but he can't
live on that. Here's a few things I know he'll eat." She handed
Pat the list and he gave her a quick nod. "Thanks," they both
murmured simultaneously.

With a general scraping of chairs and dropping of change
on tabletops, the others, concerned but grateful, exited the
café.

Charlie hung back until the place had emptied out, then
sat on the stool next to Grace. "My dad got back to me. On
top of everything else that's been going on with your leg and
Kev, I just didn't know when to talk to you. But my imagination's been running wild thinking about how you're going to
react. Then you put that sign up, so I thought . . ."

She nodded and put her hand on his shoulder. "That sign
wasn't meant for you. Knowing you were going to find out
where Annie is has kept me going. Think that's what it's like
to have a sibling?"

"Yeah, maybe so." Charles grinned. "It's been nice for me,
too, sis."

She smiled. Taking a deep breath, she balled her hands
into fists. "OK, bro, I'm sitting down. Tell me what else I need
to know."

"Well, Annie's alive, so I guess that's not bad, is it?" Charlie
inspected Grace's face.

She nodded, calm now, then raised her eyebrows. "And
where is she, Charlie?"

"She's in some kind of asylum. She's been there a long
time. She's had a hard life, Grace. She lost the baby and went
into a deep depression. That's the way she was when I last saw

her, years ago. Nathan claims he tried everything to pull her out of it. But knowing my father, I can't imagine he was very effective."

"Asylum?"

"Yeah." He was clearly relieved that Grace was taking this well. "And get this—she's in California. A place called Camarillo State Hospital. It's near Los Angeles."

Grace nodded slowly and her lips stretched in a thin grin. "She made it to LA. Good for her."

"Really?"

"Oh, yeah. There are parrots in LA."

It had taken Charlie pushing pretty hard, but Nathan finally admitted that when Charlie had visited that summer when he was sixteen, things were falling apart. Annie had been talking crazy for years; she believed she wasn't supposed to be a mother, wasn't that kind of woman. One day she'd say she knew Grace was better off without her, then the next she'd demand to see her baby girl. But after Charlie left Annie stopped talking about seeing Grace again. Instead, she became obsessed with going to LA.

Nathan wouldn't take her seriously. He'd always hated big cities. But when Annie stopped speaking entirely, he got desperate.

As soon as they arrived in LA, she wouldn't talk about anything but the parrots. She'd get up at the crack of dawn and roam the streets, looking for birds. She got lost and the police picked her up in someone's backyard. They said she needed to go to a hospital. It looked like she would be staying in the mental ward. Nathan couldn't take it anymore. He couldn't wait to get out of the city.

"That was almost eight years ago, Grace. He just left her there."

Abandoned. This was a pain Grace understood—a vein of heartache that ran through both their lives.

"So that's what I know. Right now, I just want to knock Nathan's teeth out, but I'm more concerned about you. You gonna be OK, sis?" Charlie stood up and put his arm around her shoulder.

She shook her head. "Whew. I don't really know, to tell you the truth."

He nodded. "Yeah. It's weird. A lot to take in."

Grace was quiet for a long while, staring at the stack of empty coffee cups behind the counter, stained and chipped—the same cups her mother had filled for customers years ago. Finally, she turned to Charlie.

"Thank you for all that. I don't know how I'd have ever found out if it wasn't for you."

"I won't say it was my pleasure, but I'm glad I could do it. I still can't believe all the cowards in this town, letting you believe she was dead all these years."

"It's getting harder for me to think of them as cowards." She frowned. "But I don't know what else to call them."

"Maybe it's the wrong word. I trust you'll figure it out." Charlie smiled, then he pulled a piece of paper from his pocket and handed it to her. "This is the doctor's name and number at the hospital where Annie is. I thought you'd want that. I'll need to be moving on soon."

"What's next for you, Charlie?" Grace turned her head away as she said this, not wanting him see how sad the idea of his leaving made her.

"Henry says he can get me on with an outfit up in B.C., something that doesn't have the stink of Nathan all over it." He pulled a cigarette out of the pack in his pocket and held it between his fingers. "Think I'll give it one more go as a hauler, but I know it'll never be the job I'd always imagined. Gotta start thinkin' about retooling."

"Right. Well, I hear school can change your life." She grinned at him. "Thinkin' about that for myself."

"Yeah, well, maybe I'm grown up enough to stick that out, as long as I don't end up behind a desk." He looked down at the cigarette, broke it in half and dropped it in trashcan by the cash register.

"I suspect Fish and Wildlife will be hiring. They always need guys with experience digging traps in the woods." She elbowed him lightly in the ribs.

"Thanks. I'll be sure to add that to my resume." He stood up. "Time to go."

She reached her arms out to hug him. "Don't forget about me."

Charlie hugged her awkwardly. "Hadn't pictured this," he laughed. He stood back and looked her in the eye.

"Look, there's no way I'm going to forget about you. I gotta know how it all turns out or I'll drive myself crazy imagining it. I got your number. I'll be calling." And he turned and walked out of the café.

Grace put the paper Charlie had given her into her pocket and pulled her crutches under her arms. She walked into the kitchen where Lyle was standing over the sink. "So now you know what's been going on with me."

"Yeah, well, I'd heard a few things from folks. That Charlie seems like a good guy."

"Oh, I'd say he's one of the better lumber thieves around." She chuckled.

"We've all got our shit, as they say." Lyle shrugged. "One more thing, Grace, you got a letter here from Jane."

He picked up an envelope from under the phone and handed it to her.

"Keep it, Lyle. Stick in with the others."

Too much was coming at her at once. It was exhausting. The last thing she wanted was to read anything Jane had to say.

Mary and Kevin looked like they'd been the ones lost in the woods. The pain and worry of the last days were written in the dark circles under their eyes and the deep furrows in their brows. Kev, sitting between his parents in the truck, waited as they got out, his gaze straight ahead, as if he were scanning the forest for threats before taking any chances. His ever-present, silly grin was missing.

Grace leaned on her crutches next to the truck. She gave Mary a hug and tapped on the window. Kev turned toward the sound. When he saw her, the muscles of his face began to thaw and slowly a flicker of light returned to his eyes. She opened the door and leaned in. "Hi, Kev. I've missed you."

Once the family was settled back in their house, Kevin took Grace aside. "This whole adventure has changed him, Parrot. I don't know if we're going to get him back, but I really think you can help him. I told him Pat and Charlie had found you and that seemed to make him relax a bit. He got upset again when I said you broke your leg, but he had to know." He looked over his shoulder to where Kev was sitting; then he turned back to Grace.

"Look, I know you've got your own stuff going on and you might not be able to stay in town, but could you hang around for a little while and visit with him?" He put his hands on her shoulders and looked her in the eye. "I feel terrible asking you to do this after what this town did to you."

"One thing I'm sure about, Kevin, is that I love that kid. He got himself in this situation because he was looking for me.

He and I both have some healing to do." She looked down at her crutches. "I'm not going anywhere for a while."

Her leg limited how much walking she could do, so she asked Mary to bring Kev to the cabin in the morning. When they arrived, Grace got her crutches, and she and Kev made their slow and awkward way down to the Hoot Owl for pie. This quickly became a ritual, and others took note. The folks who'd been gathering at the café while Kev was in the hospital were still showing up. That first morning Pat came in with his dad, and they both made eye contact with Grace and smiled. The next day Clett put a hand on her shoulder and nodded. These gestures were like drops of rain that sank into the brittle soil of Grace's heart. Kev softened too, a muted version of his grin returning as he stuffed big forkfuls of chocolate cream into his mouth.

"Listen, boy, before you take off, what the hell is all this stuff you scribbled on my wall?" After all the excitement up the mountain had calmed down, Walt finally had a chance to grumble at his nephew. "I thought you were a neat freak. What got into you, boy?"

"Sorry about that. Time was short." Charlie explained how he and Grace had talked.

His uncle shook his head sadly. "Oh, lordy. I knew this day was coming. She wants to find Annie, right?"

Charlie nodded. "Sure, but she's gotta heal that leg first." Charlie pointed his finger at the words he'd written on the wall.

"She asked me to call Nathan, so I did. That goddamned prick took Annie all the way to LA and left her there. Can you believe that? She's in some nut house out there. Been there for years."

Walt sat heavily on one of the kitchen chairs and rubbed his eyes with the palms of his hands. "I never could understand what that man had that made women fall for him. Seemed to me he had jerk written all over his face."

He twisted in his seat to look more closely at the wall. "You write this all down on paper?"

Charlie nodded.

Walt stood up, grinning. "OK. Now this town's gotta help her. Prosperity is so full of guilt right now I think we just might be able to pull this off."

Rose made her way to the Hoot Owl one morning. She stood by the booth where Kev and Grace were eating.

"I'm sorry, Parrot."

Grace looked up.

"Kev and I are going back to the cabin in a bit," she said. "Would you like to come with us? See what I've done?" Her anger and distrust were fading, but she wasn't ready to hear Rose's side of the story. As long as Kev was there, she and Rose could be together without that wound reopening.

As the three of them entered the cabin, Grace stepped back and let Rose take it all in, anticipating a reaction that would distract them all from any other conversation. Rose didn't disappoint her.

"Oh, my dear! This is marvelous." Rose took Grace's hand and, laughing, said, "How delightful!" Turning to the boy, she said, "Do you like it, Kev?" He nodded vigorously and pointed to the snake over the stove. "Yes, but it's not a real snake. Parrot made that up, didn't she? We don't need to be afraid." Rose had an intuitive sense of what the child needed to

hear. In spite of herself, Grace felt a wave of gratitude and af-
fection. "OK, take the grand tour—you can peek into the bath
and see Clett Tolfson's blue toilet. I sleep in the loft and you
can climb up there if you want. I'm going to give Kev a little
introduction to all the animals, so he can learn their names."

Rose took her time exploring the jungle Grace's imagination had produced, and while Grace's attention was focused
on teaching Kev what she knew about toucans, Rose let herself
out.

There is too much to say, Grace thought, *too much for either
of us to handle yet.*

Chapter 23

Grace looked forward to her time with Kev each day. His eyes were a bit brighter from one visit to the next. He'd stopped frowning at the cast on her leg and walked more confidently by her side as they made their daily trip to the café.

Wielding her crutches took both hands and Grace couldn't manage to get Kev's pie to the table on her own, so she showed him how to get it for himself. "Only very special customers are allowed back here in the kitchen, Kev. You have to promise not to touch anything but your piece of pie. Lyle will make sure it's right here on the shelf for you. You got that?"

As he nodded his head enthusiastically, Kev gave Grace a grin. In that moment, he looked almost like the old Kev. The new Kev, though, had been touched by fear and by sadness, and Grace wondered if that was a change that could ever be healed.

One evening Grace called Mary and asked her if she'd seen the change in Kev. They spoke about how he seemed happier, more relaxed. "But he's different, Mary. It's not just that he's the not talking; it's like he's not a carefree kid anymore."

"Well, that's right, isn't it? He's growing up and he's learning how the world really is. And how he really is. He's got to understand that hiking alone in the woods is dangerous!"

"I hate to see that fear in him, though."

"I know what you mean, Grace. Nobody likes to see a kid forced to face the reality of pain or loss when they're still young. We go to great lengths to protect them, don't we?"

One morning a few days later, as he and Grace were going from bird to bird around the walls of the cabin, Grace pointed to a scarlet macaw and called it a parrot. "Macaw," he said. "You're the parrot."

Grace replied with a straight face, "Maybe."

"Not maybe!" Kev yelled. "You're the parrot!"

Pretending to flap her wings, Grace asked, "A parrot who flies?"

"A parrot with a leg that's broken," Kev whispered.

She put her arms around the boy and held him close. "My leg is getting better, Kev. I'm so sorry you thought I was lost. You were so brave to go out looking for me."

"I got lost. It was dark and scary. I got hurt."

"Yes, it was a bad time. But we're not lost anymore and we're both getting better."

Kev grinned, pointing at the cast on her leg. "Maybe, maybe not!"

"Oh, Kev!" Grace hugged him tightly. Her tears confused him initially, but when she started laughing, so did he.

With Kev finally talking again, Grace found herself faced with her own confusions. She thought a lot about what Pat had said:

Was going to find her mother a kind of running away? How would she feel if Annie didn't recognize her? Before she made another decision, she knew she needed to hear what Rose had to say.

When Rose picked up the phone, Grace found herself at a loss. "I . . . um . . . Rose?"

"Grace?" The older woman sighed. "I've been hoping you'd call. Shall I come down there?"

"Actually, could you come and pick me up? I'd like to do this at your place, but I can't get up there on my own."

"Good idea. I'll be there in a half hour."

Neither woman spoke until they'd arrived at the Dyers'. Grace found it difficult to look at Rose; she walked over and sat down at the dining room table. Keeping her head down, she ran her finger along a scar in the polished wood. The old table had witnessed some of her happiest days and held this souvenir of one of her saddest.

"That was a bad day," Rose said as she pulled out a chair and sat opposite Grace. "I'd never seen such pain in your face. I don't think you even realized what you were doing when you dug your knife into the table. But you wouldn't talk to me about it. And by then I'd gotten used to letting secrets lie." Rose reached over to take Grace's hand, but the younger woman pulled back. "You were the one thing Jackson and I never could agree on."

Suspicion pinched at Grace's eyes and buzzed in her ears. She could barely look at this woman she loved so intensely and who had disappointed her so deeply.

"He didn't believe we should keep the truth from you. But I couldn't imagine how to tell you, how to explain it to a child." Rose was pleading.

"Did you imagine I'd never find out?" Grace tasted the bitterness.

"I suppose I thought some miracle would happen. That Annie would wake up from the nightmare she was living and come home to get you. But part of me dreaded that possibility too." Rose clasped her hands and rested her elbows on the table. The tiny diamonds in her wedding ring glimmered in the pale light. "Jackson was as devoted to your father as I was to your mother. When their marriage fell apart, we were both unmoored for a while."

Grace's chest tightened against the pain. "Why"—she swallowed—"did she leave me?"

"It was a terrible time, Parrot. Your father . . ." Rose planted her hand flat on the table and pointed to the wound in the wood. "Jackson always blamed the war. 'Those guys saw ugly things in Vietnam. Who wouldn't be angry?' he'd say whenever Annie spoke about your father's behavior." She looked up at Grace. "Your momma was a sweet girl, but she wasn't strong. Warren's demons were more than she could handle. Maybe more than any woman should have to handle. He hurt her, but Jane convinced her he'd never hurt you. And, of course, she trusted me and Jackson to watch out for you. But I know, too, that Annie believed Warren would eventually let you go to her." Rose pulled a tissue from the sleeve of her sweater and blew her nose. "Then you started talking about her being dead, and I got scared. Annie called me every week or so at first." Rose picked up Grace's hand. "I told her you needed her, that she had to come back and see you. And she did, you know."

"Those weren't dreams, then?" Grace asked, allowing her hand to rest in Rose's. "She really came to me in the night? She sat on my bed?"

Rose nodded. "It was the only way. Warren would have . . . well, we were all afraid of what he would have done to her if he knew. Jane and I arranged it. Brought you up here. You remember how you used to spend the night here when you were little?"

Grace gave a single nod of her head. "It was here. She came here to see me." She pushed back her chair and walked to the window that looked out on the garden. "That's why I remembered the smell of lilacs, even in my dreams. It was your lilac bush—the one that always smells so strong and blooms so late. I dreamed about those visits later—I wrote about them in my diary."

"It was all we could think to do. Let Annie at least see you while you were asleep. But then she lost the baby and she stopped calling."

Grace nodded. "Charlie told me."

A few of the threads that had tangled into a stubborn knot in Grace's mind were beginning to pull clear. Charlie's report of what Nathan had said about Annie's change after the miscarriage. The way the letters had stopped abruptly. The dreams.

"Are you saying she never came back after she lost the baby?"

Rose nodded. "We lost her then. I think she must have gone out of her head with grief, after losing you and then the baby, she just couldn't cope. I tried to stay in contact with her, but she never responded and eventually my letters were all returned and her phone was disconnected. I didn't know what else to do."

"I had those dreams—her sitting by me, holding me—for years. Even after Daddy was killed. They seemed so real."

"When we need comfort, we can fool ourselves into believing a lot of things, Grace."

Rose got up and walked into the kitchen. She leaned against the sink. "Jackson should be here. He should have to tell you."

"But he's not." Grace looked at a photo of Rose's husband that sat on the windowsill. Grace had been so afraid that Jackson would blow up when he saw what she'd done to his table, but he hadn't. He'd been sad about it, she knew, but he'd told her it wasn't her fault. That had never made sense. "I need to know all of it, Rose. You have to tell me everything now."

"Yes. OK. When your mother left, I insisted Jackson have a talk with Warren. Tell him we knew he'd been cruel to Annie and we wouldn't stand for any of that with you. I don't know what he actually said, but when he got home Jackson told me it was going to be OK. I wanted to believe him, I guess." She turned to Grace. "It was just that once, wasn't it? That one time when you were fourteen? When you came here and sat there carving up my table with your anger?"

Slowly Grace shrugged. Could she trust her own memories of her father anymore?

"I loved him. He was gruff and all." Her eyes filled and she let the tears fall. "All the guys are like that. But he taught me to love the woods, the birds, all this . . ." She spread her arms to encompass the whole of the mountains and the forests that surrounded Prosperity. "He was a good dad." She fell down into the chair again and put her head in her hands.

Rose swayed and then walked over to the young woman she'd always thought of as her granddaughter. She wrapped her arms around her. "Oh, Gracie. I'm just so sorry for all of it."

After several minutes, Grace wiped her hand across her eyes and looked up at Rose. "How did you know he hit me?"

"He told Jackson. He was beside himself, Jackson said. He'd lost control. Something about how you kept asking about Annie. I don't know. But Jackson made him swear he'd get help, right then. And he did." Rose put her hands on Grace's shoulders and stooped to look her in the eye. "Your father went to the V.A. and talked to someone. He didn't want you to know. Another secret. They put him in a therapy group."

"Wow. I can't picture my dad in a therapy group." She chuckled and shook her head. "I hope it helped him."

"Oh, I don't know, Grace. But just knowing he was going was enough for Jackson. He told me it wouldn't happen again. I have to say, I was grateful you would be out of that house soon." Rose pulled a couple of tissues from the box on the table, handed one to Grace and wiped her own eyes with the other. "But then the forest intervened, didn't it? It's a terrible thing to say, but I felt some relief when your dad was killed."

"Oh!" Grace's eyes widened as she threw her hand over her mouth. The pain of Warren's death shocked her heart as it had that day three years before. It was almost too much to feel all at once, but there was a part deep inside her that knew what Rose had said was true for her too. She'd called it gruffness, but it was more than that. When she saw the way Jen's dad treated her, though, Grace had told herself, "I'm so lucky. My dad would never hurt me like that." But she had been afraid. Even as a little girl, something about being alone with her father had always made her uneasy. And when Jane told her he'd been killed, a tiny part of her relaxed. It was true.

With that realization, she lost the strength to fight off the tears. She put her hand over her eyes and wept.

Rose let her be for a while. As the tears subsided and Grace sat up and blew her nose, the older woman sat down next to her.

"This is an awful lot to absorb, sweetheart. You need to take your time."

Grace gave Rose a weak smile. "You knew I fed those protestors camped in the woods, didn't you?"

"Oh, I suspected something like that was going on. You did what you had to do."

"Maybe. Or maybe it was my twisted way of getting back at my dad."

Crumpling her tissue into a ball, Rose said, "Well, a few sandwiches and pies aren't going to make any difference in the end. And if any of those hardheaded loggers in town act all put out about it, I'll say the same to them. Those kids camping in the old growth can see the future better than any old coot in Prosperity. This town just hates to face reality."

"That's why you let them cut the trees in the preserve? So they wouldn't have to face reality?" This final point of bitterness still rankled Grace.

"It's what Jackson would have done." Rose stepped over to the windowsill and picked up his picture. "I told myself I would give in to him this one last time. But it was a fool's game. I let my grief make me blind."

Grace absorbed this. "I guess we all wear blinders at times. Something I've been learning about myself."

Rose smiled. "You hungry? I think it's time I fixed you a meal."

After that talk with Rose, Grace's anger started to melt and was replaced by an insistent restlessness.

In another week the doctor had removed her cast. It took some work to get her footing back; she started by pacing around the cabin, then took short strolls outside. She was still slow, but it felt great to walk with Kev to the café.

Grace was coming back to the cabin from one of her walks when she saw Pat leaving the mill office. He raised a hand to wave. "Can we talk?" he asked.

She nodded and motioned him to come and sit with her on her front step.

"I owe you an apology," he said as he settled beside her. Grace waited silently, not sure if she was ready to hear this. "I put you in a tough spot, making you choose between me and the promise you made to your dad. Shouldn't 'a done that."

She nodded slowly. "It wouldn't have worked, you know."

"Yeah, well, it was more about me acting like a jerk and grasping at straws. I'm not good with change. A little like Kev, I guess."

"True." This made her smile. "Now what, Patrick? You're done stealing trees from the preserve, right?"

"We only did that with Rose's permission," he said, picking up a pebble from the ground and throwing it hard toward the woods. "I actually hated doing that, but I couldn't see another way. Once we started, I felt like we'd crossed some sort of line and there was no point stopping. My dad was the one who made me face reality."

"Really?" Grace had a hard time picturing Burt Samson talking about saving trees.

"He's a practical guy. He doesn't like the government setting limits, but he respects the law and he told me I was stupid to think I could get away with ignoring it. Plus, he admitted he's seen changes in the mountains that worry him. He's not ready to say logging caused the salmon runs to shrink, like your aunt says, but he made me think."

She looked at him. This was the Pat she'd fallen for so long ago. "And do you think the mill's never going to be profitable again?"

"Oh, I don't know. The guys have some pretty good ideas. A small mill like ours, we'd have to cut way back on the crew and target our jobs, do more selective cutting, but we might stay alive." He sounded more resigned than enthusiastic.

"Hm. So, you'll stay on?"

"Can't think of anything else I'd want to do," he said. "You stayin' here or going off to find Annie?"

"I'm still working out where I'm going, but staying here doesn't feel right." She realized how grateful she was to be able to talk to him about this. "Annie's in a mental institution in California. I talked to her doctor."

"Whoa. That's heavy. What kind of crazy is she?"

"She's been depressed for years, I guess. Sometimes she doesn't talk for weeks. The medicines don't help much. The doctor wasn't sure if she'd know me. He said a visit from me might help her or it might make her worse." Without saying anything about it, they'd gotten up from the steps and begun walking toward the forest trail. She reached out and took his hand. "Honestly, I don't know if it would help me or make things worse for me either."

Pat stopped and pulled her to him.

"Yeah, if you aren't sure, maybe you just need some time. Maybe you don't have to decide right now. About anything."

The nights had turned chilly and the maple leaves had begun dropping their green masks. In front of the Bullhook, Pat watched Walt lower the hood of his truck, slapping it down hard till the latch caught.

"I checked her over good. She shouldn't give you any trouble. She'll make it to the airport and back fine." Walt reached out to drop the keys in Pat's hand.

"I can take her in my truck, Walt. There's no need for this." Pat kept his hands tucked in his pockets.

"Lordy, boy, you got to let me do this. Every other person in this town scraped the bottom of their wallets to give Parrot the money for this trip. This truck is what I got."

"Yeah? But you organized this whole thing. Blew her away how you did that. Handing her the check and all. If you got to do something more, how about you weather-strip those windows in the cabin while she's gone? That'll make it easier for her to stay through the winter. Don't you think?"

Walt folded his fingers over the keys and put his hand in his jacket pocket. He squinted up at Pat. "You think she'll come back? After she gets a taste of the tropics?"

Pat laughed. "I don't know. But, if she does come back, I want her to be warm."

Mexico City. Wasn't it always hot and sunny there? Should she even pack her jeans? After fretting all day over what to take, Grace tossed a few T-shirts and a couple of pairs of shorts, along with her underwear and toiletries, into the largest compartment of her backpack and cinched it up. Into the front pouch, she tucked her current diary, a pencil case with a selection of colored pencils, her Spanish-English dictionary, and the new binoculars Rose had given her.

Shauna and Jenn had been checking on her over the last month, trying to keep her spirits up. When she told them about her decision, they hadn't hesitated.

"Well, it's about time," Shauna joked.

"You deserve this, Parrot. You're gonna make us proud!" Jenn's voice had a catch in it and Grace thought for a second that she might be crying.

"You're not mad?" Grace asked. "Oh, that is such a relief. I was so afraid you'd be furious at me."

"Are you kidding? We've always known you're a fantastic artist. You were the only one who was in the dark about that."

Shauna sounded honestly happy. "I'm just relieved you haven't decided to move in here with us, 'cause we're full up now. Jenn's boyfriend is moving in."

"Really? Wow, Jenn!" Grace felt a twinge of regret at missing out on the next steps in her friends' lives. "I hope he's a good guy."

"Oh, Shauna's checked him out. He wouldn't be moving in if she had any doubts. Plus, he's studying to be a vet and not remotely interested in logging. I'm so happy!"

They'd wanted to take the day off work and meet her at the airport, buy her a drink, and send her off in style. But she told them she needed the time with Pat; saying goodbye to him was complicated.

"I'll send you guys lots of letters. I promise. I'll be back at Christmas, but you've got to write and tell me everything!"

Now Grace took a look around the cabin. Lyle had dropped off a bundle of get-well cards and laid the letter from Jane prominently on the kitchen counter. Reluctantly, she reached over, picked it up, and stuck it in her pocket.

How would this place look next time she saw it? A fantasy of showing it to her mother one day had begun to play in her mind. But Grace would not let her imagination spin that story out—she wanted to stay in the present moment for now. Inhaling Prosperity deep into her lungs, she whispered her thanks. Then she picked up her suitcase and walked out of the cabin.

Grace had had another conversation with Annie's doctor. Then she'd called Rose.

"She says they tried shock therapy a couple of years ago; it didn't work. Her memory hasn't been good since then. The whole thing sounds awful."

"Well, your life doesn't have to be about Annie, dear. It needs to be about Grace."

"What does that mean? That I should abandon her, now that I know she's alive? Just forget she exists?"

"Of course not. But you don't have to rush to her side, either. Didn't the doctor say this has been going on for years? She might not even know you. What do you *want* to do? Ask yourself that first."

It had surprised Grace when the answer to that question came to her almost as soon as Rose posed it. "I want to paint. I want to go to art school."

"Ah." Rose's voice on the phone was a soft murmur, hard to distinguish from the one inside Grace's head. "That sounds right."

"And I don't want to go to Seattle. I want to go somewhere away, far away. Maybe I should go to the tropics."

"Grace?" Rose spoke louder now. "Is that *your* desire, or something you picked up from Annie?"

This question shook Grace's confidence. All the rest of the day it nagged at her. She studied the walls around her; her fingers curled as they reenacted the process of painting each creature; her mind filled with faint echoes of the imagined conversations she'd had with Annie as she'd worked. That Annie, that fantasy mother, had guided her. But that Annie didn't exist, probably never had.

When Pat came over that evening, she told him about her conversation with Rose and the one she'd had with herself.

"I made her up in my head. She was never the mother I believed she was. She liked that bird book, but she didn't show me how to draw those birds."

"No, Parrot, she didn't. You did that yourself." He gestured around the cabin. "And you did all this yourself."

Grace rubbed her finger over the green head of the first frog she'd painted, the one in the corner by the door. She tapped the dot of white that animated its eye. "It's still hard for me to believe that, even though I know you're right. I was so convinced it was her spirit guiding me. But I painted it, all of it, myself." She looked over her shoulder and smiled at Pat. "I'm not ready to meet her yet. I have to know what's real first before I can step into her crazy world."

He nodded. "Good plan."

After she tucked her backpack under the seat in front of her and fastened her seat belt, Grace pulled Jane's letter from her pocket and read the short message:

> *Parrot,*
> *I believed what I did was the best thing for you*
> *and for my brother. We don't get a rule book for how*
> *to decide the hard stuff.*
> *We just have to trust our instincts.*
> *Love,*
> *Jane*

Grace smiled and tucked the note back into the envelope. Her dad told her the same thing a long time ago. It had taken a while, but she was beginning to understand what it meant to trust her instincts.

She stuck Jane's letter into her back pocket. Then she checked again to assure herself that she had the other envelope, the one she'd stuck in her front pocket along with her passport. The letter of acceptance to the *Instituto Allende,* the art school in Mexico City, the letter offering her a full scholarship. It was a crazy idea, but she was betting on the possibility that sometimes crazy isn't bad.

When Walt explained how the town had chipped in the money to pay for a trip to L.A. to see Annie, Grace was stunned. The people who had fostered a fiction in order to protect her from the truth now wanted to help her find it. This gesture of love brought tears to her eyes, and she hated to think that she was going to disappoint everyone. It had taken all her strength to tell him, "I can't take it."

"But why? You want to find Annie, don't you?"

"No, not yet, Walt." Grace could only hope that he would understand. "I need to find myself first."

He put the check in her hand and nodded. "You take this, kiddo, go where you need to go and come back to us when you're ready."

The flight attendants gave their safety announcements and the plane headed down the runway. Grace held her breath as they left the ground. She looked out the window, expecting to be terrified, but the bird's-eye view calmed her. The world was both bigger and smaller than she'd ever imagined.

Acknowledgements

The writing of this book has taken me on a long journey and many people have aided me as I traveled it. I'm sure I will inadvertently leave out some of you without whom this story would never have seen the light of day, for that I apologize sincerely.

My deepest thanks go the Northwest Institute of Literary Arts for existing when it did. I will be forever grateful for the stellar, supportive faculty, especially Wayne Ude, Bruce Holland Rogers, Kathleen Alcala, and Sarah Van Arsdale, my fiction mentors (wasn't I lucky?), as well as Ana Marie Spagna, Carmen Bernier-Grand and Bonnie Becker, all of whom made this manuscript better. My cohorts and writing buddies who kept the fire going year after year: Frances Wood, Connie Connally, Iris Graville, Stephanie Barbé Hammer, Jackie Haskins, Janet Buttenweiser, Kim Lundstrom, Mattie Wheeler, and Sandy Sarr; my most generous readers, Molly Gloss and Karen Fisher; and my writing partner, Vicki Robin, who watched this thing grow from a seed and nourished it with her support the whole way. Thank you to my cousin, Cheryl Sindell, for writing alongside me and believing in me. Thanks to my friends who have watched me morph from a psychologist into a writer as my hair got grayer, and who never doubted I'd get a book published one day (or if they did they never told me), especially my book group of 30+ years who kept me reading widely and wildly.

The research aid I got from Cristy Lake at the Snoqualmie Valley Historical Museum was essential, as were the personal histories of the many woodsmen and their families I was privileged to interview and to treat. Thanks to many others for sharing their experiences, including Tom La Bell, Mike and Marsha Bartholomew, Jim Ward, Dan Brisbin, Eric Warren, Bill Denzel, and Randy Peak.

My offspring, Aaron Casson Trenor and Eden Ruth Trenor, have been essential guides on this journey; their reverence for the earth continues to inspire me.

All that said, I could not have written this book without the limitless support of my husband, Mel Trenor, who read every revision and kept on loving me.

About the Author

Deborah Nedelman is a graduate of Bryn Mawr College, University of Washington, and the Northwest Institute for Literary Arts. She holds a Ph.D. in clinical psychology and an MFA in creative writing. Co-author of *A Guide for Beginning Psychotherapists*, and *Still Sexy After All These Years: The 9 Unspoken Truths About Women's Desire Beyond 50*, her short stories have appeared in many venues including *Concho River Review, Literary Orphans*, and *Contemporary World Literature*. *What We Take for Truth* is her first novel.

Deborah first saw the Pacific Northwest in 1969, when she drove up I5 from Los Angeles. It was on that drive that the early seeds of this story were planted. Sharing the highway with logging trucks whose beds were filled with enormous logs, captivated her imagination. Soon after settling into her graduate work she began spending as much free time as she could hiking in the forests of the Cascade Mountains. Years later, when Deborah worked a therapist in Everett, Washington, families whose stories centered around those forests began to show up in her waiting room. While the newspaper headlines filled with stories of the conflicts between loggers and environmentalists, Dr. Nedelman was learning about the deeply painful toll the families of woodsmen and millworkers were paying as our society's values shifted. *What We Take for Truth* is her exploration of the human side of this shift and the attempts we make to shield ourselves from the consequences of change.

The town of Prosperity, Washington does not exist but is based on the small logging towns established when the giant trees of the Cascades were considered a limitless resource and logging was a highly valued industry. The characters in this novel have lived in the author's mind for years and have long backstories only alluded to in this book. None of them is based on a real person, but their individual attitudes and agonies are drawn from the many people who have passed through the author's world.

CPSIA information can be obtained
at www.ICGtesting.com
Printed in the USA
LVHW111602061119
636549LV00005B/910/P